love on the rocks

JUDI FENNELL

MERJINN PRESS

PHILADELPHIA, PENNSYLVANIA

Books By Judi Fennell

Royally Sunk
In Over Her Head
Wild Blue Under
Catch of a Lifetime
Love on the Rocks
~Making Waves ~ outtakes

Bottled Magic
I Dream of Genies
Genie Knows Best
My Fair Genie
~Your Wish Is His Command ~ outtake

Once Upon A Time Romance
Beauty and The Best
If The Shoe Fits
Through The Leaded Glass ~ prequel

BeefCake, Inc.
Beefcake & Cupcakes
Beefcake & Mistakes
Beefcake & Retakes
Beefcake & Snowflakes

Manley Maids
What a Woman Wants
What a Woman Needs
What a Woman Gets
What a Woman
What A Guy Wants

*A colossal wave hits the shore
when an overachiever who wants to carve a name for
herself
meets a hero who needs to keep his name under water.*

After a famous Mer art critic pans her work, sculptor Mariana tritone decides to create something to make a splash—right on the face of a volcano. The iconic sculpture will cement her reputation as a serious artist and not just a member of the Mer royal family 'playing at' a career.

Jace Pacifica was forced to fake his death eons ago because his brother, Thaumus, the deposed Mer ruler, mistakenly believes Jace cost him the throne and he wanted revenge. Jace has been hiding out ever since on a deserted Pacific island.

But then Princess Mariana shows up, putting his sanctuary at risk when she figures out who he really is. He'd cast her out to sea, but she could betray his secret and cost him his life. It doesn't hurt that she's gorgeous, smart, and talented—a trifecta that makes her impossible to resist…

Until an avian spy takes the scuttlebutt to Thaumus, putting everything at risk.

Romance is rough enough, but when there's a tsunami in the weather forecast, love is on the rocks.

To my kids… and theirs. It's always about you.

Many thanks to Rachell Nichole for the title.
I love it as much as the others. Thank you!

"Legends exist for one reason:

*To explain something Humans saw
that they can't make head-nor-tail of.*

*Or as a reason to be frightened
of things that go bump in the night."*

~ Mariana's Great-Great…Grandfather

Chapter One

N ow *that* is what I call a woman." Jace Pacifica swept the branch aside and adjusted his binoculars to watch the woman climb up the rock face with a macaw for company and an interesting array of equipment around her waist.

And not a stitch on.

He didn't know who she was, but he intended to find out.

Right before he kicked her off his island.

He let the branches fall back into place to adjust himself inside his shorts. Gods, how long *had* it been since he'd been with a woman? Consuela on the beach that night in San Diego? Or was it that villa in Curaçao— the one on Mambo Beach where the rum had been better than the sunrise, which was saying something.

It didn't matter. San Diego… Curaçao… Nova Scotia or South Africa; he'd traveled every coastline hundreds of times. His reputation made those Human sailors with women in every port look like monks. As a prince of the

Mer race, he'd been alive for longer than a few of the civilizations on the planet and had been with a lot of their women. Most tended to blend together over the centuries, though a few did stand out. Helen of Troy, for one. She'd launched a thousand ships in more than just the literal sense, and the woman had reveled in that knowledge.

Jace smiled. So had he.

A long, pale leg swung wide off the rock as the naked woman scrambled to regain her hold.

Jace caught his breath, not releasing it until she had all four appendages firmly attached to the hunk of earth she was set on conquering for gods-knew-what reason. Didn't she know how dangerous this was? Sure, he was a creature of the sea, but if he could see that she was way out of her element, why couldn't she?

He'd be doing her a favor, really, getting her off the island. Win-win for both of them.

Yeah, that's it. His good deed for the century.

Question was, how to do it? As the centuries had progressed, Humans had become quick to dismiss the old stories and mythology, so rustling up some Polynesian god to wreak havoc on her wouldn't do the trick. And since he, as a second son, who, like any other ruling family's second son, wasn't blessed with a tail, well, he couldn't lure her out to sea by claiming to be what she'd call a merman.

He'd have to think this through. He didn't want to end up piquing her interest instead of scaring her off.

With one last look, Jace backtracked down the path until his feet hit the cool sand around the edge of the freshwater pool that was hidden in the island's interior. The canopy of palms kept it algae-free and off Human's radar—or satellite, as it were.

Whatever they were called nowadays, those things

had been the bane of his existence ever since they'd come *into* existence. He'd assimilated into the Human world rather easily, the perfect cover to stay off his brother Thaumus' sonar and avoid the confrontation that had set him on this solitary life in the first place. But now that he'd seen his brother's henchfish patrolling many of his usual haunts, he'd been planning to stick close to this place for the time being. No one would ever expect a de-throned Mer *spare* to be hanging out in this desolate place, which made it the perfect—and, frankly, *only*—place to be.

It was a sub-par existence, but at least he was existing. And he didn't have to constantly be careful not to give himself away as a non-Human. That's why this place had been such a boon: out of the main current of ocean life where he could be himself, and one of the few islands Humans hadn't decided to erect an all-inclusive getaway on—*yet*. But, in the meantime, it was the perfect hideout for a Mer on the lam for whenever the song of the sea beckoned.

But with *her* here, that sanctuary had gone belly-up. Damn.

How had she found this island? And why *this* one? And what was with all the equipment she'd been toting to the summit?

And why was she naked?

Jace splashed some water from the pool onto his face at that image. Long, muscled legs, a perfectly cuppable ass, and yards of curly, gorgeous green hair that brushed it… He could think of something far better than that rock for her legs to be wrapped around.

Speaking of rock, he was harder than one. Which posed a huge problem. And, yeah, he was vain—and proud—enough to enjoy that double entendre; women certainly didn't complain when he set out to satisfy them.

He shook his head. Gods, he was pitiful. His sanctuary had been invaded and here he was, wanting to invade hers in the metaphorical sense.

Hades, he didn't even know if he *could* invade, er, seduce her. Just because she was here alone didn't mean she was alone in life—

Wait. *Was* she here alone? Getting to this remote island wasn't exactly a piece of kelp; she'd had to have had help.

Hades. He hadn't thought of that.

Jace ducked behind the closest pineapple grove, cursing the mess he'd left scattered around the hut. Living alone didn't lend itself to picking up after himself. And the hut… Not exactly something someone would expect to find on a deserted Pacific island.

If she and whoever was with her caught sight of that, he could kiss the island paradise goodbye.

Though he'd rather kiss *her* goodbye.

He was going to do whatever it took to get her off this island.

~~~

"I don't get why you feel the need to risk your life like this, Mares," Tahiti squawked as she landed right where Mariana was reaching for a handhold. "Honestly, it's just a hunk of lava the gods stuck here, not some thing of beauty you keep goin' on about."

"Tahiti." Mariana huffed between repositioning all four of her limbs. *Four.* Ugh. "You might not think falling off this rock is all that big of a deal on account of
~~~

your wings, but me? Won't be pretty. So, could you *please* get out of my way?"

Mariana wedged her fingers beneath the bird's talons, praying to the gods that her strength wouldn't give out on her. The anchor's worth of tools strapped to her waist wasn't helping matters.

When she'd first come up with this idea, it'd seemed like a good one, but now? She wasn't so sure.

No—it *was* a good idea. It *had* to be. It was the only hope she had. Well, either that or endure *selinos* of commissions under an assumed name or bad reviews—or, worse, being ignored and/or not taken seriously as an artist.

Tahiti nipped a pointed piece of lava off, the grit raining down on Mariana's head. "Couldn't you have done this in the water? It'd be so much easier and a lot less dangerous."

A line of sweat ran down Mariana's forehead, over her cheek, and dripped off her jaw onto her chest. Another *lovely* part of this world; she never sweated in the ocean. Ugh. "To have the effect I want, Tahiti, this sculpture has to be visible, and if I made it in the water, news would get to the palace in no time, so I'd never get to finish it. The Council would be swimming all over me to stop the project lest Humans find out."

"And you don't think they're gonna find out *now*?" The bird spread her royal blue wings and flew up the last ten feet to the top. "Hello? This lump is visible from the water. One curious sightseer and word's going to get out."

Mariana pulled herself up another foot or two toward the brow ridge she'd been working on. "All anyone will see from there is just a smooth version of the natural rock. Not the face. That's on this side."

"Humans are going to be crawling over it once it's discovered thousands of miles from those others."

"Good. Then no one will be able to ignore it." And by *no one*, she meant the most influential art critic in her world, Helmut Conch, the guy who just *loved* to disparage her work.

"I don't get it, Mares. The Mers can't see it from the water and Humans won't know who did it. And that's supposing this volcano doesn't blow its stack. Where's the win in this for you?"

"The PR factor, Tahiti. Haven't you ever heard that there's no such thing as bad publicity?"

"Sweetie, in case it's escaped your notice, I'm an avian. We don't get involved in advertisin' campaigns."

Mariana wasn't going to waste the time or her breath discussing it. It was what it was, and, really, Tahiti's opinion didn't matter. The only one's who did was Conch.

She swung her other arm up to grab a handhold, then hoisted herself up, using her legs for extra push. She really should exercise her thighs like this more often, but she'd never had the need in the sea. Swimming with a tail used different muscles.

"You *do* know The Council is *not* going to be happy with you when they *do* find out, right?" The macaw lifted one foot, then stepped onto Mariana's wrist, grasping two fingers with the other set of talons. The bird needed a serious manicure.

"The Council has bigger fish to fr—er, things to worry about, Tahiti." That was an awful saying. Her entire family had been horrified the night her younger sister, Angel, had shared it with them. But it did come in handy…

"Shrimp strikes are not the pressin' matter they used to be." Tahiti flicked her talons.

"I meant Angel's reformations." Angel had finally

gotten the job she'd been after to facilitate an understanding between their world and the Humans, but trying to implement the Mer-Human Coalition she'd proposed had sent Council sessions into overtime.

The perfect excuse for Mariana to swim away unnoticed.

At least, that was the hope.

Mariana wedged the toes of the left foot into the crevice she knew was somewhere below the knee. How in the sea did her siblings manage this? Not one but *three* of her four siblings had married Humans—okay, her sister-in-law, Valerie, was only half-Human, but still… Rod had had to go on *land* to find her. And Reel… He and his wife actually *lived* on land for most of the *selino*. She didn't get it. Who'd want to live like this, with the pull of gravity and being limited to moving only forward, backward, or sideways, but not up and down? Sure, her brothers and sister were in love with their respective spouses, but she was of the mind that they could have fallen in love with a Mer just as easily.

Not that it mattered. She wasn't going to marry. Look at what each of them had given up—their world, their tail, their place in Mer society. Immortality wasn't worth that price. So her art had to be it. It had to live on for her. *Its* immortality would be hers. She didn't have time for love.

Love. Mariana cursed as her hold slipped. Her siblings had gone through Hades for the four-letter word.

She knew a lot more four-letter words that were a lot easier to deal with. *Work* being one of them, and that's what she was here to do.

Though, with the cuts, scrapes, and the serious gash on the right knee from climbing this gods-forsaken volcanic mound, maybe she was going through her own Hades.

"You really think this is gonna make your career?"

"It has to. It will." Mariana gritted her teeth as another layer of skin was surrendered in sacrifice to her art. She'd had to start with the head because once she began freeing the figure inside, smoothing out the rough edges and claiming the beauty beneath this rugged exterior, there wouldn't be anything to hold on to.

The metaphor for her career was too close for comfort.

"So, if you want this to be such a big splash, why all the secrecy?" Tahiti, the show-off, was walking up the rock backward, those talons coming in handy for gripping the pockmarked rock.

"Not until I'm finished, Tahiti. If they get wind of it before then, The Council will be all over this."

"But isn't Conch, the preenin' idiot, headin' this way? Didn't you specifically tell him to be here on a certain date for the unveilin'?"

"I did, but no one's going to expect me to be carving *above* the shoreline."

"Ahhhh. Gotcha. But Humans can see it. What is it you hope *they're* going to do when one of them *discovers*—" Tahiti air-quoted the word with one talon from each foot while fluttering her wings— "this thing?"

"Validate it." And, therefore, give her the legitimacy she wanted—no, *needed*—as an artist, so she'd be seen as more than just a princess of the realm "playing at" being legit. Her art was the only thing she had, and if it wasn't a success, what did that make her?

Mariana refused to go there. She'd always been a superstar in school—on the playing field... socially... She *would* be with her art as well. If not, then, yeah, she was going to have to rest on her royal laurels because those and her art were the only things she was qualified to do.

But her art was the only thing she *wanted* to do.

"Are you sure you don't wanna do somethin' else?" Tahiti stumbled as a hunk of lava bent her tail feathers to the left. "I mean, these giant heads are pretty ugly. Why not go for a big giant sculpture of a Mer?"

"Because—" She cursed as her fingers slipped, then shoved herself onto the tips of the toes to reach the next handhold. "Because that'd be too obvious."

Tahiti gently wrapped her talons around Mariana's wrist and guided her arm to the perfect handhold, complete with a little divot to wrap her fingers around. It was a kind gesture, but the bird's big, beautiful wings weren't strong enough to save her if she fell.

Again, the metaphor was too close for comfort.

Mariana swung her leg over the next outcrop, her perch for the next few hours. The head was almost free of the rock. She'd like to finish the chin by the end of the week to keep herself on schedule since she didn't know how much longer Nalu and the other albatrosses she'd hired would be able to keep the rest of the seabirds— otherwise known as the Mer Messenger Service—from discovering what she was up to before Conch arrived.

Gods, she hated this. Hated the secrecy and the necessity for it. If only the giant shell she'd created for the Royal Atlantian Hotel's grand opening had blown the fins off Conch she wouldn't have to prove herself like this. But Conch had a thing about *noblesse oblige* being contraindicated when it came to legit art, no matter how talented she was—not to mention, he didn't *have* fins to blow off. Then, there'd been the whole drunken idiot who'd managed to knock it off its stand, and, well, Conch's comments about what'd been left had been kinder than his review of the original piece and her reliance on being royal.

But she wasn't relying on that to make a name in the art world. Didn't want to, either. She never had, and her family wasn't like that. They never put themselves above others or thought they were any better. They'd been granted the right to rule when Thaumus, the last of the Pontus rulers, had turned his reign into one giant hedonistic fiesta, forgetting the gods and the need to stay out of Human sight. Thaumus had gotten too big for his fins and the gods had put an end to it, turning the reins of government over to the Tritone family.

Mariana would bet Conch was descended from that exiled ruling family, but since no one in their right mind would make that claim due to the disgrace associated with it, she couldn't prove it.

Not that it would change anything. Whatever the cause, Conch was a tough shell to crack when it came to her work. That's why she had to go big or go home, and, really, she couldn't get any bigger than a Moai statue in the middle of the Pacific, thousands of leagues from those others. Conch *couldn't* ignore this.

"So... shall I be off to fetch you some water?" Tahiti waddled along the top of the sculpture, her bright yellow chest feathers looking almost neon against the glistening black rock.

"Thanks, Tahiti, that'd be great."

"The fresh kind, right? You're sure you don't want salt water?"

Mariana undid the belt buckle that she had Angel's compulsive Human-paraphernalia-collecting obsession to thank, and hooked it onto the piece of rock she'd carved for this very purpose. Gods, it felt good to get that weight off her body. She so missed the buoyancy of the sea. "Of course I mean fresh water, Tahiti. Salt water will bring my tail back and then how would I get down?"

Tahiti shrugged. "I dunno, but then, I think this whole thing is a pretty stupid idea anyway. Rock-climbin', dust and lava chips everywhere... Good thing you don't sunburn or you'd look like a lobster right now. And you're just goin' to annoy everyone with this anyway: your parents for being disobedient, The Council for the interest it's going to bring to the area, and Humans because they really hate having somethin' they don't understand starin' 'em in the face. And in this case, I mean literally. But, hey, it's your tail on the line, not mine."

With those parting words, Tahiti swooped off the rock, the last fifteen minutes of Mariana's climb being erased in all of about five seconds. The bird scooped up the plastic child's bucket they'd found floating on the current and headed toward the grove of palms that had prevented Humans from detecting the freshwater pool on the island from the sky.

Mariana slid her chisel and hammer from the loop on the belt and set to work. A few more weeks and that pool wouldn't be the only thing Humans would discover here.

Chapter Two

Jace scooped up the folding shovel from the beach and kicked the bucket across the sand toward his hut. Damn, he shouldn't have left everything scattered all over the place, but, in his solitude, he'd gotten sloppy.

Last time that would happen.

He dragged the sea kayak from the water's edge to beneath the hibiscus hedge, hoping the neon yellow color wouldn't show through the matching flowers. He kicked some sand over the fire pit, then scattered the rocks that ringed it to keep up the pretense that he'd landed here recently.

But while it didn't *look* as if the Human had found this place because everything was as he'd left it, if the bird *had* seen it and blabbed, his story would be shot to Hades.

Hopefully, the bird was keeping to The Code and *not* speaking to the Human. Still, the very act of hanging with one was skirting the edges of compliance.

Traitor. He couldn't believe a bird had gone over to the Human side. And was probably working for peanuts. Or bread crumbs. *Literally*. What was the world coming to?

And therein lay the question. What *was* the world coming to? Jace had been around since Humans had begun building their great societies, tearing up the land, blocking the sun, and clogging the waterways. Now, they were dumping barges full of their refuse into the precious, beautiful ocean and depleting its resources—just like his brother had done with the royal coffers for his so-called Endless Party. Jace could see the same end looming for this world if the Humans didn't get a clue. And, now, a member of that race was invading one of his few remaining sanctuaries in all the oceans, and there wasn't a damn thing he could do about it. Not if he didn't want to clue Thaumus in to the fact that he was still alive.

Jace grabbed the machete and kicked the empty coconut gourds into the hedge alongside the kayak. This place had been his sanctuary for hundreds of *selinos*; he wasn't going to give it up for some female. No matter how beautiful—and naked—she was.

How long had she and her little friend been here? He'd only been gone a week, but she'd made some serious progress on that lump of lava. And that worried him. A lot. If she continued at this rate, he'd be homeless in less than a month. Then where would he go?

He *had* to get her off the island.

Jace grabbed his clothes that were drying in the sweet-smelling breeze, the hibiscus and lime and pineapple giving them a scent they'd never had under water. He'd never been aware of the power of scent so much as when he'd lived in that gods-forsaken medieval British town. That stench had almost killed him. He'd high-tailed it (well, figuratively) back to the Pacific as fast as he could swim—*after* he'd hired a sailor to take him beyond the Thames. He'd never willingly put his body in *that* filth.

He shook the hibiscus stamens off the white shirt, grimacing at the streaks of yellow and pink. Ah, well, it'd still pass for island wear. Not that there was ever anyone around to comment.

Until now.

He grabbed the two pairs of cargo pants he'd hung up to dry, then shoved all his shorts and t-shirts to the end of the line where they fell into a heap. There was no time to be picky over the sand in them. He sliced the end of the clothesline, scooped up the pile, then entered the hut.

Short of tearing the structure down, there was nothing he could do about hiding it. He'd purposefully made it look ramshackle so that anyone who might happen by would think it'd been there for decades and was on the verge of collapse.

One of the good things about Immortality was the time it'd given him to study up on things, and architecture had been a particular favorite. And not only had he had him the time to do that, but also to experiment by building hut after hut until he'd discovered how to make a typhoon-resistant one. This place stood testament to how well he'd learned his lessons.

He brushed the netting in the window aside and looked out. The beach was as near to empty as could be expected with the ten minutes he'd had since branding the image of her naked backside onto his brain.

He let the netting drop back into place to cover the window. Unlike his brother, he liked to live minimally, so there wasn't a lot inside the hut. But he still had his tools, blankets, books, and other daily minutiae that one built up after thousands of *selinos* of hiding out.

He packed everything into a steamer trunk he'd rescued from a shipwreck a century or so ago, then shoved it out the back of the hut into an opening in the hedge he'd created for this purpose. He'd only ever had to clear house once before, but those pirates had been drunk on the rum that'd been the only thing they'd saved when their ship had gone down, and scurvy or pox or some other ailment had gotten them before the madness that came from claiming to see a man emerge from the sea had.

He replaced the door in the back wall of the hut, then looked around. Deserted. She'd find nothing to show he'd been living here as of fifteen minutes ago.

Question was, where *would* he be living until he got her off the island?

Maybe he should leave the kayak out. Give her the means to get off.

But how had she gotten on?

A flash of blue-and-yellow caught his eye through the window netting. The bird was circling the beach. Probably scavenging. Birds were good for that, which was why he'd hired Kama, a frigatebird whose dedication to duty was matched only by his lung capacity, to keep other flocks away. The fewer beings who knew he was here, the better.

The macaw landed on the hammock. Shit. He'd forgotten to cut that down.

"Hmmm," said the bird. "This is convenient. I wonder if Mariana knows about this? It's the perfect place to hang out while The Council wonders where she's gone."

The Council... Mariana...

Oh *shit*.

Jace might not have been living among Mers for the past few thousand *selinos*, but he certainly knew who the ruling family was.

And he *definitely* knew who Mariana was.

That explained the green hair.

He shook his head. Mariana Tritone. Eldest daughter of the ruling Tritone family. The Brain, as she was known, for her legendary straight As throughout school and being class president, valedictorian, magna cum laude... The woman was the Mer world equivalent of Humans' Einstein.

And she was an artist, too. A sculptor, if he wasn't mistaken. And he didn't think he was; royal gossip was always a topic of discussion among seabirds from different oceans whenever they met up—typically at Humans' seaside restaurants. She'd been a topic of conversation the last time he'd been in the Canaries. Something about a giant shell sculpture that hadn't gone over well. Or maybe it *had* gone over and that was the problem; he couldn't remember the specifics. But he *did* remember hearing about her. He was always careful to keep the fact that he understood bird speech from the gossips, but he sucked up their knowledge for all it was worth. And this was worth a lot. Especially with her being here.

How far behind would her brother Rod, their ruler, be?

And behind Rod, *his* own brother? Thaumus still hadn't given up the hope of getting the throne back.

And what was a Mer princess doing *with legs*?

A crab scuttled beneath the front door. "Hey, Jace. We got company." Merc clacked his claws together like an old man's dentures.

"I know, Merc."

"It's a Mer princess."

"I know that, too."

"Well, gee, aren't you just a smart guy?"

Jace didn't answer. If he *were* so smart, he wouldn't be in hiding from a brother who no longer ruled the seas. But that only made Thaumus more dangerous since he no longer had to answer to anyone on protocol. Taking out a second son of a now non-ruling family wouldn't garner so much as a flip of a fin—*if* anyone even noticed he was gone. Especially since he'd made it seem that he had been gone for a long, long time. He ran a hand through his hair. Ah, well, if Thaumus *did* end up finding out about this, he'd cross that isthmus when he came to it.

"So—" Merc bounced off the table leg as he scuttled sideways. That missing eye had thrown off his peripheral vision ever since he'd lost it in an attempt to escape the fishing nets. "Whatcha going to do about it? About her?"

Jace knew what he *wanted* to do about her. Which had him shaking his head. Yeah, it'd definitely been way too long between shore leaves if he was more concerned about *taking* her to bed than *losing* his bed. "I'll think of something, Merc."

"Well, if it were up to me, I'd be thinking quickly. She's set up at the crater and I heard she ain't leaving until she's carved the whole rock into one of those Moai head statues. Yuck. What do we need one of those here for? Ugly suckers."

His thought so, too, but art was subjective. And he didn't care if her statue was the most beautiful thing on the planet; it could *not* happen on his island.

"So I'm thinking," said Merc, clacking his claws, "if you want, I could round up a crew and we could scare her off the island by overrunning it."

Jace peered out through the window netting. The bird was filling the bucket with water from the pool. "No self-respecting Mer is going to be afraid of crabs, Merc."

"True. I forgot she wasn't a Human for a second. It's the legs, you know—uh, I mean—" Merc's lone eye stalk drooped. "I wasn't saying legs are bad, Jace, it's just—"

"I get it, Merc." Jace's legs were no longer the sore subject they'd been when he'd been growing up in Thaumus' shadow. Second sons of ruling families got legs; it was the way it was and no amount of belly-aching could change it. He'd accepted his lot in life a long time ago—and was glad for them, actually, since they enabled him to hide in the Human world, but, still, this was who he was. And right now, those legs would come in handy for having her think he was a Human. Because, just as he'd known who she was from her name, so, too, would she know who he was from his. And that was the *last* thing he needed. "Okay, Merc, here's the plan. I'm going to go talk to her and—"

"*What*?" The crab almost pinched his remaining eye stalk in half with his left claw. "You *can't* talk to her. You'll blow your cover. She's going to know who you are."

"No, she's not. There's no reason to suspect I'm alive." And, actually, Jason Pontus *wasn't* alive; it was Jace Pacifica who'd escaped Thaumus' net and survived all these many centuries who was.

"Look, Jace." Merc was waving his claws in the air like a hula dancer. "I know you're all ladies-man and everything, but you gotta consider the logistics. What's she going to think when some random guy walks up to her on an island in the middle of the Pacific as if it's the most normal thing in the world?"

"That he's been shipwrecked. Given that she isn't going to want me to find out about the Mer world any more than I want her to know who I am, she's either going to find some way to explain what she's doing here or leave. I'm betting on the latter. It's easier and no one would believe me if I'm ever 'rescued.' Just, whatever you do, don't let her know you know who she is."

Merc scratched his carapace. "I dunno. I think you ought to dive back into the ocean and let the whole thing flow over. Once she finishes, she'll be gone."

The macaw flew away with its bucket.

"But others will come after her. I'm not ready to give up my island yet." He was tired of having to be on the run. He'd done it for eons and was fed up with not getting to live his life. Bad enough he had to swim in the shallows in the rest of the world, but this was his *home*, dammit. The one place in the world he felt safe and could be himself. She wasn't going to take that from him. Not when there were hundreds of other islands just as well-suited for her purpose. Whatever that was. "Don't worry, Merc. If the fear of being found out doesn't do it, I'll try some other way."

While classic over-achievers like Mariana Tritone didn't let anything get in their way, she didn't know who he was. What he was capable of.

If there was one thing Jace had learned over the *selinos*, it was what women liked, regardless of how much they'd achieved. He knew what he was doing.

He was going to seduce Mariana. Either she'd run— er, *swim*—screaming from him, or she'd succumb and they'd spend the rest of her time here keeping each other immensely occupied so he could keep her from doing whatever it was she was doing. He'd hope for the former, but, actually, wouldn't mind the latter.

After all, sometimes, you had to lose a couple of battles to win the war.

Chapter Three

The war was over almost before it began—because the woman dropped an anvil on him.

Jace rubbed his toe. Thank the gods it was the smallest toe and the sand had absorbed some of the impact, but, dammit, an anvil? Even if the thing was only the size of his fist, what in Hades did she need an anvil for? Did she have a forge up there, too?

Jace glanced up again. Maybe that was the way he should walk around while she was here. If he hadn't been looking up and seen the anvil heading in his direction, it could've killed him instead of breaking a toe.

Luckily, he saw no sparks coming off the top of the lava, but he took two steps back anyway—well, one step and one limp. His toe fucking hurt.

And now he had to be *charming*. That was the *last* thing he felt like being to her. He'd rather wrap her up in a fishing net and set her adrift on the next wave off the island. But he couldn't because that'd be murder to a Human, and if he wanted her to think he was merely Human and not a sociopath, that idea was out.

Still, he could fantasize about it…

In the meantime, it was time for the charm. "Hey, lady! Lost something?"

Again, good thing he was looking up. A chisel came hurtling over the edge and embedded itself in a coconut. Which fell out of the tree, hit a rock, then shot straight at him, clipping him mid-thigh.

The woman was a menace.

And then her bird-brained friend dive-bombed him from the top of the rock. He almost shouted at the thing, but then remembered a Human wouldn't expect a bird to understand him.

Instead, he dodged behind a palm tree, cursing when the bird's wing tip skimmed across his eye. Great, now she was going to blind him, too.

Gods, he just wanted this to be over with.

"Who are you?" Long, green tresses obscured the woman's face as she leaned over from her perch, her toes gripping the lava.

Oh, sure. *Her* toes still worked.

Jace blinked the pain from his smarting eye. No way was he telling her who he was. Might as well walk a gang plank while he was at it. Though, as a Mer, that wasn't such a terrible fate. But the meaning was the same.

So, he opted for pasting on his sexiest smile and hoping she wouldn't realize he didn't tell her his name. "Aren't *you* the prettiest sight for sore eyes—" he meant that literally, unfortunately— "that I'd never thought I'd see."

She sat back. "How'd you get here? We're in the middle of the Pacific Ocean."

So much for the charm. "A boat. It took on water and I had to escape in my kayak. I rowed ashore and here

I am. You wouldn't happen to have a boat around here I could get back to civilization with, would you?"

She shook her hair over her shoulders.

Very good thing he was looking up—he got the perfect view of an upturned breast, curvy waist, and enough thigh to get his mouth watering. Yes, Mariana Tritone was one Hades of a looker.

"I, uh, don't. No."

"Really? Then how'd you get here?" Let her squirm a bit over her answer. Served her right for invading his privacy.

And breaking his toe.

The bird coasted back onto the rock with something streaming from its beak, and Mariana looked down at him. She must have figured out the view he was getting and quickly brushed her hair forward again, taking all that delectable flesh from his sight.

But then she shifted her toes under her and disappeared behind the rock, giving him a perfect parting shot of that heart-shaped backside he'd seen on her way up.

"Um, give me a few minutes and I'll be down."

"Sure thing. I'm not going anywhere."

He hobbled over to the palm tree, checked for falling coconuts, then leaned against the trunk, his injured foot resting against it in a quintessentially relaxed pose that showed off his abs really well as he tossed the anvil in one hand, flexing those aforementioned muscles in ways women liked. Jace wasn't conceited, but he knew—and enjoyed—the effect he had on the fairer sex, and, yeah, he might enjoy it a little bit more with Mariana.

A long, white leg swung off the top of the rock, but a piece of fabric covered everything else from view. That annoying bird had stolen one of his shirts. He must have missed it when he'd scooped his clothes off the sand. He'd love to know how Mariana was planning to explain *that* to him. Eh, let her sweat about it. Just like she could sweat it thinking he'd want her out of it…

That idea was getting better by the minute as he watched her climb down the rock. She'd never know who he was, so why *couldn't* he enjoy some time in her company? He could be exactly what he said he was; a shipwrecked Human with no hope of getting off this island unless he wanted to brave the sea in a ten-foot kayak. No Human was that insane.

Well, okay, yeah, there were a few. Seriously, some of the crafts Humans decided to try to brave even normal swells with were just, well, insane.

"You need some help getting down?" He should get off the tree and help, but the view was sweet from here. His shirt had lost a few buttons scraping against the lava and the gaps were at just the right place…

"No help needed; I'm good."

She certainly was. It was a damn shame that the woman was a full-blooded Mer because those legs of hers were sexy as Hades. Perfectly shaped, strong, long… He wouldn't mind nibbling the entire length of them.

He grimaced and adjusted himself right before she leapt the last five feet to the ground.

About five-three to his six-two, with hair that went on and on and on, the woman was a knockout even without the anvil. His shirt looked like a dress on her, a boring, bleached-gray dress with missing buttons, the only shape to it the colorful length of fabric she'd tied at her tiny waist.

She looked sexier than Helen ever had.

He'd forgotten what Mer women were like. Petite

but strong, with long hair that could ensnare a man—or a Mer—and let him die happy. Their song could lure even the most stalwart sailor to the depths and entrance a Mer so that he'd give her anything she wanted.

All this one had to do was smile at him and Jace felt his knees tremble.

He shook his head. Gods, he was being an ass. His knees were trembling because of the damn coconut and the anvil. Both legs had taken direct hits, and if her violet eyes swirled like a tropical whirlpool, inviting him into their swirling depths, well, he ought to be immune.

Ought to be, but… wasn't.

"Missing something?" He held out the anvil.

She looked at him warily, like he'd bite.

Only if she asks nicely.

"Thanks." She grabbed the tool from him, then repositioned his shirt on her lithe frame. "Did you have the chance to send out a distress signal?"

What, she couldn't hear the one his libido was screaming? "Nope. Didn't even think about it. The boat went down too fast." Something else, however, was doing anything *but* going down.

"So no one knows where you are?"

"You do." He worked his devil-may-care smile back onto his face, turning the charm way up. By now, most women would be eating out of his hand. Literally, if he asked them to.

This one just rolled her eyes. "Cute. So, what's your plan? Hang out on a deserted island on the off-chance you'll be able to flag down a passing cruise ship?"

"I could ask you the same thing. You're not exactly jumping up and down with joy that someone's found you."

"Perhaps I didn't want to be found."

"Which opens the door to some very interesting questions."

"Here. Let me shut it for you." She spun around, tucking her hair behind her ears, and started walking away. Which, truly, was no hardship to watch. "You have to leave this island."

He pushed himself off the tree trunk and walked behind her. His fingers twitched above her shoulder, but Jace put a stop to that. He shouldn't touch her. There was no need to freak her out. "Hey, sweetheart, I'm with you on leaving. Question is, how?"

She looked over her shoulder. "You have that kayak."

"Seriously? You want me to set out across this ocean in a kayak? Sorry, sweetheart, but I don't have a death wish." If he had, he would have surrendered to Thaumus *selinos* ago.

She spun around and thrust her hands to her hips.

Which made her breasts thrust against his shirt, a sight Jace was all for.

"Well, you can't just stay here," she said, her agitation doing delicious things to those breasts.

Jace forced himself to keep his eyes on hers. "Why not? You have a special claim to this place I don't know about? Last time I checked my charts, this island was uninhabited. Do you own it or something?"

She muttered, "Or something," but obviously hadn't intended him to hear it, so he let it go. Sometimes ignorance was the better part of intel.

"So, what *are* you doing here, Princess? Aside from being the Welcome Wagon, that is."

"What did you call me?"

Shit. He'd forgotten she actually *was* a princess. But he'd use it to his advantage. He hadn't stayed alive and undetected all these *selinos* by not thinking on his feet. "I called you *princess*. You prefer something else? Girlfriend, perhaps? Lover? Sexy *thang*?"

She rolled her eyes again. "Funny." She fixed the neckline of his shirt—actually, she *un*fixed it, making the collar on the left side stand up, and he had to stop himself from straightening it solely for the chance it would give him to touch her. "You're handling being shipwrecked better than most Hu—people I know."

"Know a lot of shipwreck-ees, do you?"

This time she added a heavy sigh to the eye-rolling. "You know what I mean."

He crossed his arms, adding a little pec-flexing just because he could. "Sorry, *Princess*, but I gave up trying to figure women out eons ago." Literally. "Why don't you tell me and we'll avoid a whole bunch of misunderstandings that way. And pardon me for pointing out the obvious, but you don't seem all that excited for me to be here."

"I'm not, if you must know." She threaded her fingers through her hair, pushing it back in one long, tumbling mass of sex appeal down her back. "This was my getaway. My chance to… well…"

"Get away?" He arched an eyebrow.

She glared at him, a little too immune to his charm for his liking. "To be alone. And now you've ruined it."

"Well pardon me for having a leaky boat. Trust me. If I'd known it was going to leak, I wouldn't have bought it. I was trying to get off the grid for a bit—a vacation, if you will." He fought the urge to run his hands through her hair. And pull her against him and cover those pursed, plump, disapproving lips with his and kiss the sense out of both of them. "Look, if you want to call your boat captain or whoever brought you here and arrange for me to get off this island, I'm more than happy to leave you to your solitude."

"I… can't. I'm um… incommunicado for two more weeks."

Two weeks? Good gods, he'd have the entire population of the whole Pacific Ocean here by then. Thaumus would get wind of it for sure. "You're saying I'm stuck here for two more weeks?"

"It's better than indefinitely."

Not in his book. But he had to play along. "So, what happens in two weeks? Your knight in shining armor rides in on a white yacht and rescues you from your island tower?"

"Where do you get this stuff? No, in two weeks, my project will be done and I'll leave."

"Just like that?"

"Just like that."

Jace's mind was going a league a minute. *Could* his secret stay hidden for that long? Could *he* stay hidden for that long? What would it take to make Thaumus suspicious? Maybe he was being too paranoid.

No, paranoid was what had kept him alive all these *selinos*. It paid to be paranoid. "And then what?"

"What do you mean?"

She licked those plump, pursed, disapproving lips and Jace had to catch his breath when his cock reacted. This woman was dangerous on a lot of levels. "What I mean is, I'm no art connoisseur, but it looks to me like you're carving something. You're just going to leave it here when your two weeks are up?"

She blanched, which, considering that her skin was untouched by the sun, was a telling reaction. "Yes, I will."

"Seems kind of pointless if you ask me."

The hands were back on the hips, this time in fists. And anvil. "Well, I didn't ask you."

"Whoa, okay, lady. Whatever you say." He put his hands up in mock surrender. "Carve your hunk of lava and have a blast. In the meantime, I guess I'll get my stuff out of the hut so you can stay there."

"Oh, there's no need for that. I don't need it."

"You brought a tent? I mean, I know it's not the Ritz, but the roof doesn't leak during a storm. I'm more than happy to switch with you."

"There's no need. I'm fine staying outside."

Knowing who she was, this made sense. But he wasn't supposed to know who she was, so it *shouldn't* make sense.

"Look, Princess, my mother brought me up to be a gentleman." He *ought* to get an award for saying that with a straight face. Oh, his mother had *wanted* him to be a gentlemer, but it had been far more fun to *not* be. "I can't, in good conscience, take the hut and leave you to the mercy of the elements."

"Trust me, I'll be fine. You said you needed a vacation; what makes you think I don't, too? It's not as if I get to sleep on a deserted island every day, you know."

Uh huh. She could have her pick of islands, but, again, he wasn't supposed to know who she was. "Well then, you definitely need to keep that." He nodded at the shirt she was wearing.

She turned around to look behind her, then back, her long hair swishing over his arm as she did so. "Keep what?"

"My shirt. You were pretty naked up there."

Ah, *there* was the color in her cheeks. All it'd taken was a mention of nudity. He'd have to remember that.

"I wasn't expecting to share this place with anyone else so I wasn't exactly prepared."

He crossed his arms, enjoying watching her squirm to come up with plausible explanations. "I get that. Still, seems kinda… I don't know… *dangerous* to go rock-climbing in the nude. Not that I'm complaining, mind you. Feel free to do it anytime you want. Just be careful you don't scrape yourself." He fingered one of the tears in the sleeve.

She looked up at him, her violet eyes staring into his.

Interest warred with common sense, a look he'd seen from countless women through the ages… usually right before they capitulated. *Finally,* his charm was getting through to her.

Jace leaned in. Only a few millimeters, but enough that if she wanted to say no, she had about ten seconds to do so.

It only took her two.

"If you wouldn't mind, then, yes, I'd like to keep your shirt. I can pay you for it."

Oh she'd pay all right. "No worries. It's yours." But he did figure that her owing him gave him the right to at least straighten her collar—with both hands and close enough that he could almost feel the tips of her breasts grazing his chest. The fact that they were grazing the inside of his shirt would have to do for now. "Just let me know when you want to get rid of it, okay? I'll be more than happy to help with that." Considerably *more* than happy.

Another flush covered her cheeks. Good. His charm was working.

Problem was, so was hers. He was liking Mariana Tritone's repartee a little more than he should.

Which could pose big problems in the future.

If they had one.

Why did he have to be hot?

Mariana cursed the heat that rose to her cheeks because he *had* to know that she found him attractive.

Which was INSANE. He was HUMAN for gods' sakes.

Not to mention, he was an intruder. Maybe even a spy…

Damn. Had Rod figured out where she was and sent this guy—

No. He wouldn't send a Human to do his dirty work. Well, it wasn't really *dirty* work; she was the one out of line for risking exposure to the Human world, so he could just send out a few deputies and take her into custody and no one would flutter a fin.

"Princess? You okay?"

Something was fluttering all right.

"I'm fine." She jerked the collar out of his hands and herself out of his reach. *Fine* was a relative term and, right now, she was relatively *not* fine, but he didn't need to know that.

Damn. She needed to get away from him.

But she couldn't. He was stuck on the island, and unless she wanted to explain her little, um, *secret*, by asking a pod of dolphins to escort him back to the mainland—thereby *definitely* sealing her fate with Rod and The Council—stuck was where he was going to stay.

With her.

She had a headache.

"You're, uh, looking a little green around the gills, Princess. Want me to make you a piña colada? Minus the rum, of course. Unless you know of some pirate booty around here. Or you have some on you."

Gills? Her hand slapped to the side of her neck. She didn't have gills. She'd *never* had gills. That was just a stupid Human misconstruction. Mers were perfectly capable of breathing through lungs that could adapt to both air and water; they—*she*—didn't need gills. Figure of speech, that's what that was.

She exhaled. Heavily. "No rum. No piña colada. I have to get back to work."

And away from him.

She spun on her heel, pleased that she kept herself upright.

"So, you're okay with me taking the hut, right? What are you going to do? Sleep in the hammock?"

She paused and made the mistake of glancing over her shoulder.

No one should be that good-looking. It wasn't fair. "I'll handle my own accommodations, thank you. You just stay on your side of the island, and I'll stay on mine."

"Ah, man, where's the fun in that?"

"You know, for someone who's been shipwrecked, you have an awfully good disposition about it." Other Humans had been screaming their bloody heads off the few times she'd run into them. Angel had been all about helping them, but Mariana had been the one to remind her that they couldn't get involved. On pain of death.

Yet, here she was, doing just that.

Damn. All she'd wanted to do was carve a statue and make her mark, not start an interspecies incident.

Chapter Four

The sand was uncomfortable.

So was the hammock.

And forget about knocking on the door to that ramshackle hut for a mattress or something in the middle of the night last night; no way had she been planning to get anywhere near that guy.

Mariana pounded sand—ha!—and rolled over. Gods, what she wouldn't give for her nice comfy lair, but it took too long to dry her tail out to get legs if the guy—what was his name anyway?—came looking for her, so she was stuck sleeping here.

When she'd planned this project, she hadn't counted on a shipwreck-ee she'd have to hide her true self from. Yet, somehow, she *was* going to have to go back in the water within the next few nights or risk being stuck with these legs forever and *that* wasn't happening. Last night, she'd used some of the gods' oil she'd borrowed—okay, *stole*—from Rod that had allowed him to keep his legs for an extended period of time when he'd gone after

Valerie on land, but she was going to have to ration her supply judiciously.

"Maybe you ought to just call it quits." Tahiti dropped a Brazil nut onto the sand beside her from her perch on a palm frond. "Breakfast of champions for you."

Mariana raised an eyebrow. "I don't have a beak, if you recall."

"Yeah, but that tongue of yours is awfully sharp." Tahiti squawked with laughter so much she toppled out of the tree.

Breaking her fall with a furious pounding of wings sent the sand scattering all over the place—including into Mariana's eyes, which made Mariana jump to her feet.

"I guess I'm up now."

"Didn't you want to be?" Tahiti brushed her breast feathers with the tip of her wing, sending more sand flying. "I thought the sooner you were done, the sooner you could get away from Lover-boy over there." She cocked a wing feather like a thumb toward the hut.

"Shhh, Tahiti. I don't want him to hear you. I could explain a word or two, but not full sentences. Birds don't talk to Humans."

"With just cause. Do you know how stupid most of them are? 'Polly want a cracker.' Puh-leaze!" The bird shook her feathers, sending a few floating onto the sand.

"Shhh. Don't let him hear you."

"You know, this isn't going to be quite as much fun as I imagined if I have to play dumb around him."

"It'll be *less* fun if I have to go on trial for outing our race and the gods call you in as a witness."

"True." Tahiti picked up a feather and poked it into her back. "I don't do under-the-sea well."

"So let's remember that and keep your beak shut."

"Whoa, chicky. No need to get all dictatorial. I've got enough of a survival instinct that I know when to can it."

The door to the hut opened.

"Like now!" Mariana hissed as she gathered up the other half dozen feathers and practically shoved them into Tahiti's beak. "Here. Go put these back where they belong."

"Mmmburmbmph," Tahiti replied before launching herself into the tree.

Mariana didn't have the heart to tell her that she wasn't blending in with the green fronds. Maybe the guy—what *was* his name again?—wouldn't notice.

"Trained parrot?" he asked as he walked toward her.

So much for that.

"Um. Sort of."

Tahiti choked on a feather.

Which was better than spouting her opinion.

"Hey, I'm sorry, but I've forgotten your name. I'm Mariana." She held out her hand. Best to come clean about her faulty memory instead of trying to figure out his name for the next two weeks. Not that she should really care what his name was, but it would make conversation between them easier.

He put a hand on his heart and shuffled backward. "Princess, you wound me. Am I not memorable enough that you need a name?"

She rolled her eyes. "Let me guess. Hollywood heartthrob."

"You think so?" He stood straight, losing the injured look quickly enough.

She wasn't going to pander to his ego, however. "I'm guessing the overacting isn't getting you many roles."

He fist-thumped his chest. "Overacting? Me?"

"If they gave an award for worst impersonation of a

wounded hero, you'd win. But, too bad, they don't." She flicked her fingers and turned away. "Now, if you'll excuse me, I'm heading back to work."

"But what if I don't?"

She glanced back. "What if you don't what?"

"Excuse you."

"Excuse me?"

"No problem."

"What?"

He had the most annoying grin on his face. "I said, 'No problem.'"

"What's no problem?"

"A phrase?"

"Huh?"

"Princess, are you sure you're okay? Didn't hit your head on that lava, did you?"

"What are you talking about?"

"I know what I'm talking about, but I'm seriously concerned that you don't."

She shook her head and patted the side of it with her palm. Her hearing had to be off because he was making zero sense.

"See? I thought you might have done some damage." He rubbed the spot she'd just patted. "I don't feel a lump."

"You will if you don't back off." She didn't know what game he was playing, but she wasn't in the mood. She had work to do. Rock to carve. Bigger fish to fry than him—in this instance, that idiom worked. "Look, I'm fine, but I have to get to work. Have a nice… um, day. Whatever." She stalked off toward the rock, the bird trailing after her.

"You know? *Princess* suits you. I think I'm going to keep calling you that. At least until I know you better."

She wasn't going to respond because the last thing she needed was for him to get to know her better because then he might find out that her title actually *was* Princess.

She looked as good going as she did coming.

Jace chuckled. Double entendres always made him laugh and that one especially because he was actually wondering what she *did* look like when she came.

Maybe, with a little luck—and two uninterrupted weeks—he'd find out.

"What's with that look, Jace?" Merc scuttled over half of a giant clam shell.

"What look?"

"The goofy one on your face that looks like you ate some bad kelp or something."

"Or something." He dragged his eyes off her backside to look at the crab. "What's up? Why are you back?"

"What? A guy can't hang with his buddy for no apparent reason?"

"No. It's too much of a coincidence."

Merc sighed, his eye stalk swaying in the breeze. "There's a flock of albatrosses about seven leagues away. In every direction."

Shit. Not what he needed to hear. "Who are they?"

"I didn't want to go asking and draw attention to myself. They might be hungry." Merc's eye stalk dipped as if he was ducking for cover.

"Albatrosses don't eat crabs."

"That we *know of.* They *could,* which would mean the crab wouldn't be able to tell anyone. I'd rather not take the risk. I grabbed hold of the first sea turtle I could find and hung on to his plastron as quick as possible to get away."

Jace shook his head. Merc was a worry wart, a fact that grated on Jace's nerves, but, in this instance, he was glad for. He didn't need the birds to know he was here, and if Merc started asking questions, they might wonder why the crab cared.

Jace sure as Hades cared, however. What were albatrosses doing so close to this island? It wasn't a nesting site; they liked the cooler waters of the Southern Ocean. Which is why he'd thought Kam and his posse were the best option for patrolling the skies here. But since albatrosses could take off and land on water— whereas frigatebirds would sink—the larger birds were able to catch food in place instead of having to rely on the assistance of dolphins and whales to school their prey or catch flying fish on the fly, as it were, like frigatebirds had to. Albatrosses were definitely the better choice for surveillance, but they were also majorly connected to the undersea world he was trying to avoid, so they hadn't really been an option for him.

But they obviously were for someone—and he bet he knew. Dammit. "Did you hear anything they said?"

Merc clacked his pincers. "Yes, that's why I came back. They're on her payroll."

"The princess'?" Jace glanced back to where Mariana had disappeared into the underbrush. Dammit again. He didn't want to be right in this instance.

"Ain't no other *her* here that I see." Merc's eye almost did a three-sixty. "You?"

"Uh, yeah. I mean, no. I mean, yeah, she's the only *her* here. But what would she be doing with albatross spies?" Spies spoke to her *vacation* being more than she'd said it was. And that worried him. Something else was going on.

"I got the impression they were more guarding her than

spying on her. Which fits with her being royal and them hanging offshore for a while. They're kinda just hovering there, making big ol' circles as the wind blows. You know how lazy albatrosses are when it comes to flying."

Just because the birds rarely flapped their wings didn't make them lazy. Albatrosses were able to stay aloft for days at a time by riding air currents. Lack of flapping was a huge conservation of energy so they could stand guard for long periods of time. As far as Jace was concerned, albatrosses were the perfect stealth flyers. Their vision from the heights was part of the reason he rarely hung out on beaches and had constructed the hut, though he hadn't expected a squadron of them to be in the area. And if they got a little too curious about him…

Hades, he hadn't told any of the frigatebirds who he was—only Kam knew and ran interference because, if Thaumus got wind that he was alive—

"What else did they say?"

Merc shrugged his carapace. "I dunno. Something about taking bets on who'd find out she was here first, The Council or Humans. And what's going to happen to the Moai she's making."

Moai. The statues on Easter Island that weren't found anywhere else in the world. Putting one here would bring Humans out in droves, and their field study of the damn thing would go on for decades.

Damn. She was putting them both in danger once someone noticed her statue.

Forget getting her off the island quickly being his sole focus; he was going to have to make sure she was too occupied to have the chance to *finish* it in the next two weeks.

No one was going to take his sanctuary away from him, by royal decree or otherwise.

Chapter Five

Are ya done yet?" Tahiti landed on the statue's brow just as Mariana swung her hammer.

She jerked it away at the last second, taking a chip out of the bridge of the nose that she hadn't wanted to. "No, but *you're* going to be if you don't get out of my way. I almost hit you."

"But ya didn't."

They'd been friends all of Mariana's adult life, but because Tahiti was almost twice her age, the bird thought she knew more. Mariana thought Tahiti was verging on senility—and this latest maneuver only upped that belief. "Is there something you need, Tahiti?"

"I could go for a backrub. My left shoulder has some arthritis." The bird canted toward her. "Do you think you could just, you know, a little… right there?"

Mariana held up her chisel. "What part of 'I need to finish this before Conch gets here' do you not understand, bird?"

"No need to get nasty." Tahiti ruffled her feathers. "And it's *avian* to you, fishy."

Mariana gritted her teeth against the insult. She did have it coming since she'd insulted Tahiti.

"Besides, I was just comin' up here to give you the lowdown on Lover-boy down there. I think he's losin' his marbles."

"Why do you say that?"

"He's talkin' to a crab. Been doin' so all day. Which is better than, oh, I don't know, maybe, say, a volleyball, but… still. The sun's fryin' his brain. You might want to do somethin' 'bout that."

"What am I supposed to do?"

"You might try talkin' to him. If he has you to talk to, it could keep him sane."

Or she could tell him she was a Mer and really send him over the edge. That could solve her problem for her. "I don't have time to play tour guide. I'm on a deadline."

The bird shrugged. "Fine by me, but when you're sharin' the sand with some whack-a-doo, don't come cryin' to me if he starts chasin' you around with a club or somethin'. I'm just lookin' out for you."

"And I appreciate that, but if you wouldn't mind getting off the brow ridge, I can smooth out this chunk you made me take out of it, then get back to work so I can get off this island on time and not have to deal with him."

"Oh, sure, blame me." Tahiti's crown feathers flared. "I get no respect 'round here, I tell ya. No respect."

"You'll get some when you leave," Mariana muttered as the bird fluttered upward. She pulled the tooth chisel from her workman's belt, then worked the bridge into shape again.

"You know the wind and elements are gonna give him enough dings and pockmarks that no one's gonna notice that one little slip o' the hammer, right?"

Mariana didn't reply. What Tahiti said was true, but she was going to put her best work out there. What Mother Nature did was up to Her; Mariana would only be satisfied with her work being as perfect as possible.

Not that that seemed to carry weight with Mr. Conch-on-High.

Gritting her teeth, Mariana worked the chisel across the stone until the contouring was smooth.

"You want me to sing or somethin'?" Tahiti tapped her claws on the top of the statue.

"No."

"Tapdance?"

Gods no. "No."

"Recite a poem? 'The Iliad' maybe?"

"Studied that ad nauseum in school, thanks. No rendition required."

Tahiti sighed. "This isn't very fun."

Tell me about it. "You could always take a nap in the top of a palm tree down there." The closest fronds were at least fifteen feet below her. That would keep Tahiti out of her hair.

"I'm all about gettin' my beauty sleep, but in a palm? I'll fry my beak for sure." Tahiti did a flamenco dance as she turned to face out to sea. "I *could* always check up on the advance team. See if they've seen anythin'."

"Sounds like a good idea." Too bad she'd only set up sentinels *away* from the island. How'd they miss Mr. Gods-Gift-To-Women down there? A shipwreck ought to have caught their attention, or, at the very least, his arrival by kayak.

Or… maybe he'd already been here before they'd set up camp and it'd been sheer luck that she hadn't run into him yet. After all, it was a big-ish kind of island and she hadn't gone touring. The volcano face had been her focus.

Well, whatever the reason, she couldn't worry about it now. He was here and she had a job to do. She'd worry about the rest once she finished.

"Alrighty then, I shall return." With a salute that would have made any general proud, Tahiti took flight eastward.

Mariana didn't watch her go. Instead, she took out her chisel to work on the crease where the eye met the nose, trying to keep another set of eyes and the slope of his nose out of her brain. Of all the islands in the Pacific, why'd *he* have to end up on this one?

Sigh. As if carving a face from a hunk of lava wasn't tough enough—an ironic term since this lava was actually called *tuff*, which was softer and more easily sculpted than lava—now she had to figure out how to get this guy away from the island before Conch showed up.

She chipped at the statue's face again, the tuff giving way beneath the Human steel tools Angel had scavenged for her. They made the process easier than if she were using native stone ones, a fact *Monsieur* Conch had pressed home on many occasions. While she would actually like to use authentic artifacts, she didn't have the luxury of time. Hence the reason she'd pre-made the obsidian-and-coral eyes and brought them with her. She'd done that to save herself time so she could focus on the rest of the work so Conch couldn't disparage her any further. The fact that he'd actually agreed to come out here—probably already gleefully anticipating another evisceration of her work—had been a coup, but her funds were going to *just* make it through her schedule, so it was sink-or-swim time. She *had* to be finished. But now she had something else to worry about.

She stared out at the sea while shaping the slope of

the nose. Sculpting usually relaxed her, but even the view couldn't take the edge off. Pity, because the sunlight was trickling over the wave crests like diamonds spilling from kimberlite tubes onto the ocean floor, and the breeze lifted the hair from her nape, the perfect temperature to do what she loved most. It was interesting how she'd never appreciated the sea breeze's coolness until she'd started spending hours on land. The sun, too, was more of a factor than when she was in the water, sweat being one of the more uncomfortable facets of this project.

Gravity, too, as she adjusted her seat on the rock, then twisted her back to get out some of the kinks. She couldn't wait to be finished and get back into the ocean where she belonged. *Away* from the Human.

She looked at the slab of coarse stone where she sat. It was too much effort to climb down to pour fresh water over herself to cool down. The trip back up would undo any benefit.

She sighed and smoothed a divot on the curve of the cheek. Artists suffered for their art, and she was most definitely doing that. Conch would *have* to see that when he looked at this piece. He'd *have* to give her her due.

"Hey, Princess!"

Her hand slipped, giving the statue a scar. Damn. More things to fix. This guy was causing her all sorts of extra work.

She adjusted her hold and ignored the pain-in-the-butt—the one on the sand.

"Yoo hoo, Princess!"

She gave the chisel an extra hard tap, taking another chip out in the quest to smooth over the scar—*and* take out her frustration on being interrupted.

"I know you can hear me. I can hear you muttering."

"No you can't." Damn it; she shouldn't have replied. "Because I wasn't muttering."

"Hmmm. I could have sworn I heard it."

"It was me," came a whispered squawk from the top of the palm tree.

Apparently, Tahiti was not only a fast flier, but a silent one.

"Okay, okay, you caught me. I was muttering." Mariana slid the chisel back into her tool belt, catching some of his shirt on its way there.

Thank the gods Tahiti had swiped the clothing, and thank the gods he hadn't asked how she'd come by it, but he would at some point. She needed a failsafe story.

"Well, now that that's cleared up, Princess, how about some lunch?"

She glanced down at him, but the sun bounced off the sand, blinding her. She shielded her eyes. "Not hungry."

"I'm not buying that. You gotta keep your strength up to climb mountains, you know." He waved his arms. "I've got an assortment of fruit and fish on the grill down here."

She followed where he pointed and, sure enough, there was smoke. "How'd you make fire?" Did Humans carry flint around with them? "Did matches survive your sinking ship?"

"Waterproof. Genius invention."

Did the guy have an answer for everything? Well, everything except how to get *off* the island.

Maybe they could work on that. The sooner he was gone, the sooner she could work uninterrupted.

But lunch wasn't a bad idea actually. It'd be quicker to eat what he'd prepared than find and make her own food. Not to mention, she could get some fresh water to cool down, plus, this would be the perfect opportunity to put a barnacle in his ear about finding a way off the island. That kayak wasn't a bad option—especially if she rounded up a few dolphins to ensure he made it back safely. He wouldn't have to know; dolphins befriended Humans all the time in the so-called wild, so it wouldn't be odd. "I'll be right down."

"You will?"

Ha! She'd surprised him. Good. It was never a good idea to be predictable. "Don't sound so surprised. You did invite me, after all."

"That I did. Be careful getting down. Wouldn't want you to scratch those gorgeous legs."

There was nothing gorgeous about legs and she had half a mind to tell him so, but it would mean more explanation than she wanted to give, so she bit back the words and worked on climbing down without injuring herself—

Not because she took his advice to heart.

Call him shocked; she'd actually taken him up on his offer.

Good thing he'd actually caught a few fish.

Good thing she hadn't seen him do it, because, let's face it, it was far easier to grab them when he didn't have to keep coming up for air every thirty seconds like a Human. He'd gone after an assortment, considering she was used to eating like a, well, princess.

"I can't believe you went hunting," Merc said as he side-scuttled across the sand, following Jace back to camp. "Don't you feel bad? Those are your constituents you're eating."

"Says the guy who picks apart dead things on the ocean floor." Jace ran a tattered t-shirt through his hair to dry it—didn't need any seawater getting on Mariana—

then picked up the stick to poke the mackerel to make sure it was done. So much easier to cook on land than with magma wells under the water. Here, when the cooked fish fell apart, it didn't float away.

Merc huffed as he made it back to the fire. "At least they're already dead. And mostly unrecognizable so I don't know who I'm eating. That's more than I can say for you."

"Not having this discussion, Merc. It's called survival of the fittest for a reason." He flicked a charred tail toward the crab. "Here you go. House specialty. Enjoy."

Merc's eye stalk swung from the tail to the sea, then back again.

"Seriously, Merc, it's okay. Everyone's gotta eat. And better to eat than be eaten."

"True that." Merc snapped up the tail in his pincer, then scuttled off behind a clump of coconut husks.

Jace, enjoying the peace and quiet from the over-judgmental crustacean, pulled out the palm frond mats he'd woven and slid a banana tree leaf under one of the fish, transferring it to the coconut bowl he'd hollowed out. A second coconut shell held a mix of local island fruit, and the spork he'd made out of a tree branch was pretty decent if he did say so himself. He could have pulled the dishware and utensils out of the box he'd buried under the hut, but that would involve an explanation he wasn't planning to give her because he doubted she'd believe that cookware had been on his mind as his supposed ship had been supposedly sinking.

An abandoned sea turtle shell he'd found on the beach made a decent table and an old tarp would do as a rug to keep the sand from creeping where she wouldn't enjoy sand creeping. A set of coconuts with a hole knocked into them to provide liquid refreshment, and it was a pretty decent meal if he did say so himself. It was too bad, though, that he didn't have any candles or a bottle of wine to really set the mood for seduction.

Then again, this was lunch—not exactly the best time to seduce someone. Especially someone who was intent on getting back to work. He couldn't believe she'd actually agreed to come down for this meal.

And he couldn't believe how gorgeous she was as she walked out of the vegetation. True, the royal family was known for being pleasing to the eye, but Mariana? She was beyond *pleasing*.

"You've been busy." She pointed to the table.

He slid a coconut drink closer to the middle so it wouldn't slide off. "*Inspired* is more the term."

She cocked one of those luscious hips and arched an eyebrow. "Uh huh."

He bit back a smile. She was as female as any he'd ever met and there'd been a flash of appreciation in her eyes before she got all *bored* on him. She wasn't as disinterested as she wanted him to think.

Or as she wanted to be.

Now, to get her *more* interested. Well, more interested in *him* than that statue.

It *was* a tough job, but someone had to seduce the princess.

He held out a hand. "My lady?"

She rolled her eyes.

But she did take his hand.

And, holy monkfish, he was *not* prepared for *that*. *Day-um*, the woman was packing some serious heat. And all with just the touch of her fingers.

He was majorly looking forward to other body parts if he reacted like this to fingers.

Yeah, seriously tough job he had ahead of him.

Or maybe that was a *hard* job…

"Quite the spread you have here." She crossed her legs under her as she sat at the table. "You have fishing gear?"

"It was in the kayak." Damn, he hadn't thought about the logistics. Still, that was as good a rationale as any.

"And some seriously good bait it seems." She reached for the spork and studied it. "This is an interesting thingamabob."

Probably had never seen one.

"It'll work in a pinch." He took the seat opposite her and picked up his drink. "Here's to many more lunches."

She arched an eyebrow. "Why do I get the feeling you're not in any hurry to get rescued?"

He took a sip, then shrugged as he set the drink back on the table. "I've got two weeks 'til your boat shows up. Being shipwrecked could be a whole lot worse because, call me crazy, but I can use the vacay. I mean, I might not have room service, but I also don't have a hotel bill or have to deal with crowds, and the views are to-die for. Present company included." Without giving her time to respond—or scoff—he slid the banana leaf cover from the fish he'd cooked over some old metal grillwork he'd salvaged eons ago (but would claim came from his ship if she asked). "Bon appetite."

Her eyes widened. "So, if you're not Hollywood, are you a chef?" She tentatively poked at the fish as if it'd leap up off the "plate" and bite her.

He bit back a smile. He could cook himself a decent meal, but chef material he was not. "I got lucky and caught this guy early on, so I had some time to prep him. Not like I've got anything else to do. Unlike you." He scooped up a helping for himself then let himself enjoy it—giving her the opening to respond.

She didn't take it.

"So… this big carving project." He cut into a rambutan, peeling back the spiky, hairy covering, then removing the pit before popping the grape-sized white fruit into his mouth. Some of the best things about living *out* of the sea were the different fruits, some of which he'd imported ages ago. Anyone discovering the island would think seeds had been carried by sea birds. "Why are you doing it? Someone commission you or are you just into hard rock between your legs?" He tried not to smile, but that was one of his better double-entendres and he couldn't *not* gloat.

She, however, just raised an eyebrow. "Ah, I get it now. You're the product of some weird, socio-science experiment that's made you a teenaged boy trapped in a man's body."

At least she'd noticed it was a man's body.

He licked a drip of rambutan juice from the corner of his mouth with his tongue.

She stared at him a second too long—long enough to make the corner of his mouth twitch—but he didn't smile. Nope. Let her think she was calling the shots.

"So where did you learn to cook on a deserted island?" She helped herself to a slice of pineapple.

"But I'm not on a deserted island. You're here."

She took a bite out of the circle, *rind included.* "Are you always going to answer my question with a question?"

"That wasn't a question; it was a statement."

"A contrary one. Which is what you seem to come up with."

"Maybe I'm a contrary sort of guy."

She pulled the half-circle of pineapple out of her mouth. "Are you?"

"Am I what?"

She huffed and tossed the fruit onto the table. "Never mind. You just answered it." She dabbed the corner of her mouth with a banana leaf. "So… dude." She arched an eyebrow, but he didn't fill in the blank with his name.

Just to be that contrary sort of guy he'd said he was.

He didn't really care if she knew his name or not—his *current* name. The real one? The one he'd been given at birth? Yeah, that one was staying under wraps. No one knew that one except the head of his security and Merc—*and*, of course, his brother and every member of the civilization he'd left behind. No, Jason Pontus was dead to that world and it was best he stayed that way.

She glared at him. "How did you happen to come to be in this part of the world?"

"Boat. I don't see a landing strip around here, do you?" The island wasn't big enough for one, which was an added reason he'd set up shop here. This place was a mere speck in the Pacific Ocean and far enough from any land or shipping lanes that it'd been the perfect set up for, like, ever. At least, until she'd come along.

"You know what I mean."

He shrugged. "I thought I did, but given that look you're leveling at me, I guess I don't." He helped himself to a prawn. He'd thought about saving them for dinner since he wasn't sure he'd have the time to do some surreptitious fishing, but, well, he liked prawns. He'd found the troupe of them in a sandbar offshore, and one thing had led to another and voilà! Prawns for lunch.

He'd really like a nice sav blanc to go with them, but there was no way he could explain a bottle of wine. Maybe he'd have to "find" some rum tonight hidden in one of the caves around the island.

Mariana took a deep breath—which did all sorts of nice things to her chest. (Yeah, he was a dogfish for noticing.) "Okay, Mr. Picky, what do you do for a living that you're sailing around the Pacific in a boat small enough to wreck?"

"Hey, it was a pretty rogue wave."

"Oh, really? When? Because I haven't heard of any in this neck of the coral reef lately."

Ha, with her trying to pass for Human, that sentence gave her away because, the fact was, Mariana Tritone *would* have heard about a rogue wave since things like that tended to get around. While body-surfing was fun, no one—Mer or Human—enjoyed getting caught in that undertow, so the news of a rogue typically traveled faster than the wave itself. Which was saying something.

He sliced open another rambutan. They were so much better out of water than under it. "Honestly, I'm not quite sure when it all happened. I was on vacation and tried not to keep track of time, just enjoying being one with the scenery, you know?"

"Sounds pretty irresponsible to me. I'm guessing you're not an America's Cup champ then?"

"Funny." Not. She had a tongue on her.

Wouldn't you like to find out…

He ran a hand through his hair, tugging a bit to get his focus where it needed to be. "All I know was that I was in the kayak for a while after the boat sank. Days. Not quite sure how long. I landed on this island more dead than alive, and thankful for it, but I kind of lost track making shelter and getting food. You know, that survivalist sort of thing."

He liked her wearing his shirt. Maybe more than he should if his plan was to seduce her into not finishing the statue. He didn't need any emotional entanglements; he hadn't survived this long by getting emotionally involved with anyone, *especially* someone of the current royal family.

Still, his shirt hung on her, and with a couple of buttons missing, provocatively so. Besides, sexual attraction did not mean emotional entanglement, and he'd better remember that he knew that.

She cocked her head and her lustrous green hair spilled across her breasts. "You're avoiding my question."

Yes, he was. "No, I'm not. I just don't know the answer so…" He picked up a prawn and waved it under her nose. "Moving on."

She snatched it, looking angry enough to bite the head off.

Which is what Mers did, but that would be a dead giveaway that she wasn't Human, so he had to hand it to her when she set the thing down and used the scallop shell he'd put at her place setting like a knife to detach the head.

Still, using that shell was another giveaway of her heritage.

She removed the exoskeleton and legs as if she'd done it for a lifetime—which she had—then tossed the prawn into her mouth, chewing furiously.

Her cheeks blazed in anger, and her eyes seemed to become so purple they were almost black. She really was a pretty little thing.

He bit back a smile. She'd kill him for calling her that. And he wouldn't blame her. No Mer wanted to be called tiny. Or a *thing*, but that was a whole other kettle of fish.

It wasn't that she was tiny that attracted him—though she was—but being a Mer meant she was strong in ways Human women couldn't be, no matter how often they worked out. He had first-hand knowledge of the differences. Swimming through the seas required muscles Humans couldn't develop without the aid of steroids, but, even then, the muscles wouldn't be as sleek as Mariana's.

He probably shouldn't be thinking about that now. Not if he wanted to get her off his island with his anonymity, his heart, *and* his life intact.

Right. He had one job to do and that was to seduce her until she couldn't see straight enough to finish her statue by the time her rescue mission returned to get her.

Not a bad gig if he could get it.

Chapter Six

Who did this guy think he was?

Mariana tried to keep her eye-rolling to a minimum, but, seriously, he thought he was the gods' gift to women. And, in his world, maybe he was, but where she came from? Notsomuch.

Sure, he was good-looking—if she cared to look. Which she did not. She had too much on her banana leaf to care what some guy looked like or if he was built nice—damn, he was.

She shook her head. Sure, she had needs, but those were momentary itches—and something she didn't really need a man to scratch if she were honest. But none of that mattered until she finished what she'd come here to do, so why was she lollygagging around lunch when she ought to be on the rockface? She was not here to be charmed.

"You know… you're really beautiful."

Someone needed to tell that to her ego.

She swallowed the final bite of the prawn. "And *you* are avoiding telling me anything about yourself."

He leaned back onto his hands, his ab muscles contracting way too nicely for her peace of mind.

"Me? I'm an open book. Ask away."

She tapped the turtle shell table with the fork/spoon thing. "What's your name?"

A sexy smile slid across his face. "What do you want it to be?"

She tossed the utensil onto the tabletop and got to her feet. "Okay, that's it. Thanks for lunch. I have to get going."

"Hey, wait a minute." He stood much faster than she had. She'd have to work on that. "You don't need to go anywhere."

"Look, Whatever-Your-Name-Is, I don't have time to be chasing my tail—" oops, bad idiom choice, but since he didn't know about Mers, he'd take it as a figure of speech— "with someone who's about as substantial as St. Elmo's Fire."

"Hey, St. Elmo's fire is a real thing."

She tugged the shirt—*his* shirt—back into place. "And it's fleeting. Which is the best description I can come up with for any sort of honest conversation with you, and, frankly, I don't have time for it." She spun on her heel—not an easy feat in sand—then headed back to the lava.

"But we haven't talked about dinner."

That stopped her because it was so unexpected.

She turned around. "*Dinner*? What is this, a restaurant?"

He shrugged. "It's not like I've got anything better to do."

"But *I* do."

"I know, and I'll let you get back to your work if you just want to give me a rundown of your likes and dislikes. Any allergies?"

Was he for real? Mariana glanced up at the sculpture. She really needed to get back to work. Her momentary thoughts as to eating while she was here had been to take a swim each night and gather what she could, then let her tail dry out by moonlight so she'd be ready to work in the morning. But since she wasn't going to be able to do that every night with him around, this conversation was actually an important one to have since Mers needed a lot of calories. Already she could feel her abdomen contracting.

She put a smile on her face and turned around. "Um, no allergies, and honestly, I'm not picky about food. We have a limited selection here, so whatever you can come up with is fine by me."

"Oh, so now I'm your personal chef?"

She felt herself blush. She *was* presuming a lot, wasn't she? As a member of the royal family, she was used to being catered to, but this guy—whatever-the-Hades-his-name-was—didn't know that. "Well, I just figured rescuing was a good exchange for meals?"

"Ah, that's how you're going to play it, huh?" He brushed off his legs and she caught herself staring at them. They were different than hers. Longer, more muscle, hair. Not bad, actually.

He was far too attractive for her peace of mind.

She *did* roll her eyes at that thought. Her career was on the line and she was noticing his looks? That thought, alone, ought to have her swimming for the seamount. She wasn't going to put any man above her career. Her future. "Look, I really have to get back to work, and since I can only work in the daylight, dinner's not really a consideration for me until sundown."

"Hard to go foraging by moonlight, though."

But not under the sea… Which he couldn't know about.

Damn, he was messing with her timeline—and when he smiled like that, her nerve endings.

She exhaled. Avoiding the conversation wasn't going to make it go away. The guy was fixated on dinner and she was fixated on him not finding out she was a Mer. "Um, okay. There's always coconut."

"You know, for someone who's carving a mountain, you really don't think all that big about anything else, do you?"

Um...

She forced her gaze to stay on his face. Why was it she heard suggestive talk where none should be? The sun had to have done a number on her brain if she was going *there* about him. "Then what do *you* want?" Damn, her voice was husky.

His eyes narrowed.

Gods, had he noticed? Did he have an inkling what she was thinking? She'd die of mortification if he did.

But not until *after* she finished the sculpture. If she was going to leave this world, she was going to leave her mark on it beforehand.

"What I want and what we can have are two very different things."

Was there an underlying meaning to that sentence?

Gods, she just wanted off this island and out of his presence. He could completely derail her plan. Stop her from achieving her lifelong goal. For what? A pair of sexy legs and a smile that could outdo the sun for its shine?

Oh good gods, she was losing it.

"Look… whoever-you-are. I honestly don't care what we eat. We're only here for two more weeks, so sustenance is fine. More of that fruit, any left-over fish, whatever. I wasn't planning for this to be a stay at the Royal Atlantian." Oh, crap. That hotel in the Bahamas was called Atlantis; the one she'd named was the one actually *in* Atlantis. Thank the gods he didn't know any of this.

"Didn't you bring any food?" He crossed his arms, a little smile playing about his lips.

He had nice lips. That bottom one was plump enough to…

She exhaled. Sunstroke, that's what this was. And it needed to stop. Now.

And she needed to come up with a believable reason for not having the typical Human food. "Actually, I didn't bring food with me because of storage concerns. I knew there was enough here to get me through, and I brought fishing gear, too." She crossed her fingers behind her back and made a note to have Tahiti send one of the albatrosses on a mission to find a rod. Too bad Tahiti couldn't fly far enough; it'd taken a lot of driftwood, some obliging dolphins, and a floating island of plastic which was so sad that Mariana could barely think about it to get Tahiti to this island since she couldn't make the full distance in one flight. "And there's the fresh water pool, so that's covered."

"Thought of everything, have you?"

She cocked her head. "You make that sound like a crime."

"Did I?" He picked up his coconut and took a sip. "Sorry about that. I guess I just wasn't expecting to have someone show up on the island. Talk about a relief."

He sounded anything *but* relieved. He actually sounded annoyed.

She picked up her own coconut. "So, we're good on the dinner thing then, yes?" Without giving him the chance to answer, she turned away to head back to work. "I'll see you at sunset."

But then she'd have the night to contend with…

Chapter Seven

Four hours later, she threw her tools down in disgust.

What was it with that guy? The entire time she'd been working this afternoon, all she'd been picturing was *his* face. *And* the fact that she didn't know his name. He needed a name—if only so she could curse him because the nose she'd just honed didn't look like it should.

The Moai had long, broad noses which was what she'd been going for. *Until him.* And now she was going to have to figure out how to re-work this nose to get it back to what it should be. Which was going to wreak havoc with her proportions, and then her timeline would be shot.

She'd like to shoot him. Why'd he have to be here? When she'd found the island months ago, the shack had been a cyclone away from demolition, the remnant of some long-dead lost seafarer, and no one had been here.

She should have checked it when she'd come back this time, but who would have expected a shipwreck survivor? The odds had to be astronomical.

Thank the gods he hadn't caught her in the water or drying out her tail. When she thought of what could have happened if he had...

And now that he knew *she* was the artist, the Human world would learn its origins. That wasn't what she'd wanted; only Mers could know, otherwise Humans would want to know all about her. They were like that, those Humans. Too damn inquisitive for their—and her—own good. Maybe she *should* have dolphins escort him off the island—right into a hunting pod of hungry orcas. That would take care of the threat of him telling what he knew.

Thankfully, though, that was *all* he knew. If he knew she was a Mer...

She'd have to kill him. Either that or she'd be sent to trial, which meant she could forget making her name with her art. The one thing she definitely did not want to be known for was breaking the most important law of her world.

"You done yet?" Tahiti landed on top of the head, adding a squawk on the off-chance Mariana didn't recognize the voice.

"I wish." She set her tools in the belt then scrubbed her face. She had another hour until sunset, but with the way today's work had been going, she'd probably end up elongating the eyes and making the brow less broad, maybe adding some long lashes that would make any woman envious, and give the cheekbones an added sculpting to capture the way they narrowed down to those lips— "Did you have Nalu send someone off for fishing gear, Tahiti?"

The macaw flicked her feathers like fingers. "Of course. Don't I always do what you ask?"

Mariana raised her eyebrows. "Um... need I remind

you of the time I'd told you to put the diamonds back in the kimberlite vein—"

"Hey, if that stupid moon jelly hadn't drifted off course past that Human's boat, they'd have been back where they should have been and he never would have seen them."

"And yet, it did and he did."

"Yeah, well it's not my fault moon jellies are directionally challenged." Tahiti angled her wings as if she were resting them on non-existent hips. "Besides, Reel ended up getting the woman of his dreams, so all's well that ended well. You ought to be thanking me—"

"*Thank* you for setting up my brother to get mortality and leave the sea? I love Erica, but she's not worth losing my brother."

Tahiti leaned so far down Mariana was surprised she didn't slip off the rock face. "What about those babies of theirs?"

Mariana couldn't stop the smile that sprang to her face. Reel and Erica's kids were perfect. And the fact that they could breathe underwater only had a little bit to do with that.

"See? Humans are good for somethin'. Well, besides popcorn, that is." Tahiti had mastered the art of playing up to Humans just enough to have them feed her but from far enough away that they couldn't touch her.

Mariana exhaled, a much more cleansing action on land than in water. She was tired; dealing with a contrary macaw wasn't high on her list of Likes. "That's all water under the bridge, Tahiti, since what's done is done, but you didn't answer my question. Do we have a fishing rod or not?"

"*We* do not. You, however, do." Tahiti nuzzled her

back with her beak, then withdrew the one purple feather she had. "Now look what you made me do. I'm so riddled with guilt, I'm molting. And my pride-and-joy feather, too." She tried to poke it back into its place. "Ouch. That hurts more than plucking." She extended it to Mariana. "Will you hold onto this in case it doesn't grow back? I want to remember how I used to be."

Forget What's-His-Name; *Tahiti* ought to head to Hollywood.

Mariana stuffed the feather into her work belt. "I'll guard it like it's my own. Now, where's this rod?"

"Back in Atlantis on the throne?" Tahiti smacked the tuff with a talon, chinking a small—thankfully—piece away as she guffawed. "Get it? Fishing rod… your brother Rod?"

Mariana rolled her eyes. As if the puns were anything new. She'd grown up with them. "Tahiti. Get a hold of yourself. Where's the fishing rod?"

"Down there." The bird swept her vibrant wing toward the pool. "Outta sight like you wanted."

"Okay. Good. Thank you."

"Sure thing. Now, about my feather." Tahiti paced, tapping her beak with one of her primary feathers. "Do you think if I found a bower bird, he could give me a weave? They do such beautiful work on their houses. Well, except for Horace. That last abode he made had looked a little too lean-to-ish for my tastes—and the rest of the bower population's as well apparently, since he ended up a bachelor."

Mariana held out the feather. She knew where this conversation was headed. "Do you want me to arrange transport to the closest colony?"

Tahiti plucked the feather from Mariana's fingers, thankfully a little more circumspect with her beak around digits than her talons were around rock. "If you wouldn't mind."

Which meant Mariana had to get down to the ocean now to contact a messenger to find a pod of pilot whales heading to Polynesia—both the islands *and* Tahiti's great-aunt.

Mariana swiveled the tools into place around her waist for climbing, then swung a leg out of her straddle. So much for hitting her daily goal, but she really wasn't feeling it anyway.

A professional artist might have the luxury of waiting for inspiration to strike, but you do not. *You have a limited amount of time, a limited budget, and a limited shelf life to accomplish this. The longer you go without producing anything worthwhile, the more it'll reinforce Conch's estimation of your talent.*

Or maybe she just didn't have enough talent.

She plunked her butt onto the rock, which should have hurt more than her self-doubt… but didn't.

What if she *didn't* have enough talent? What if Conch was right? What if all her accolades *were* because she was a member of the royal family and most of their population wouldn't disparage the daughter of their ruler? What if she wasn't as talented as she thought she was?

No, that wasn't it. It *couldn't* be. She *was* good. She knew her stuff—the nose debacle notwithstanding, and *that* she blamed directly on What's-His-Name. Now, if she could just get him out of her head, she could laser her focus back onto this hunk of lava and get the job done without these stupid head games or wasting time.

If only she didn't have to keep running into him, but the island wasn't big enough to avoid it now that each knew the other was here.

And she did like having him prepare meals for her—ones better than she'd been planning on…

Too bad there *wasn't* any rum here; she could at least have him passed out for a good portion of the day.

She looked out at sea. *Actually…* there were more than enough shipwrecks around here that a bottle or two—or twenty—could wash up on shore for him to partake…

A bit of scavenging, some wave action… It wouldn't take much at all…

She grimaced. Not one of her prouder moments, but if she didn't pull off this sculpture, she didn't have a future in the art world, and if she didn't have a future in the art world, she didn't have a future, period. Sculpting was the only thing she wanted to do. The only thing she *knew* to do. It was her calling. More than that, it was her legacy. Her siblings had chosen love and marriage and the Immortality that came with it. She'd chosen differently. The art would outlive her. Its immortality would be hers. It had to be enough.

And since she didn't want to trade in on her family's name to earn her career… Well, if it involved a little too much rum for her island-mate, he was, after all, the one who'd suggested it. It wasn't as if she could force him to drink it—not that she would if she could—but having the option available to him might be the thing she needed to enable her to fully focus on her work.

Okay, then, she had work to do. "All right, Tahiti, let's get you on your way."

The bird looked up from where she was trying a one-beak weave with the feather. "Mfwfwh?" She spat it out. "Um… okay? I thought that was the plan."

It was for Tahiti, but Mariana had a whole other one.

Chapter Eight

Jace scanned the beach one more time before he walked out of the ocean. Not that his nudity was a problem; he was more concerned that she'd taken note of how long he'd been out there or that he hadn't surfaced for air.

Since she was nowhere in sight, he dove under once more, stashing the bottle behind a triton shell—ah, the irony—he'd jammed into the sand. With luck—and his extensive knowledge of wave effect on sand—the shell should dislodge just as they were finishing dinner. Then the bottle would wash ashore so they could enjoy it.

He'd made sure he'd found a full bottle; Mer tolerance to alcohol was higher than Humans', so they'd need a lot to put his plan in motion.

He winced. He'd never *had* to get a woman drunk to get her into bed, but desperate times called for desperate measures and her statue had to go. This wasn't one of his prouder moments, but he wasn't going to do anything she didn't want him to; he just needed her to relax a little. Let her guard down. Get comfy with him.

Then they could get comfy together.

This time, he grimaced. Maybe this wasn't such a good idea. Maybe he ought to just tell her who he was and explain the situation, and then she'd take pity on him and stop sculptin—

There were so many things wrong with that thought, he didn't know where to begin. He didn't like to be pitied; there was no way she'd keep the secret if she knew who he really was, and he didn't want to put himself at anyone's mercy.

Plus, he *wanted* to get comfy with her.

That was the truth and why he'd gone for the rum in the first place.

He took one last look at the triton shell. All he'd done, really, was set up the possibility; it was up to her if anything happened. After all, it wasn't as if he was going to force her to drink it.

He made it halfway up the beach when he admitted that he couldn't live with himself if he went through with this setup. This wasn't who he was. He could rationalize it all he wanted, but, in the end, he had an ulterior motive, so that made any move he put on her suspect.

In his real life, his day-to-day, he wouldn't have come in contact with her. Even if it'd been a normal meeting on the beach on the island where her brother Reel lived with his wife Erica and the royal family made pilgrimages to on occasion (if Humans only knew!), he always stayed far away from those meet-ups. All it would take would be one little inconsequential mistake of saying or doing something a Human wouldn't know, and they'd pick up on it. Like he had when she'd eaten the pineapple rind. Humans didn't do that.

And *he* couldn't do this.

Sighing, Jace turned around and strode back to the bottle of rum. Nothing good ever came from a bottle of rum; hadn't he seen enough proof over the centuries?

He grabbed the bottle neck and pulled it from the sand, then heaved it over his shoulder, tossing it far enough that, if the waves *did* happen to bring it back to shore, it'd be long after tonight's dinner was over and the temptation removed.

He'd find some other way to get her to stop carving that statue.

~~~

Mariana waved goodbye to Tahiti as the bird flew off into the sunset. The pod was close enough for Tahiti to make it before nightfall, and Shauna, the matriarch, had personally promised to keep Tahiti above water for the night. Between Tahiti flying and the whales resurfacing every fifty miles or so, the macaw would get to where she wanted to be.

The bird out of sight, Mariana glanced behind her. No sign of What's-His-Name. Perfect.

Keeping behind the water line, Mariana scuffed through the dry sand, keeping an eye out for any creature she could find that wasn't an avian. Birds were the biggest gossips on the planet and with their wing speed, word would get out before she could get back to work. She didn't need every flock knowing her business.

Luckily, she saw a marine iguana sunning itself on a chunk of lava instead.

"Aloha, e kōkua mai," she called, waving when it
~~~

opened the eye on this side of its head. "I'm wondering if you could give me a hand?"

The lizard snapped its jaw. "I don't have hands, Human—*espera*. How did you know the code for speech? Humans don't know that."

"Because I'm not a Human."

The lizard turned its head, looking her up-and-down. "You appear to be one."

"I'm a Mer. I'm just, you know, in disguise at the moment."

"Ah. *Comprendo*." The lizard went back to sunning itself, as if seeing a landed Mer was a normal occurrence.

She might want to ask him about that. Rod would like to know who was being so cavalier with their hidden-from-Humans status. "I was wondering—"

The iguana snorted salt out of its nose. "And I was sleeping. Looks like we're both left wanting."

He adjusted his grip on the rock and flicked his long tail to the other side.

Rude. If he knew who she was—

But she couldn't tell him. With that attitude, he'd leak the news just to piss her off. Maybe she should find another creature to help her.

Problem was, the beach looked deserted and he really was perfect for the job: able to swim quickly while holding his breath for a while and had claws to grip a rum bottle if there were no octopi about.

But, yet, he shouldn't even *be* here. Marine iguanas lived on the Galapagos Islands and those were thousands of leagues away. "What are you doing here?"

He snorted out another round of salt. "*Dios*. I *was* trying to warm up, but I guess that will not happen now." He hefted himself to face her. "What is it you need help with so I can go back to my nap? And if it's food you want, scavenge around on the ground. I'm not up to climbing a palm tree for coconuts. They fall on their own anyway when they're ready."

"That's okay, I'm good with coconuts. No, I need you to get a message to an octopus for me."

"*¿Yo?* You're the one who lives in the water. I just visit it." He shook his back. "It's going to be a bit *frio* this evening for a swim. In case you aren't aware—and seeing that you're not typically on land so I don't know why you would be—I need the sun to warm myself back up. It's going to be going down soon. That's called a sunset."

He was speaking to her as if she were a child. "I know what a sunset is."

"*Claro que si.* I have seen your kind surfacing to watch them. *Muy hermosa,* you know. The sunset, that is, not the Mers. Though I don't have anything against Mers, *¿comprende?*"

"*Sí, comprendo.*" She lifted her hair off the back of her neck. He might be chilly, but hair got heavy and hot on land in the sun. "But I can't go in the water for reasons I'd rather not go into at the moment. I could make a fire to warm you back up when you return." Thankfully, she'd brought flint on this trip, so that, along with her chisel, kept her from having to search for What's-His-Name's stash. "I wouldn't ask if it weren't important. Please. It shouldn't take long."

The iguana snorted twice as much salt. Really a gross habit, especially since he wore half of it on his head. And yet, some female iguana would find this sexy. Go figure.

"I can see that you are not going to let this go." Another snort. "*Bueno. ¿Que quiere?*"

"I'd like you to locate an octopus and ask her if she could find a bottle of rum from one of the sunken ships around here, then have her bring it around to the western beach and let it wash ashore. As soon as possible, if you wouldn't mind."

The iguana flicked the tip of his tail. "What do you need with a bottle of rum? Most people would give their right eye—and full wallet, which men do—to be on this beautiful island away from the hustle and bustle of real life. I'm telling you that you will never see a sunset as *bellisima* as one from this island. You should stay sober for it."

She refused to let his words guilt her into not doing this. She just needed the Human to be hung-over tomorrow. And the next day and the one after that. That's all. Besides, *he* was the one who'd said he wished he'd found some. Where was the harm?

Yes, she was swimming a thin crevice, but this was all about the greater good. Her artwork needed to be seen and appreciated. She needed to touch her people with her work to leave her mark, otherwise, she'd just be some hanger-on member of the royal family. Reel was on land, no longer a part of royal life, Rod was the ruler, Angel was providing a societal service, and Pearl would probably do something equally beneficial, but all Mariana had to offer the world was her art. "I'm not going to drink it. It's for my… work. The sculpture."

"Oh, so *you're* the one defacing the island?"

"I'm not defacing it. I'm sculpting a face into the rock."

"Because this *isla* needs one of those? Aren't there enough on *la Isla de Pascuas*?"

Easter Island's statues had all been toppled due to intertribal warfare over two hundred *selinos* ago. The ones that were currently standing had been uprighted by an archaeological team in the past fifty *selinos*. *Her* statue would be the first upright one the world would find.

"It's an important sociological work the world needs."

"It will bring Humans out in droves."

That was the exact thing What's-His-Name had said. Was this some mantra being echoed in the caves on this island?

"Perhaps, but the Mer world will appreciate it." She crossed her fingers. At the very least, *Conch* needed to appreciate it and her commitment to her art.

The iguana rotated one eye her way. "Which means *your* people will come around then, *¿si?* Do you think any of them might help a displaced iguana out? I'd like to return to *la Isla Española*. There's a certain lady there that, well, you understand, *¿no?* If it hadn't been for the sudden waterspout when I'd been searching for a tasty morsel to win her favor, I wouldn't have gotten swept out to sea. I'm sure she's incredibly worried."

Talk about serendipity… His plight would work with her plan. "I will personally escort you there myself if need be once I finish the sculpture if you'll help me with getting the message to an octopus."

He raised his reddish head. "*¿Verdad?* You give me your word?"

She nodded, tapping her heart since she couldn't do a pinky-swear with him. "I do."

"*Bien.*" He ambled off the rock. "I happen to know of a wreck not too far from here and, with all the gold spilling from its hull, I'd venture a guess it belonged to a pirate. They were known for carrying quite a bit of rum. Would you like a casket or two if our octopus *amiga* finds them?"

Tempting as that was, she didn't want What's-His-

Name to drown not only his troubles but also himself. "A bottle will be fine. Thank you so much."

"Just have that fire waiting for me when I get back, *¿vale?*"

She "*vale*-d" then watched Part One of her plan go into action.

"Do you smell smoke?" Jace sniffed the air. He'd extinguished his cook-out fire over an hour ago and doubted the smoke had lingered this long. Not with these ocean breezes.

"Smoke?" Mariana sniffed the air—she probably had a lot of practice with royal sniffs. "No, I don't. Do you think there's a fire? I could go check."

"And let all my hard work go to waste?" He flourished a hand over the spread he'd prepared, pretty darn proud of himself if anyone asked. Sweet potatoes had been a surprise find, and between them and the breadfruit, he'd filled the underground fire pit he'd had going at full force. But he'd smothered that fire and the wind hadn't shifted, so maybe the smell was just lingering on his shirt. He'd thought about not wearing one, but decided manners dictated he did.

His libido demanded he not button it.

He caught her noticing.

Points to his libido, but maybe he should have kept the rum—

No. He wasn't that guy.

"So, how'd sculpting go today? Did you give the guy an earring? Nose ring?"

"That wouldn't be culturally correct. At least, not according to the current Moai, so no. I wish I could find some scoria and make an authentic pukao for his head, but lifting it into place would be an issue. And not all of the Easter Island statues have them anyway."

"Are you talking to me or to yourself?" He voilá-ed a large elephant ear leaf off the specialty of the day with enough fanfare to get her attention, but not enough to pat himself on the back.

"What's that?" She pointed to a sweet potato.

He almost told her she was giving her Mer-ness away, but why ruin a moment? "Sweet potatoes. And I infused them with some sugar cane." He doubted she knew what that was. Sugar tended to dissolve in water too quickly to be of any use in a Mer household. "Try it. I guarantee you'll like it."

He split open the skin then scooped out a sporkful and held it to her lips.

When her lips closed around the utensil and tugged, Jace felt an answering tug in the one article of clothing he was *fully* wearing. And what a pity that was.

Maybe *he* should have had some rum; looked like he might need it.

"Oh, wow. That *is* wonderful." She held out her hand, the shirt she wore gaping a bit near her shoulder. "I *can* feed myself you know."

But it was so much nicer for him to do it—

"Uh, sure. Here you go." He handed over the utensil, then sat back and dug his butt into the sand so he wouldn't be tempted to lick the fleck of potato at the corner of her mouth.

Instead, he picked up his own spork and made himself concentrate on his own sweet potato. "So, Mariana, why the Moai? Why here?"

She tugged the shirt back into place, then glanced away, a sure sign she was about to tell a whopper.

Which meant he was going to have to work out the real reason.

"They've always fascinated me and they're indigenous to the area."

"Um, not really. They're only on Easter Island."

"I mean the Pacific as an area."

"Pretty big area."

"And yet we both ended up on the same island, so maybe it's not as big as you think."

Spoken like a true Mer who had the oceans at her disposal. As one on the lam, he needed the ocean to be big—the better to hide in. The Atlantic was a little more heavily traveled with all the cruise ships doing their island-hopping thing. Which was also the reason he stayed away from French Polynesia; this island was the last empty outpost before things got busy in the South Pacific.

None of which he could use as an argument.

Not that he ought to be arguing with her anyway. He needed to get on her good side. To intrigue her. Let his natural charm do the work it'd been doing for him for centuries.

He offered her some breadfruit. "Here, try this. Breadfruit crisps." After baking it, he'd dipped slices of it in a mango/banana puree and sautéed it on a hot rock. He'd bet she'd never had *this* in Atlantis.

"Oh my gods, this is heavenly." She closed her eyes and licked her lips, a soft "mmmmm" coming from the back of her throat, and Jace got a flash of what it'd be like to have her under him on the sand, bodies touching in all the right spots, murmuring that "mmmmm" for him.

Thank the gods for the shorts. They'd keep him from embarrassing himself way more than scales could.

He gulped and picked up his coconut milk, taking a healthy swallow as he stared inland—anywhere but at her. Gods, what he wouldn't give for a bottle of rum.

"Oh, hey." Her voice got him to look back at her—not that he really needed any reason. "What's that?"

He followed her pointing finger to see…

The bottle of rum washing up on shore.

He looked heavenward. The gods were either sending him a signal…

Or laughing their asses off.

Chapter Nine

Mariana got to her feet and grabbed the elephant ear leaf before Jace even thought about moving.

He was thinking about what that bottle of rum could represent. And why he should throw it right back into the sea.

But then she held it up—wrapped in the leaf which, as a Mer himself, he understood the no-touching-saltwater thing—as she walked back, and that idea went out of his head because who was he to question the actions of the gods?

Especially when those actions benefitted him.

"It's rum!" She held it out to him. "Want some?"

More than she could know.

He should have taken a nice long swim out to the current to deposit it there instead of merely tossing it into the waves. "You know, I think I'm going to pass."

"You're kidding me." She looked like she was about to cry.

Didn't want to drink alone?

Hmmm. He looked skyward. Never let it be said that he wasn't a gentlemer. "Well, we do have coconut." He held up his drink. "All we need is some pineapple. Too bad there's no ice."

This better be in the gods' divine plan… otherwise he might come to regret this moment.

~~~

Hera waved a hand in front of the tablet propped in front of Her husband so that clouds floated over the scene of the beach below, then She narrowed Her eyes at Zeus. "Is this some Divine Plan You like to think You can control?"

Zeus yanked the mini lightning bolts He'd been fashioning off the dining room table. She didn't like when He brought his work home with Him. "Of course not, Honey. You know I don't like to interfere in the lives of My—I mean, *Our*—creations. I gave over Free Will eons ago."

Had cost Him a really nice garden, too, dammit.

"And all it took was an apple and a snake to get you to do so." Hera brushed some cloud mist off Her *chiton,* Her eyes lingering on the tablet a moment longer than necessary. On the beach below, Jace had said something that made Mariana laugh—really laugh—and his face had done something complicated in response. Something unguarded.

Something He'd seen on Hera's face too often of late.

He watched Her watching them. "Hera—"
~~~

"Don't." She moved to the china cabinet and pulled two fluted glasses from the cabinet. "So, this isn't your doing? You're not misdirecting the waves or placing marine lizards where they shouldn't be to affect a realignment of royal Mer houses?" She raised an eyebrow as She set the glasses before Him.

It was pretty annoying that She knew Him so well. "Hera, I swear on My mother's grave that I am not doing that." No, the waves were definitely not being *mis*directed and that lizard was exactly where he should be.

But… wait. How did Hera know that Jace was from a royal house? He'd been sure to let everyone think Jason had died.

He shook His head. He'd never understand women.

"Your mother is the mother of all gods, which means that she can't die. Therefore, she can't have a grave. I wasn't born yesterday, *Dear*." Hera glared at Him. "If this is Your work and it ends badly, I am going to say, 'I told you so' for the next fifty millennia. Just so You understand the stakes."

Zeus crossed the thunderbolts under the table. "I understand, Dear. I will not interfere in whatever relationship these two have going." Well, not much. But the truth was, Jace deserved more and since Pele had come to Him to see what could be done about getting her life back, He'd had time to reflect on the whole situation. Jace had done a good deed by helping her around the turn of one of the centuries—there'd been so many Zeus couldn't keep them all straight—which had been the right thing at the time to fake her death to keep her sister, Nāmaka, off the scent. But Pele wasn't happy hiding in the shadows, sleeping in her volcano, never able to bask in the sunlight, float among the waves, go where she wanted—as any goddess wouldn't be. She wanted her life back and she was entitled to it. While Nāmaka hadn't been prepared to accept that her husband hadn't loved her, Pele—who'd caught him with a few too many Humans to believe his, "It was just this time," speech— had wanted her sister to see the truth. Her mistake had been in using herself as the setup.

Unfortunately, Nāmaka had only seen what she'd wanted to see, and anything that set Pele in a bad light had won out over the truth.

But enough was enough. Zeus agreed with Pele. And Hera would, too—if She hadn't already—and, well, even for a god, it was easier to beg forgiveness than ask permission since He'd done all of this without alerting the rest of the Pantheon—including His wife.

And, besides, while He might have put that "enhanced" rum bottle in Jace's sight in the ocean, He'd had nothing to do with it showing up on the beach. That was all Mariana's doing.

Which He found fascinating.

He stuffed the lightning bolts into His toga, then jumped onto a Roomba-like Segway made of cumulus clouds to zip into the kitchen. He passed the fridge and headed toward the pantry. He was going to need some popcorn for this show.

~~~

Mariana should probably regret this moment. After all, it really wasn't fair what she was about to do to him since Mers could drink Humans under the pier. And while
~~~

there might not be a pier here, at least there was some nice soft white sand where he could sleep it off.

"I don't think ice is going to happen, but I'll go look for a pineapple." And make a quick run back to extinguish the fire she'd made for the iguana. She hadn't figured the winds could carry the scent this way.

"Or…" He cocked an eyebrow, which was just too sexy a look on him. "We could just do shots."

Or they could do shots. It'd get him to sleep that much faster. Then again, it wasn't as if she could work on the sculpture at night. And it *would* be rather lonely with him sacked out early… "No, I'll get some pineapple. Might as well enjoy the rum." *Really, really enjoy it, dude.*

She handed him the bottle—all the better if he started without her. "You stay here. I'll be back."

It didn't take her long to make the trip back to the fire, scuff some sand over it—the iguana had already burrowed in beside it since the warmth would keep his body insulated during the night—then hurry back with a pineapple.

The bottle was still sealed.

Waggling it, he grinned. "Didn't want to start without you."

She hid a grimace. "Well, aren't *you* the gentlemer—man." Oops. Shouldn't slip up like that.

"I like to think so." He took the pineapple from her. "Have a seat. I make a mean piña colada."

She shook her head. "I was thinking it'd be nice to have a fire and sit on the beach and watch the sunset." It could be a while 'til the rum kicked in, so they might as well get comfortable.

"Whoa!" What's-His-Name made a quick dive for

one of the coconut cups as it started to roll off the shell table. "Oops. Almost knocked that off."

His smile of apology would have her forgiving him anything.

Among other things...

Oh Hades no. She headed to the small grove of coconut trees to gather dried fronds instead. The man was way too good-looking for her peace of mind *and* for her plan.

But no one would have to know...

No no no no no. *Not* a good idea.

She scooped up an armful, then tossed her hair behind her shoulder, before heading back toward the table, arguing with herself the entire time. She was *not* going to take advantage of the him.

The situation on the other hand...

She dropped the fronds by the table. No, she wasn't going to do that either. It wasn't right and it wasn't who she was. She'd make her career on honesty and integrity and ethics; anything else would be a fraud and she'd never be able to live with herself.

Still, she took the drink he handed her. One drink wouldn't hurt, after all. Not to a Mer, and, presumably, not to a Human. Especially one of his size—

Okay, she didn't need to start thinking about *that*.

"Cheers." What's-His-Name raised his cup.

She raised hers. "Ditto."

"So?" He walked around to the side of the table. "Am I right or what? I make a mean piña colada."

She licked some froth he'd somehow managed to make off her lip. "Yes, it's very good. But there's just one problem."

His left eyebrow arched—right back to being sexy.

She looked down and shuffled her feet. Dammit, she didn't want him to be sexy. She had a sculpture to finish and her career to make, and him being sexy made imbibing alcohol with him dangerous.

"And that is?"

"And what is?" She didn't remember what they'd been talking about. His sexy eyebrow had distracted her.

Oh, for Olympus' sake; since when were eyebrows sexy?

He raised the second one.

Apparently when they were attached to his face.

This was definitely *not* going how she'd planned. And thank the gods the sculpture already had eyebrows.

He raised his cup. "The problem."

"The problem?" She still didn't know what he was talking about.

"You said there was just one problem with the drink. What is it?"

That she couldn't lick it off him?

She slammed her hand over her mouth. *Please don't let me have said that out loud.*

"What's wrong?" He set his drink onto the table and got really really close to her.

Boy, was he tall.

"Did you bite your tongue? Break a tooth? I know I didn't get any of the skin in the mix when I squeezed the juice from the pineapple."

Oh thank the gods, she hadn't said it. "No, I, um..." She took a step back because she really couldn't think straight when he was standing in her personal space. "Sensitive tooth. The rum hit it and..." She shrugged, having no idea if this was even a thing.

But he seemed to buy it, so *phew*.

He exhaled. "So, the rum's the problem?"

Maybe she should take that excuse and leave the bottle for him.

But him being a gentlemer—man—he might not drink it.

Decisions, decisions. What was the problem again?

His eyes searched hers and she couldn't look away. Whoever he was, he was potent.

Whoever he was… Right. He didn't have a name. That was it. *That* was the problem.

"The problem is…" She raised the drink and nodded at him. "I'm not sure who to thank for this wonderful concoction."

A V formed between those sexy eyebrows. "Me. You thank me. Unless you see someone else around here who made it for you."

"I know *you* made it, but I don't know your name. *Still.*"

The V went away and the smile came back out. "Ah, yes, that's right. My name. You want to know it."

"I do."

"Why"

"*Why*? What kind of question is that? We're stuck here together for a while. Why *wouldn't* I want to know your name? I need something to call you."

"Call me whatever you want."

"I *want* to call you by your name. What is it?"

"Why is it important?"

"It wasn't until you refused to tell it to me."

"Now I'm wounded." He put his free hand to his chest.

And what a chest it was.

Oh for Poseidon's sake.

"My name wasn't important until you didn't get what you wanted."

It took her a second to refocus on the conversation. "I didn't say that."

He tapped his chest. "Oh, but you did."

She was really trying to get the image out of her head of *her* hand on that chest. "No, I didn't. I said—"

"That you didn't really care what my name was until I wouldn't tell you." He took another sip of his drink. "You know what that tells me about you?"

She didn't like where this conversation was headed. "What?" She raised her own eyebrow.

"That you are someone who likes getting what she wants."

"Doesn't everyone?'

"Sure, but not everyone *does* get what they want. Your irritation with me tells me that you are one of those who does."

"You make that sound like a bad thing."

"Depends on what it is you want."

Why did she get the feeling they were no longer talking about his name?

She shook her head. "What I want are two things. One, a fire, and two, your name. Why is it such a big deal?"

"Fire? Because it took man thousands of years to learn to make it and, once he did, it changed the face of evolution."

"Are you ever serious?"

The teasing light left his eyes and the smile became a flat line. "Trust me, when I have to be, I can be *dead* serious."

Again, why did she feel as if there were two meanings to his sentence?

This was getting her nowhere. "Okay, then. How about we make a bet? I win, you tell me your name."

"And if I win?"

"I'll answer a question of yours."

"What's the bet?"

She wagged a finger. "Nope. You either agree or disagree, *then* we'll discuss terms."

"You drive a hard bargain, Princess."

She couldn't hold back the wince. "Are you in or out?"

"Oh, I'm in."

He wasn't talking about the same thing she was; she knew it.

And he knew that she knew.

Maybe this wasn't such a good idea.

He crossed his arms over that really nice chest. "Unless you're changing your mind?"

"Of course not." She'd never backed down from anything in her life. Not The Council when they'd tried to hook her sister, not Conch when he'd disparaged her work, and definitely not this guy who thought he could outsmart her.

"Good. So, what's the bet?"

She brushed back her sleeves. "That I can get a coconut to go farther than you can."

The V showed up again between his eyebrows. "I have to warn you that I've got a good arm."

"And I have two of them."

That got a chuckle out of him.

Which got a different reaction inside of her.

"You're sure you want to do this?" he asked.

"Positive."

"What's the catch?"

"What makes you think there's a catch?"

"There's always a catch."

"That's rather jaded of you."

"It ought to be my middle name."

"What *is* your middle name?"

He chuckled again. "Nice try, Princess." He rubbed his hands together and cocked his head. "You're absolutely certain this is what you want to do?"

She just looked at him. She wasn't going to repeat herself.

"Okay, but I get to pick the coconuts."

She swept her hand. "Be my guest."

He jogged to where the hammock was strung between two thick palms, searched around the base, then returned with two big green ones. "I'll open these for the nut inside."

"No, these are fine."

"Princess, these are difficult for *me* to heft and my hands are bigger than yours."

She shrugged. "It's fine. Actually, better that way. I can use two hands."

Looking at her warily, he handed one over. "You want to go first?"

"Nope. You go right ahead. I want to see what I have to beat."

"Okay, then. It's your funeral." And with that, he headed toward the water.

Then he swung the large nut between his legs and sent it hurling into the ocean—

Exactly as she'd been planning to do because any distance he'd throw it on land would have been outdone by where the waves would carry hers.

He'd seen through her plan.

He turned around. "Beat that."

"You figured it out." She didn't even bother throwing hers; it would be pitiful and they both knew he'd outplayed her.

He jogged back to her. "Come on, Princess. I knew there had to be a catch so I replayed how you phrased it. You never said anything about who could *toss* one farther. Distance is a big deal on this island, so it wasn't that hard to figure out." He tapped her coconut. "Aren't you going to try to beat me?"

"We both know I won't. I'm not going to embarrass myself any more by trying." She tucked the nut against her hip. "So… you win. Congratulations. Ask away."

He put *his* hands on *his* hips and studied her. So much that it made her squirm.

Truly, it was only the fact that he was studying her like a scientist studies a subject, not the fact that his bare chest was within touching distance, nor that his forearm brushed hers ever so lightly—and the goose bumps were caused by the wind—or the fact that he smelled of the sea and masculinity, always a powerful combination on a good-looking male. Especially one she was alone with on a deserted island, thousands of leagues from another being, with the promise of a fire, and the sun spreading a rainbow across the sky as the light hissed below the horizon.

"Do you want to kiss me?"

He said it so softly that it took her a few seconds to register what he'd asked.

Yes. Say yes!

It was truly amazing how part of her was ready to fling the collective *her* off a cliff without considering the consequences.

Consequences be damned. The hot guy is asking if

you want to kiss him. Only an idiot would say no, and we're no idiot.

"Mariana?" He leaned closer, his lips inches from hers. "I asked you a question."

"I know you did."

"And what's your answer?"

She bit back a smile and tossed his words back at him. "Why is it important?"

She almost laughed at the flash of irritation that disappeared as quickly as it'd started. Two could play his game.

"Because it is." He moved closer. "*Very* important."

More goose bumps flushed over her skin. Crap. He was much better at this. And he was too sexy for her own good.

"Answer me, Mariana. That was our bet, remember?"

And she'd thought she'd been so smart suggesting this game.

But while he'd outplayed her—she'd never say he'd *outsmarted* her—she still had one ace up her sleeve. He'd been studying her mouth from the first sip of her drink… so she licked her lips. "Yeah. I remember our bet. Whatcha gonna do about it?"

Jace closed his eyes briefly and groaned. Damn, the woman knew how to play him.

And he wanted to play with her.

Deliberately, he reached for the coconut cradled in the curve of her waist on her hip.

She didn't flinch when he took it from her.

But her belly contracted when the back of his fingers skimmed her skin.

She wasn't as in control as she made out.

Made out was an interesting choice of phrase…

He tossed the coconut away, vaguely registering when it hit the sand by the spray of grains on his ankle as he cupped her cheek.

"What I'm going to do about it, Mariana, is…" With the barest of suggestions, he urged her toward him. "This."

The kiss exploded between them.

Chapter Ten

She made it a rule to never kiss anyone whose name she didn't know, yet here she was doing that very thing. And why? Because of a pair of sexy eyebrows and a bottle of rum?

Sounded like some pirate's really bad sea shanty.

Oh, gods, she was a lightweight when it came to spirits. It'd been a long time since she'd imbibed anything besides kelp wine so the rum had to have gone straight to her head; it was the only logical explana—

"Hello? Are you with me?" Mr. Hottie pulled back, his gaze all concerned and his finger tapping her temple. "I'm not used to women going blank on me while I'm kissing them."

"Maybe that's because they know your name." She was quite proud of herself for being able to look into those eyes of his and still speak coherently.

Not that she was feeling particularly coherent.

The rum must be really potent—which wasn't that difficult to believe since it'd been sitting at the bottom of the sea for a couple hundred *selinos,* which could increase the fermentation process—

"And there you go again."

"Come again?" She winced. *Really* bad choice of words—

That he'd caught onto since he looked like he'd swallowed his tongue.

That's our *job, sista.*

She shhhh'd that voice in her head. She didn't need any help with any images when it came to this guy. "Please tell me your name." The words came out in a whisper before she'd even thought them, and they sounded needy. Begging, almost.

"It's Jace," he answered just as softly, almost as if they were each speaking to themselves and didn't realize they'd said it aloud.

"Jace." She rolled the sound of it around on her tongue. He looked like a Jace. Strong, yet not overbearingly so, a hint of softness in there, but uncommon enough that you'd remember him. Yes, he looked like a Jace. "Thank you."

That seemed to bring him out of whatever rum-induced stupor *he* was in. "Damn, woman. You played me good."

"I wasn't playing."

Wouldn't mind, though...

"So you always sound so breathy and pliant when someone kisses you?"

Just you.

Thankfully, she had enough self-preservation to keep *that* little tidbit to herself.

She cleared her throat and shook her head. "Look, I just wanted to know your name, Jace. I don't get why it's such a big deal. It's a nice name." Probably would be going too far to ask his last name so she'd be content with his first. After all, that was the most personal anyway. "It beats calling you, 'Hey You.'"

"It's just a name. It doesn't define me."

She shook her head. Sounded like he had some issues when it came to his name. "Is it a family name?"

He barked out a laugh which didn't sound amused. "No. Definitely not."

She was just going to let that stay there and not push for an explanation. It'd have to do that she'd gotten his name out of him. They had almost two more weeks together; she'd find out more before then. And figure out what to do with him when Conch showed up.

"So." He stroked the back of her hand. "Now that you know my name, shall we go back to making out?"

She curled her fingers into her palm to resist returning his caress. Much as she wanted to, that was not part of her plan. "I kinda think the moment's lost."

Damn if he didn't arch that eyebrow again—and the flutter in her belly said that maybe the moment *wasn't* as lost as she thought.

"I'm all about trying to find it again. I think it started with this last time." He cupped her cheek.

Yup. That had started it.

"And then I did this." His fingers whispered along her jaw, the slightest urge for her to move closer and—

Bam! The moment was back with a resounding *crack!*

Along with thousands of droplets of rain.

"Damn it!" Jace said what she'd been about to. "A storm? Where did that come from?" He grabbed her hand and started running toward the shack.

Mariana had to concentrate on staying upright as he dragged her with him because she wasn't as coordinated with these legs and feet as he was.

Another *crack!* and a flash of light split the air beside her, and the next thing she knew, Jace was scooping her up in his arms, getting her off her feet in the nick of time as a giant palm pummeled the sand where her butt had just been.

Her butt was in a much nicer place now, bouncing along beside his abs as he sprinted the last few yards to the shack.

He kicked the door open, set her on her feet, then had the door closed right before the heavens unleashed a deluge.

"Where the hell did that come from?" Jace brushed the hair off his forehead, then leaned against the window frame. "The weather was perfect today for miles."

"You'd be surprised at how deceiving the horizon can be, distance-wise." She wrung out the tails of his shirt she was wearing in case any ocean spray was mixed in with the rain. "You wouldn't happen to have another shirt I could wear, would you? This one is soaked."

He spun around faster than a water spout.

And his eyes turned as dark and stormy as the sky behind him.

Then she looked down and saw why.

She might as well not be wearing anything for all the coverage his wet, plastered-to-her-skin shirt provided.

Good gods, she was practically naked.

Another flash of lightning only made it more apparent.

Or, rather, *trans*parent.

"Jace?"

He sucked his brain out of his shorts and back into his head at the sound of his name, and somehow managed to drag his eyes back to her face.

Just as she wrapped her arms around all that goodness.

"Uh." He cleared his throat. Twice. "What?"

"I asked if you have another shirt I could wear. This one…"

She let the words trail off because they both knew what "this one" wasn't capable of.

"Hold on." He averted his eyes, then dragged over the wooden chest of things he figured would be appropriate for him to have on the island after his supposed boat supposedly sank.

It wasn't a lot.

Thank the gods there were two shirts.

But no more shorts. Which meant a towel was going to have to suffice or nudity would come into play. While that worked for him, he had a feeling she wouldn't be jumping on that bandwagon any time soon… if at all.

If he played his cards right, however…

He tossed her the other shirt. "Turn around. I have to get out of these shorts."

It was promising that he heard her swallow.

Hard.

~~~

Zeus looked over His shoulder as Hera was taking the moussaka out of the oven, then twiddled His fingers. Rain fell harder on the little island, and, as He brushed His lightning bolts through the air, more flashes lit up the evening sky on Earth. He loved playing with weather,
~~~

especially when it served a purpose. And this purpose was two-fold.

He swept His hand, and waves crashed onto the beach, though He was careful to end them about fifty yards from the shore. Mariana had to choose to tell Jace who she was, not have it be thrust upon her by her legs turning back into a tail; that choice wasn't up to Zeus. Just like He couldn't force the words out of Jace's mouth about his name.

Nor could He force the rum *in* to loosen his tongue, but, hey, if they wanted to imbibe His special blend, that wasn't His fault. They *did* have Free Will after all.

How many times He'd cursed himself for giving it to them, but once given, it wasn't easily reclaimed, so He'd had to live with the ramifications ever since.

That didn't mean He couldn't make things easier or more difficult for them.

He puffed, and a couple of palm trees keeled over— oops, better dial back the wind gusts. He didn't want to destroy the island, just make it more desirable to be inside than out.

And, yes, *desire* was a key word for the evening.

He liked both of these beings. They were good at heart and it wasn't fair that the actions of others were directing their lives. They deserved to have their lives under their control.

Well, except for tonight. And maybe into tomorrow, too, because they were, after all, very stubborn.

He just had to make sure He didn't forget about them like when He and Hera had taken a five-week vacation a few millennia ago. If He hadn't given Noah that busy-work of building an ark, it would have been more disastrous than it had been. As it was, it'd cost Him a lot of species, and He'd had to congratulate Noah for the remainder of the man's life which hadn't been as genuine as the man had thought. But that had been what Noah had been about all along. Poor guy had had a complex about not being able to do anything right, so the ark-building was supposed to have helped him feel better about himself. Who knew he'd be the one to save the Human race in that part of the world?

Zeus shook His head. He didn't want to go through that again. Hera still didn't let Him forget that He'd been so self-indulgent on their trip that He'd forgotten all about His responsibilities.

He checked his Apple watch (He'd had the same idea, but Jobs had come up with it first, so, hey, if He didn't have to reinvent the wheel, why bother?), then snapped His fingers for the necessary *accoutrement* to make it into the shack. "Siri, set the timer for twelve hours."

That ought to give them enough time to get acquainted. Couldn't do that with Mariana up on her rock—His rock, actually, but He wasn't going to squabble about ownership—and it was about time that Jace had something good happen to him. Like Hercules, the guy was a hero, and, again like Herc when he'd first started out, no one knew it.

That was about to change. After all, if He, the head of the gods, couldn't help the guy out, no one could.

Well, except maybe Mariana.

Chapter Eleven

Jace secured the towel around his waist, then slicked his hair back one more time before exhaling and turning around.

He sucked his breath right back in.

He'd never seen a more beautiful pair of legs.

Or a sexier woman wearing his shirt.

And her hair… It was wind-tossed and as riotous as the weather outside, and he just wanted to sink his fingers into it and haul her up against him and devour her until the storm abated.

He wasn't sure the one inside of him ever would.

"What are we going to do about dinner?" She fiddled with the collar of the shirt as if food was the biggest of her problems.

Food? *That's* where she was? He was so far from food he couldn't remember the last time he'd had any.

Calm down, asshole, or you'll get her running right back out there.

Right. He didn't want to do that. He needed her to

like him. To be charmed by him. To do anything *except* go storming off in a fit of anger over something Neanderthal he'd said or done.

"I guess the sweet potatoes and breadfruit are beyond salvaging," she said, sighing.

"Yeah, probably." He ran a hand through his hair again. He'd been planning to make a supply swim next week to restock the shack since he was out of provisions—which was a good thing since a full larder would be tough to explain for a shipwreck victim. "I could run down and grab the mussels—"

A laser show of lightning ripped through the sky, thunder cracking overhead like a sonic boom.

"Or maybe not." He glanced around and saw—

Funny, he didn't remember bringing the bottle of rum in with him.

She must have.

Interesting.

"Or…" He picked up the bottle, knowing what he was about to say probably wasn't a good idea, but since he wasn't driving the show here, he was going to let it play out as the gods—or Mariana—wanted. "We can just do shots and forget all about being hungry."

She opened her mouth—he thought it was to say something, but maybe it was in surprise—but then she shut it. Then she tapped her bottom lip. "Are you trying to get me drunk?"

"Will it work?" Someone else seemed to be driving his mouth, too.

Her eyes narrowed. "What's your plan, Jace? Get me drunk and have your way with me?"

"Princess, my way doesn't seem to be the issue here." But, yeah, it wasn't a bad idea. He shook the bottle.

"So what'll it be? I Spy? Truth or Dare? Or…" He lowered his voice to its most sexy. "There's always Strip Poker."

~~~

"Zeus, dessert's ready. Put Your toys away and come back into the kitchen, please."

Damn it, just when things were getting interesting.

Zeus glanced up.

Hera, arms crossed, was tapping a wooden spoon against Her bicep.

He didn't mess with the goddess when She was in this mood. Not the sharp mood—He could handle sharp. This was the other one. The quiet one. The one he didn't have a name for but recognized like a change in atmospheric pressure.

Sighing, He waved a hand across the tablet and clouds floated across the screen. He'd done as much as He could to facilitate things; it was up the two of them now. He just hoped they didn't make the same bad decisions as that other couple in the garden had. He was rather tired of trying to save the people of this planet. Most work, by far, of any He'd created. "Coming, Dear. It smells delicious."

~~~

"I wasn't born yesterday, Jace." Mariana resisted the urge to yank the bottle out of his hand and toss it outside. That's what she *should* do, but what she *wanted* to do was to challenge him. Not to any of those games he'd mentioned, of course, but a straight-up, shots-'til-you-drop drinking contest. Four shots, tops, and he'd be flat on his back.

Which is right where we want him.

No. No she did *not* and that stupid voice could just shut up. She glanced around. The pile of blankets he'd tossed out of the trunk would have to do as a bed—for him. She'd just curl up in the corner until the storm passed, then she'd head out to the hammock—or, better yet, the ocean— because, even dead drunk, he'd be temptation.

And that's a problem because…

She fiddled with the top button of her—his—shirt. A shot contest *could* set her plan in motion… But it wouldn't be right. It wouldn't be fair to him. She was better than that… Right?

Yes. She was. She, more than most, knew that helplessness of being at someone else's mercy.

So, patting that top button to leave it alone, she straightened her shoulders. "Besides, I don't know that doing shots on an empty stomach is a smart idea."

"True. But we have to do *some*thing to pass the time." He glanced out the window just as another light show went on display. "It doesn't look like this is going to end anytime soon."

She really shouldn't. It wasn't fair to take advantage of him like this. Humans just couldn't compete with Mers when it came to alcohol. But *he* wasn't letting it go so…

"Okay, but you stay on that side of the hut—" She pulled a worn steamer trunk that must have drifted onto the island at some point away from the wall to act as both a room divider and a table. "—and I'll stay on this side." She folded her legs under her and sat. Interesting pose. Not one she could do with a tail since tails didn't have knee joints.

Jace seemed to be chewing something, though it could just be the inside of his cheek. "You sure you want to do this?"

She shrugged, trying to keep the guilt off her face. After all, *he* was the one who'd suggested it and he looked like he was all-in with the idea. Plus, she really *did* need him out for the count for as long as possible tomorrow to get work done, and it wasn't as if she was planning to take advantage of the guy; he'd just have a really long nap. Besides, with him snoring away, she'd actually be able to sleep. At least, that was the hope…

She shrugged again. "Like you said, what else do we have to do?"

The look he gave her ought to have her coming up with another option, but she wasn't thinking very hard for one.

For better or worse, this was going to play out.

He set the bottle onto the trunk, then sat across from her.

She really hoped she didn't come to regret this.

Chapter Twelve

S o how *are* we doing this? Truth or Dare? Spin the Bottle?" He looked anything *but* regretful.

"I was thinking more like tit-for-tat."

Jace choked. "Tit for what? Sign me up!"

Yeah, she'd swum right into that one, so she couldn't be disgusted with him. Still… "Must everything be about sex with you?"

"What's wrong with sex?"

"Nothing's wrong with it—"

"Phew. You had me worried there for a moment. I thought you were going to say you didn't like sex."

"I like sex just fine." Wait. How had they gotten onto her sex life?

"Good to know. With men? Not that there's anything wrong if you swim in the lady pond. Even on occasion."

She picked up the bottle and shook it. Roughly the same amount as before. "So you didn't guzzle the entire thing?"

"Of course not. I'd miss out on this tit-for-whatever you want to play." He waggled his eyebrows.

Which should have made him look ridiculous, but it only made him look sexier, sitting there with his hair slicked back from a face that looked as if *it* had been carved from stone, with those cheekbones, those arms, and a very well-defined chest that rivaled those of most men in her world, plus a smile that cut through the dark stormy sky like a slash of lightning.

And, dear gods, now she was waxing poetic? *What* was in that piña colada?

"So, are there any drinking glasses in this place or are you going to have to make a run for our coconut mugs out in that?" She tossed her head toward the door where, right on cue, another boom of thunder split the sky.

"Or we could just share the bottle. One shot for you, one for me."

The alcohol *would* kill any germs…

Who was she kidding? She'd already kissed him; she wasn't worried about germs.

Plus, then she could skimp on her shots and he'd never know. Or, if he figured it out, it'd be too late. Hopefully, a few days too late.

"Okay." She held it out to him. "Here you go."

"Nope." He shook his head, sending droplets skittering through the air.

She tucked the shirt over her legs on the off chance that any of those were seawater, though, given the pounding of the storm, she'd bet on rainwater.

"I went first last time. Your turn."

She couldn't argue that without making a bigger deal out of this than it warranted, so she took a swig.

A small one.

Still… *wow*. That rum packed quite a punch. Even with the tiny sip she'd taken, she could feel its effect. Must be a really old bottle of rum. She'd have to pace herself.

"So how do we play this tit-for-tat?"

"It's easy." She handed the bottle to him. "I ask a question, you answer it, then I have to decide if you're telling the truth or not. If I say you're lying and it's true, I drink. But if I say it's true and it *is* true, then *you* have to drink. The person asking questions keeps going until they have to drink."

"How will you know if I'm telling the truth?"

She arched an eyebrow. "You mean to tell me that you're a liar?"

The corner of his mouth ticked up. "Damn, woman, you're good. Okay okay, I concede. I'm an honorable guy and will own up to any drinks I earn. As I expect you to."

"Of course. I wouldn't have suggested this if I was planning to lie. What's the point?"

"Depends on how badly you want to get me drunk and for what purpose."

Not the one he was thinking of.

Still, she had to fight a flush of guilt from showing on her face. This was for the greater good; she had to remember that. "I'm not going to lie."

"Good. Then it's settled. We shall each be at our most truthful. So." He took a swig then held out the bottle to her. "Now that we're both liquored up as it were, you want to start? After all, ladies first."

She couldn't tell if he was being condescending or the rum had already begun to hit him. She could definitely feel it around the edges of her brain, so she was going to have to take her drinks judiciously.

"All right." She propped her elbows on the trunk and held the bottle by its neck, swinging it gently, studying him, trying to figure out her strategy.

"Seriously, Princess, there are a thousand questions you could ask."

But there weren't a thousand shots in this bottle. "Patience is a virtue I guess you're lacking."

He crossed his arms—which did really nice things to his pecs. "I didn't know this was going to take all night. There are *much* better things to do all night than answer questions."

Yeah, she got that, but that was not the point of this game, so she let the comment pass, setting her strategy in motion. She had to make her questions count. "Okay, what's your favorite color?"

He burst out laughing. "*That's* your big question? My favorite color?" He slapped his palm on the trunk. "That's easy. Green."

They both knew he was lying; he, because he thought he knew her game plan, and she, because she did. And she'd counted on him lying.

Now to see if he'd own it.

"I don't believe you." She held out the bottle.

"How can you not believe me? I thought we were supposed to be honest."

She just let the bottle swing between them.

"Fine." He huffed and took the bottle. "Favorite color is purple." He took a swig.

"Uh, buddy?" She tapped the trunk. "Take two. Your favorite color isn't purple either."

Bottle still at his lips, he turned his head and looked at her with one eye.

She swept her fingers upward. "Keep going."

Rolling that eye, he took another swig.

She knew because she watched his Adam's apple as he swallowed both times—which, interestingly, demonstrated that Adam's apples became a source of female fascination after some rum on a storm-tossed deserted island.

She needed to get off this hunk of land quickly— hence the reason for this game.

"Okay, my turn." He set the bottle on the table. "What's the real reason you're carving a sculpture on a deserted island?"

Hmmm. Apparently, he wasn't as clueless about strategy as she'd hoped. So that meant she had to one-up him. Now… how to answer this without lying?

"Princess? You gonna answer the question?" He nudged the top of the rum bottle with a finger.

"Uh, yeah. I'm just trying to say this as concisely as possible."

"I'm all ears."

She could tell him enough of the truth that it wouldn't be a lie. After all, it wasn't as if he'd ever be in her world to find out the backstory, and he certainly wasn't going to be able to pick her out of the crowd in his world.

"I'm trying to make my name in the art world. There are so many artists that I need something big. Something that will stand out and get noticed. Something that will make people pay attention."

He studied her a little too long—almost as if he could see into the rest of what she wasn't willing to share.

"You know? I believe you." He walked the bottle back toward him. "Which means I have to drink, doesn't it?"

"Yup."

He took a swig, then set the bottle down with an "Ahh" as if it were the best rum in the world. "I'm seeing a pattern here. If you keep telling the truth and I keep believing you, I'm going to get very drunk, aren't I?"

"A big guy like you? I think you can handle your liquor."

He cocked his head, studying her. "Why do I think you have another agenda?"

"You *wish* I had another agenda." And they both knew what *that* was.

She picked up the bottle, pretending to study it, but, in reality, she didn't want to look at him. Didn't want him to see the truth in her statement; she *did* have another agenda—and maybe another one that didn't contradict his. But she had a job to do and that *had* to take precedence. "Ask your next question."

Oh, he'd ask a question all right. Namely, who she was. And wouldn't that be interesting to see her try to lie her way out of that one?

Except he couldn't call her on it if he didn't want her to know how he knew her identity.

What a fine kettle of fish this was. Outplayed at his own game.

How to play this, how to play this…

"Any day, Jace."

"You mean *night*, Princess." He hooked a thumb toward the door which the wind still rattled. Surprising, because he'd constructed this place to withstand a Category 5. Must be some mad storm that had sprung up out of nowhere. Hopefully, there wouldn't be a tsunami because this island wasn't big enough to withstand one.

He'd *have* to come clean about *what* he was, as well as *who* if that happened.

As would she.

Yeah, not the best of either world. Here's hoping the storm calmed down. Preferably before he got shit-faced.

She strummed her fingers on the makeshift table.

"All right, all right. I have to come up with a good one or I'm going to be having a party for one with this bottle." He exhaled. "Who are your parents?"

"My parents?" she practically squeaked.

Good. Let her squirm like a worm on a hook.

Still, he had a feeling he was going to be the one drinking.

"Um, well, they're my parents. Mom's name is Kai and Dad's is Fisher."

Damn it, she was honest about it. Of course, no Human would know Fisher and Kai were the heads of the current royal family, so he couldn't either. And they weren't strange names for Humans, so he couldn't call her on that. Not like his brother, Thaumus. Yeah, that wasn't common among Humans even when the ancient Greek guy his brother had been named for had been around.

He grabbed the bottle. "Guess I'll have to take your word for it."

"I'm not lying."

He knew that, dammit.

The rum hit the back of his throat with a burn, setting off a coughing jag that was kind of humiliating. *Big strong guy like him* ought to be able to handle his liquor.

"Careful there, Big Guy. There's more to come."

"I think we need to change the rules."

"Because you're not winning? That's not very sportsmanlike of you."

"I'm not going to be in any sportsmanlike shape if this continues," he muttered, feeling the alcohol hit his bloodstream. Damn, this was some potent stuff. Those pirates must've paid a pretty penny for this lot. No wonder their boat had gone down. Probably dead drunk and hadn't cared.

"Okay," she said, smiling a little too sweetly… which meant she was up to something. "How about we do a max of five questions in a row?"

He mulled that over. Where was the twist in that?

It would give him the chance for payback and she was smaller than him so her body would feel the effects sooner than his, which could work in his favor, even if he couldn't see her angle.

Still, he didn't need her hanging this change-in-terms weakness over his head for the next two weeks. "No, no. Those were the rules; we'll keep them."

"But it's not going to be very fun for me if you end up passed out in a few more questions."

"Mighty sure of yourself, aren't you?"

She shrugged. "As you pointed out, all I have to do is keep telling the truth and you'll have to keep drinking."

"You planned this."

"You agreed to the rules."

"You cheated."

"No I didn't. I told you how the game was played up front and you elected to let me go first. Fair and square."

His ass it was fair and square. She'd played him.

But he *had* insisted that she go first.

Which she'd probably counted on.

Yeah, she'd played him. So now he had to find some way to turn this around or he'd be out for the count before they got to ten.

Time to go for the hard answers. "Okay, next question. How did you get to this island?"

"I already told you that."

"Remind me." This ought to be interesting. "What kind of boat brought you here?"

Panic streaked across her face. Good. See how she liked losing.

But then she smiled. "A Sea Ray."

Well, damn. She knew her marine life *and* her yachts. And, with his luck, a manta ray *had* let her hitch a ride.

He sighed and picked up the bottle. "I guess I'm drinking again."

"Like you said, all I have to do is keep telling the truth."

Redacted though it was.

He asked her a few more questions that he thought were so clever, but she out-clever-ed him with her answers, until his strategic skills were as steady as the surf crashing on the beach outside.

Time to up the stakes.

He scrubbed his face. "Okay. Next question." He planted his palms on the table. "Will you kiss me?"

"What? You mean now? Or ever?"

"You don't get to ask the questions, Princess, remember? I'm asking them." And feeling pretty darn good about that one, too. "So? Answer it. Will you kiss me?"

"Are you asking permission or if I ever will again?"

He leaned forward, his elbows digging into his pecs. "I asked if you will kiss me. The interpretation is up to you." He slid his hands forward until they were almost touching her arm. "So, Princess. Will. You. Kiss. Me?"

She studied him so long his arm muscles almost began to shake.

"Yes."

She said the word quietly, but she said it.

Which was all he needed to hear.

He slid around the table and had her in his arms before she could utter another word.

Not that he wanted her to, especially because she was kissing him back with as much passion as he was kissing her.

He splayed a hand across her back, feeling each hitch in her breath.

That he caused.

He might have lost the drinking game, but he'd definitely won the prize when it came to Mariana.

She turned into his embrace and took the kiss to another level. Carnal, she gave as much as she took and somehow—Jace didn't know how, nor did he care—they ended up sprawled on the floor, a tangle of arms and legs and that glorious hair entwining them as it would if they were floating under the sea.

But lovemaking under the water could never match the push-and-pull of being on land, the pounding and the urging and—shit, if he didn't calm the hell down, this would be over before it'd begun.

She dragged her hand down his chest, shoving his shirt aside—good, something for him to concentrate on: getting the damn thing off. He needed to feel her skin on his.

He freed one arm, managing somehow not to break the kiss, but when it came time to take her shirt off, he had to pull back or he'd rip the buttons...

Hell, it was *his* shirt. He didn't need buttons.

They pinged all over the shack.

One might have hit the window.

Or maybe that was some storm-tossed debris.

Whichever, he didn't care. All he knew was that he had to get the shirt *off*.

She was more than willing to help, wiggling in the most mouth-watering way that he just *had* to taste.

Just a taste.

Quick, light, over in a fl—

Hell, no way. He needed to savor.

She moaned when he sucked her nipple into his mouth and that was all the incentive and permission he needed.

He slipped both hands behind her back, arching her into his mouth. She gripped his hair, her fingers clawing his scalp. *Mark me, Princess.* He sent the words to her because he couldn't speak them, but she seemed to understand because she dug her nails into his skull, driving her breast into his mouth.

Gods, he couldn't get enough of her.

He slid one of his hands around to her other breast. She fit his palm perfectly, her nipple hard against it. He played with it, his tongue matching the rhythm on the other.

Gods, she was beautiful. Her head fell back, strands of her hair trailing across her pale skin and he wanted to trace their path.

He reached for some, crushing it in his fist, then brushing it over her nipple.

She groaned again, arching herself this time, digging her nails into his shoulder. "Yes," she breathed, the sound low and throaty and it turned Jace on like nothing else ever had.

He feathered the ends of her hair over her skin, leaving her breast to trace down to her hip. She sucked in a breath when he released her hair to trail his fingers lower.

And then she stopped breathing.

"Like that?" he whispered against her breast.

She nodded. Furiously.

He nipped her nipple and she gasped.

Always good to get air going in; he didn't need her passing out on him. Well, not unless it was from sheer pleasure, but they hadn't gotten that far yet.

He stroked her, finding what he was searching for.

What she needed him to find.

"Ohmygods," she breathed.

Jace smiled against her skin. That one exclamation would give away her Mer status to those in-the-know.

And he knew.

Right now, he was knowing a lot of things.

He knew that she liked when he slid a finger into her.

Liked it even more when he used two.

And when his thumb got involved…

It didn't take long to have her come apart in his arms.

"Like that?" he whispered again, this time inching his way up to her neck and that sweet hollow at the base of her throat.

"What *was* that? You didn't—I mean, we didn't— Well, you know."

He chuckled. "Seriously? You can't say the words after I gave you such an intense orgasm?"

She opened one eye. "Don't go sounding all smug. It's been a while for me. Of course it would happen quickly."

"Oh, so *that's* how you're going to play this, huh?'

He sucked on her skin, purposely leaving a mark. She wasn't going to be able to diss him so easily. "I guess I'll just have to prove that it wasn't a fluke."

She stiffened. "What's not a fluke?" She wiggled her toes against his calf.

He bit his lip. She was worried that her tail—her *flukes*—had somehow appeared.

He could definitely confirm that they hadn't.

But perhaps he should inspect that area even more in depth just to be sure…

"What are you—? Ohmygods— Jace, no, you can't—ohmygods, yes… you *cannnnnn*."

He smiled against her thigh. He could and he would.

And he did.

Twice.

And then once more just for fun.

Chapter Thirteen

W ell, *that* was an interesting night," Mariana muttered against his bicep, her lips tickling his skin, the rest of her—every soft curve—not *tickling* him, exactly.

"Damn, Princess, you say the most romantic things." Jace stared at the shack's ceiling, not wanting to look at her.

Because he was afraid what he was thinking would show.

He'd slept with a member of the Tritone family. A princess. *His* princess, if he was going to get technical about that.

A rival princess.

And he wasn't a damn bit sorry.

Matter of fact, he was so far from sorry, it ought to worry him. Which it did. But not enough to regret it.

Thaumus would have a sea cow if he knew.

Jace bit back the smile. He'd love to tell his brother and see the horror that'd cross his face, but ya know? Jace didn't exactly want to be thinking about his brother when he'd just woken up with the most beautiful Mer in the oceans in his arms.

He looked at the top of her gorgeous green hair. He couldn't even tell her that he was a Mer, too.

This was *so* going to complicate things.

She sighed and it didn't feel so complicated at the moment; it just felt… right.

Which ought to scare the Hades out of him—and it probably would. Later. "I'd offer you a penny for your thoughts, but I have a feeling they're worth a lot more to you."

She sighed again. "I don't know what I'm supposed to say to that."

"How about *thank you*? You know, for the four orgasms."

She glanced up. "It was only three."

"*Only*. Jeez, I must be slacking." He kissed the top of her head because she was so darn cute when she tried to be indignant about multiple orgasms. "And it *was* four. You lost count. That last one was when I just used my—"

"Oh, right. I remember."

And so did he.

Every delicious moment and every delicious inch of her skin.

He couldn't be upset about last night. Hell, he hadn't even gotten her drunk—she'd done that to him.

And he'd gone along willingly if he were honest.

She raised her head, glancing at the window. "It's still raining out."

"How *will* I ever cope with all the sexy words that come out of your mouth, Princess?"

A chuckle rippled through her. "I didn't realize you

were the kind of guy who needed nice words and rose petals."

"I can do without the roses—allergic—but the nice words wouldn't hurt."

"Why? Afraid you didn't measure up and need some assurance?"

He winced. "Those words, Princess? *Measure up*? They're not exactly the ones a guy wants to hear the morning after."

Her hand slid to just where he needed it to. "I don't think that's something you need to worry about, Jace."

True. But there was something he *did* need to worry about: Mariana didn't seem to be in any hurry to move. Meaning, she wasn't running out of the shack to get away from him while swearing this couldn't happen again.

Meaning, she wasn't going to leave the island to get away from him.

Meaning, she was going to keep carving her statue.

Meaning, people would come here.

His truth would come out.

And Thaumus would hunt him down for eternity.

It took Mariana a few seconds to realize exactly where she was and exactly what she was doing.

What she'd done. What *they'd* done.

And that it'd been great.

Actually, *Jace* had been great. Oh, not in the World's Greatest Lover sort of way—though he actually might be (not that she'd tell him that; his ego had to be inflated enough)—but ohmygods, she'd slept with a *Human* and it'd been just like being with her Mer lovers—albeit somewhat different because legs had been involved, but, mostly, it was *really* different because of...

him. Not the fact that he was Human, but the fact that Jace was… well, Jace.

She'd never known anyone like him. That smart mouth and those sexy looks, and the way he knew a woman's—her—body…

Now what was she supposed to do?

He swelled in her grasp.

Well, there was always this…

"Ah, Princess, yeah. That feels so damn good."

She should stop.

This could lead to nothing.

It was *destined* to lead to nothing because Mers and Humans shouldn't be together.

Talk to your siblings about that.

Right. Three of the five Tritone offspring were married to Humans.

Married? My, how we've made the leap from sex to marriage. When'd that happen?

Her fingers stilled. Hades, her whole body stilled.

What was she thinking?

"Uh, Princess?" Jace's hand covered hers. "You know how I said I'm not used to women blanking out when I kiss them? That goes triple for when we're being intimate. If there's something else you'd rather be doing, don't mind me."

She winced then glanced up at his aquamarine eyes. "I'm sorry. It's just that…" What? *What* was it? What could she possibly say? He'd probably run for the seamounts if she told him what she'd thought.

Talk about humiliating. Rejection from Conch was enough; she didn't need any more from Jace. Not after, well, *that*… "I was thinking that… well…"

What in the sea could she say?

"What? That this might not be enough for me? That I might want more?" Jace removed her hand from his body. "Listen. If that's the way I thought, last night wouldn't have happened. If you recall, it was all about you. I was the very interested participant to your pleasure, remember? But there was no reciprocity requested. No ultimatum for intercourse, right?"

"Oh gods, was I that selfish?"

He smoothed her hair off her face. "Selfish? Only in taking your pleasure, but I was more than willing to give it. You were magnificent and don't go getting all screwed up in the head over it. It's just that…" He glanced down. "I figured, if you're touching me, you're interested, but then you went somewhere in your head."

"I guess I tend to do that."

"And at any other time, I wouldn't mind. It was just that I was in the moment and you… weren't."

Shame on her. He'd given her three—okay, maybe it *was* four—amazing orgasms and hadn't asked for anything in return and, now, when she'd initiated contact, she'd dropped the ball—er, so to speak. That wasn't like her. It wasn't well done of any lover and, truth to tell, she wouldn't mind enjoying him that way. "I wish we had condoms."

"You and me both," he gritted out. "But we don't and this works almost as well." He squeezed her fingers. "I'm willing to give it another try if you are."

As far as "tries" went, they were successful.

But it just left Mariana wanting more.

Which she shouldn't. But the simple truth was that Jace knew his way around a woman's body and even when it was all about him, he included her as well.

So here she was, half-wrapped around him (legs really did have some good uses), her hair a tangled mess all over them, her breath trying to find its rhythm again, and an utterly gorgeous, sated man beneath her, trying to keep that stupid marriage thought out of her head when her stomach rumbled.

"Guess I should have gone for those mussels last night," he said, making no attempt to move.

"True. You might be too worn out to move now."

"Depends on what kind of movement we're talking about." He rotated his hips in case she didn't get the message.

She'd gotten it all right. "Well, you're out of luck if that's what you're talking about because *I* can't move."

"Not even to go carve your mountain?"

"Not even for that." She should, though. She ought to get her body off of Jace, pull his shirt on, then go climb that rock.

None of that sounded appealing.

The arms he tightened around her, however, were more than appealing.

"Good. I really don't want to go anywhere either. Besides, it's still a mess outside."

She'd forgotten the storm, frankly, because of the one they'd whipped up inside this hut. Who could care about the weather outside when he'd been making her feel the earth move on sheer sensation alone inside? Nothing the gods could fashion came anywhere close.

A bolt of lightning hit somewhere nearby and the smell of ozone rushed through the shack.

"That was close." Jace made an attempt to sit up. He got to the slanting-against-the-wall stage. "I better make sure it didn't start a fire."

"The rain will put it out."

"That's true. But what if it did some damage?"

"To what? A palm tree? I'm sure it's not the first time this island has been hit by lightning."

"What if it hit your sculpture?"

Oh crud. She hadn't thought of that.

Mariana scrambled to her feet quicker than she would have thought she'd be able to. "I have to go check." She looked around for her shirt.

There. Hanging off the corner of an old harpoon. Not exactly her favorite wall décor…

"Uh, Princess?" The laughter in his voice made her look at him.

Big mistake.

Emphasis on *big*.

She averted her eyes. "What?"

"You remember that the lightning bolt you're going to investigate is dangerous, right? And it's not like the storm is over." As if on cue, another boom of thunder rocked the walls of the shack as lightning lit it up as though it were high noon. "Besides, if it *did* do damage, it might not be reparable."

Her breath whooshed out. What if it was ruined? She'd have to start over—and that was *if* the rock face had survived. If it hadn't…

If it hadn't, she'd be all washed up. She'd never get Conch to agree to travel to see her art a *second* time. This was a one-and-done. Frankly, she'd been surprised he'd been up for this journey, but, then, he was probably salivating at his next chance to pan her work once more.

And she was going to hand him that opportunity on an abalone shell.

Her legs turned rubbery—interesting concept—then she sank back to the floor.

"Hey, Princess." Jace's tone wasn't the mocking one he usually had when he called her that as he crawled off the pile of blankets and over to her. He plunked his butt on the floor beside her and put an arm around her shoulder. "It's all right if it did. You can start over. I'll even… help you."

She shook her head, not bothering to swipe the handful of hair that had fallen over her shoulder into her lap because she didn't want him to see the tears slipping down her cheeks.

This sculpture wasn't just some one-off carving to her. It wasn't just something to pass the time or make herself feel good. It was her chance to show the world—and Conch—that she didn't need to rely on her royal laurels—which included a royal allowance. The money she'd paid Nalu had come from jobs she'd taken on commission under an alias. Money she'd earned because of her work, not her name, but if she couldn't claim the work as her own, then no one would know what she was capable of. It'd taken her two *selinos* of living frugally to save that money, and Nalu didn't give refunds.

Not that she'd ask. That'd be *all* she'd need to get out to the public, that a Mer princess had asked for a refund because she couldn't finish the project she'd hired him for.

Jace squeezed her shoulder. "Come on, Princess. It might not be that bad."

Oh it could be. It definitely could be.

What was he doing? Offering to *help*? Was he *out of his mind*? The whole purpose of last night had been to get her *off* the island without her big COME TO MY ISLAND beacon intact. But he was now offering to help her?

What was in that rum?

He glanced at the bottle. Damn, there was still a little more than half left. That stuff was potent.

"Mariana?" He couldn't see through the tangle of hair that hid her face.

Instantly, the memory of how that hair had been tangled all over her—and him—in the middle of the night came to him.

Seriously, what did it say about him that he got hard from the memory while she was sitting here, all upset over a *rock*?

Last night hadn't gone as he'd planned in any aspect whatsoever. And, now, neither was today if he was volunteering to help her make his home a tourist attraction.

She sniffled and shook her head. "Thanks for the offer, Jace, but it's not as easy as 'fixing it.' If the mountain has been struck, the scale will be off. I calculated each measurement based on the height of the rock with the surrounding trees. It's pointless to carve it below the tree line because no one will be able to see it."

To him, that sounded perfect. "We could always cut some of the trees out of the way."

He heard the words but couldn't believe they were coming out of his mouth. He *seriously* needed to stay away from rum.

She tossed her head. "Really? You'd help me do that?"

"Yes" came out of his mouth while his brain was bitch-slapping the inside of his skull. What was *wrong* with him? He was trying to get her *off* the island, not keep her here.

Keep her here. That had a nice ring to it—

Ring. Shit. *Keep her* and a *ring.*

No no no no no no. *Not* gonna happen. She was royalty. The enemy of his family.

Which, actually… made her his friend since he was *also* an enemy of his family.

Damn, he really needed to stay away from rum.

Thunder crashed again, this time electrifying the ozone. "That's really close."

"Too close to be the mountain."

"Yeah." He rubbed her arms where goose bumps had risen. "So maybe your project is fine."

"But it's the tallest point of the island. Isn't that where lightning always strikes?"

"Not necessarily. Could have just been a tree that exploded or something. Let's not worry about it now anyway. There's nothing we can do at the moment because, even if we wanted to brave the rain, the lightning's too dangerous."

She swiped her hair off her forehead, her violet eyes glimmering with unshed tears.

Women's tears always did him in.

"So, what do you suggest we do until the storm stops?"

"Sweetheart, do you really want me to answer that?" Hell, it was hard enough to not look lower than her face because, while she must have forgotten that she wasn't wearing any clothes—most Mer women only wore a top, if that—he sure hadn't. He ought to get points for being a gentlemer.

She chuckled. "Seriously, is that all you think about?"

"I'm wounded that you're *not* thinking like I am. Wasn't last night enticement enough?"

She blushed. That surprised him. After all, she was a royal. She was used to being under public scrutiny so she'd had to have learned to hide her emotions. So, to see her allow one to show through… It made him feel… special.

Oh, good gods. His freaking plan had backfired.

He'd worked so hard to make her want to *leave* that he hadn't been able to see that he'd now want her to *stay*.

"Last night was…" She looked away. "Nice."

"If that's your definition of 'nice,' I'd love to know what 'spectacular' is," he grumbled. Here, he was thinking the tectonic plates had shifted on a tsunamic scale last night and she… wasn't.

Geez, talk about a blow to his ego.

The storm raged around outside the shack, but the silence inside was deafening. Had she really not felt something… different? special? amazing? last night?

"I'm sorry." She touched his arm. "It was really nice. Truly. It's just that…" She looked away again. "I don't… I wasn't planning… I'm here to do a job, not get involved."

She wasn't making him feel any better. A job—a fucking hunk of *rock*—was more enticing than time with him.

Thunder covered his curse as he stood up, which was probably just as well. It wasn't a word he typically said in front of a woman.

He grabbed the towel from the floor and knotted it around his waist tight enough to cut off blood supply to his lower region.

Which was a damn good thing because for some unfuckablyknown reason, his lower region was still fucking interested.

Gods, was he a glutton for punishment or what?

"Okay, fine. I'll go check your mountain. You stay here." Yup, total glutton.

"Oh, but I can't ask—"

"You didn't ask, I volunteered. Now, stay here. No sense both of us getting fried. Then no one will finish the statue."

"You'd do that for me? Finish it?"

He stopped in his tracks. Why in Hades had he said that? If he let her go out and she did get injured—or worse—by lightning, he'd be home free. It had win/win written all over it.

Then why did he feel as if he'd lose something?

So let her *go.*

Wow, really? Was he really *that* selfish that he'd put her at risk?

But you're putting yourself in danger by going.

He was. Which made *zero* sense whatsoever. It wasn't as if he *couldn't* die—his Immortality was conditional—longevity but not invincibility—so he *was* putting himself at risk by going out there. It wasn't even as if he'd be able to *earn* invincibility by saving her because Zeus had only been able to bestow Immortality without having to alert the entire Pantheon of gods when Jace had done his good deed for Merkind by saving Pele. Since no one else could know that Pele was still alive and in hiding, lest her sister, the sea goddess, find out and go after her again, Jace was stuck with provisional.

Which didn't protect him from his sibling either.

Jace rubbed a hand through his hair. What was with all these family members going after other family members? Were they really so caught up in their own sense of power—or lack thereof—that family became a threat? An afterthought? Something to despise instead of embrace?

Sometimes, family sucked.

But he hadn't saved Pele for the accolades, and he wasn't going to protect Mariana for them either. He just didn't want her to get hurt.

And that thought might be more dangerous to him than Thaumus could ever be.

Chapter Fourteen

*H*uh. He'd left her.

He'd actually walked out that door, into the maelstrom, for *her*.

Why in gods' names did he do that?

Mariana pulled her knees to her chest and wrapped her arms around them, staring at the door swinging shut.

Why'd he have to go and be a nice guy on top of a crazy-good lover? She didn't want to think about him like this. She didn't want to think about him *ever*. This was a one-off. A vacation romance—Hades, it wasn't even a *romance*; it was an island fling. He didn't have to go and be all nice to her, too. Do things for her. Actually be someone she wouldn't mind starting a relationship with…

Crappy. Nothing was going as planned on this trip.

She glanced at the jumbled pile of blankets next to her. *That* had certainly been unexpected—both the event itself and the… execution? of it.

She giggled. *Execution.* Well… the French *did* call it *la petite mort*—the little death. That went with *execution*.

Oh, gods, she was still rum-drunk. Which was amazing considering she didn't typically get drunk, but, then, that stuff had been potent.

Or Jace was…

Goes without saying.

But it shouldn't have happened.

And it couldn't happen again.

Right. She had a job to do and she'd merely slept with the guy, not vowed her unending love.

Which she didn't have time for anyway. She didn't even have time for relationships if she wanted her career, so, therefore, she didn't have time for these thoughts about Jace.

Thunder roared over the hut and something fell off the shelf, nicking her leg on its way down.

She also didn't have time for these legs.

Her legs. Oh gods. Her *legs*. Her *tail*. How could she have forgotten?

Mariana scrambled to her feet—which she could end up being stuck with if she didn't get into the ocean before the sun set tonight to get her tail back. It was one of the very few things that sucked about being a Mer— lose the tail for longer than two sunsets and it was gone for good. The limited amount of oil she'd used would only shield her for an extra day, two if she was lucky.

She wasn't feeling particularly lucky, last night notwithstanding.

Lightning flashed and another round of thunder rolled overhead. It really was nasty out there. Amazing that Jace had gone out in it at all, let alone, for *her*.

Hopefully, he'd find his way back quickly—

Or… not.

She glanced outside. Rain didn't bother her.

Lightning was a concern, of course, but once she hit the ocean and went deep, it wouldn't be a threat.

With Jace gone, she could do what she needed to do for her tail, and he'd never be the wiser.

If he was gone long enough.

She'd just have to pray that he was because she'd rather risk him finding her than losing her legs forever.

~~~

"Hey, Princess, where ya goin'?"

Mariana was about five leaps from the waves when a one-eyed crab popped up from the sand, a bit of seaweed wrapped around his crusher claw.

Damn. She'd been recognized.

And not only that, but he'd seen her with legs. If word got back…

There'd be Hades to pay. Excuses to be made. Rings to kiss—well, not really, but she'd be down on bended fin, begging forgiveness.

"What's your name, sir?" She hunched down to the crab's level.

"'Tis Mercutio, Your Highness." He rolled his pincer claw in front of him and bowed.

"Well, my friend Mercutio, if you wouldn't mind, I'd like to keep my presence here a secret. Can you do that for me?"

"A secret? You mean no one knows you're here?"

"Right. And I'd really like to keep it that way. Can you help me?"

The pincer swung to his chest so quickly, the crab
~~~

knocked himself sideways. "Me? Help a princess? Well, who'd'a thunk it?" He almost severed his remaining eyestalk as he smacked himself on the head. "Of course I will, milady! But of course!"

She wasn't so sure about the chivalrous posing and antiquated words, but she'd take his promise any way she could get it. "Thank you, kind sir. And if you ever need anything, you can contact me at the palace."

"In *Atlantis*?" His eye almost popped off its stalk by itself. "I've never been to Atlantis, Highness. Is it as magical as they say?"

Depending on who "they" were… "It's lovely. Truly." What was with *her* speech pattern now? She was sounding just as ridiculously archaic as he was.

Ah, well, whatever kept the guy's crab trap shut.

"Well, then, I shall look forward to renewing our acquaintance at the palace." His carapace puffed up a little bit.

"Thank you, my good crustacean. I appreciate your loyalty." She patted him on the closest approximation a crab had to a shoulder.

"Think nothing of it, my liege."

Okay, that was taking the obeisance a bit too far. Still, the guy was obviously an ardent monarchist, so having him in thrall of her royal status was going to work to her advantage. "Now, I have to pop into the ocean for a quick, um—" Probably not the best idea to tell him she was going to grab a bite to eat because crab was, after all, a staple— "exercise." She tapped her legs. "Not quite as good as fins."

"I know. My buddy, uh—" The crab clipped his mouth with his pincer.

That had to hurt.

"I mean, that my buddy and I always say we don't know how Humans do it with only two, ya know?" He danced on his eight walking legs, waving his two clawed ones over his head like he was going to throw a fishing net—dastardly inventions.

"I agree." She was going to pat him again, but those waving claws were dangerous. "Well, then, um… Carry on." She did a royal wave, then headed toward the ocean. A few hours and all would be back to normal.

Well, *island* normal.

~~~

Jace trudged back to the hut, slogging through dripping wet vegetation that still had the ability to slice through his skin if he wasn't careful. Whoever called the Pacific islands *Paradise* had never run through a jungle. Even Mer skin wasn't immune.

He swiped a streak of blood off his bicep. Damn pygmy date palm. Good fruit, but spiky leaves. He'd imported a few to *up* his food choices, but he hadn't counted on trying to navigate them in a hurry. Mainly because *no one ever came here*. And yet, now, someone had.

He shook his head, flinging rain droplets off his hair into the… well, rain. Buckets and buckets of the stuff. Funny thing was, he was the one out here getting soaked, checking on her damn rock, but Mariana was the one who wouldn't mind the rain. He hadn't either when he'd been sea-dwelling; it'd been just a different form of his daily environment. Now, however, after living on land for so long, rain was annoying.
~~~

And so was the fact that Mariana was nowhere to be found when he got back to the hut.

Also annoying was that Merc had gotten into the rum.

"Hey, Merc. Make yourself at home."

Merc waved a piece of the cork at him. "Don't mind if I do. Good rum ya got here."

Totally missed the sarcasm. "So, Merc. Any idea where Mariana is?"

Merc took a swig. "Who?"

"Mariana. You know, the princess?"

Merc looked to be a little green around the gills. "Prin—" He spit out some rum. "Cess?"

"Yeah, you know. The one carving the rock? She has legs? Remember?" How much rum did it take to get a crab drunk? Especially stuff that potent. He still felt its effects.

"Uh, yeah. That one." Merc was about to take another sip off the piece of cork, but Jace swiped it.

"Where is she?"

"Who?"

Jace exhaled. Loudly. "Mariana. The princess. She was here when I left. Any idea where she is?"

"Uh, nope." Merc shook his carapace so vehemently his eyestalk almost touched each side. "Nope. Can't say."

A little too vehemently to be believable. "What can't you say, Merc?"

"Un, can't say—*hic!*—what I can't say."

"How much rum have you had?"

More than enough—a good portion of the cork was in shreds and Merc was almost a match.

"Can't say."

Of course he couldn't. Amazing he was able to say

*any*thing. "Look, all I want to know is if you saw her go somewhere."

"Saw who?"

"The princess."

"Which princess?"

"What do you mean, *which princess*? How many princesses do you know?"

"Well, are we talking *actual* princesses, like Kate or Eugenie or Tatjana or Catharina-Amalia or Stephanie or Charlotte or Caroline?" He hiccupped. "*Or…* are we talking social media princesses like Brittany or Miley or Paris or Beyoncé—though I guess she's a queen. Like Latifah, right? I'm sorry, what were you saying?" Merc's eyestalk was spinning around and the four right legs were sliding out from under him.

Jace sighed. He wasn't going to get a straight answer out of the crab. The guy was barely coherent when he was sober; a couple drops of that rum *would* make his eyestalk spin.

Jace ran a hand through his hair, flinging a bunch of rain around the hut. Too bad he couldn't have Kam track her down but that would give Mariana's secret away and if he asked the albatrosses if they'd seen her, that would give *his* secret away.

Gods, he was tired of hiding his existence. Tired of living a lie and pretending to be someone other than who he was.

Especially now, with Mariana. After all, the enemy of his enemy was his friend, right? The Tritones had zero interest in Thaumus making a comeback, so, theoretically at least, he and Mariana were on the same side. That could be a good starting point.

Starting point for what? Where ya going with this

thought, idiot?

Right. He *was* an idiot. If he came out of hiding—even to be on Team Tritone—Thaumus would make sure he didn't last long. It wasn't as if the Tritones would have any reason to want to keep him around; he was, after all, still an heir to the house of Pontus, and, therefore, a possible threat to the current royals. It wouldn't matter what he'd say.

Except, now, the only royal he had any interest in was missing.

Gods, it felt good to be free.

Mariana undulated through the water, her iridescent green scales shimmering beneath the waves. It might be storming above her, but, here, under the sea, the roiling waves felt like a comforting embrace rocking her to sleep.

How could Reel and Angel give this up?

An image of last night popped into her head, but she shook it away. Sure, sex with Jace had been good—what they'd been able to do of it because *no way* had she been willing to risk creating a baby—but that feeling wasn't worth giving up *this* one.

She dove into a shallow trench, skimming her fingers along the bottom, feeling the smooth sand dance off her skin. She loved the texture of it and had been trying to figure out how she could become the first Mer artist to work with it without having water ripples carry it away as she was doing so. Maybe if this lava rock sculpture did what she hoped it would, she could earn enough from sculpting commissions to build a tide-free studio where the water only moved when she wanted it to. She'd have to come up with some way to keep the sand particles together, though—

Maybe Jace could help out with that.

Now why'd she have to go and think that? Jace had no part in her life—last night notwithstanding—but these past few days here were an idyll not to be repeated. She certainly couldn't ask him how to build a waterless shelter under the sea for an art studio; he'd think she was mental.

Besides, she didn't need a man to help her. She was certainly capable of coming up with something. After all, Humans had managed to build their bridge support structures and some hotels under tidal waters, so if she studied their building techniques, she ought to be able to figure something out.

Mariana grabbed a fistful of the grains. Yes, that was an idea to consider once she finished this sculpture. She could be the only Mer artist to create with sand itself instead of having to carve sandstone, and then it wouldn't matter what Conch thought of her work.

She tossed the grains into the current, a few pinging against her teeth as she smiled. Think of that; she would be recognized as creating a new medium along with her art, and then commissions—under her own name— would go through the porthole.

That would certainly show that ol' critic just how talented she was.

She squared her shoulders and shook her hair over them—not that it stayed. But one thing at a time, though. To prove her talent, she needed to finish the sculpture by the time he arrived, *then* work on the new medium afterward.

She also needed to get back onto land and dry out her tail for her legs to come back so she *could* finish on time.

With that thought, Mariana flicked said appendage powerfully enough to propel herself right onto the beach, then pulled on the shirt she'd left there. Luckily, the rain would help with the desalinization of her scales, so it shouldn't take as long as a non-weather-event transformation. It just had to be long enough for Jace to not find her.

"Mariana?"

Which, of *course*, didn't happen.

Chapter Fifteen

Mariana curled her flukes under her tail.

Not that that would hide them. They were pretty hard to miss.

And Jace wasn't missing anything.

"I… I can explain."

She soooooooooo couldn't explain. Not with a *tail*.

Oh, gods, she'd blown it. The one—*ONE*—main rule of her world and she'd just tossed it out like an empty clam shell.

Jace didn't move. He just stood there, his eyes bugging out.

She'd seen the look before.

"You. Are. *Gorgeous*."

But not accompanied by those words.

Well, at least he wasn't freaking out.

Maybe she could work this to her advantage. She *did* have a few tricks up her scales. After all, her kind had been singing sailors into a stupor for eons, making them forget even their own name.

She inhaled. She hated to do this to him, but he *couldn't* know about Mers.

She opened her mouth and the first note emerged—

"Don't bother. It won't work on me." Jace waved a hand.

She choked down the note. "Wha... *what*?" How did he know what she was even going to do?

"Your siren's song. It won't work. I'm immune."

"How do you know that?" Like, *seriously?* The first note was supposed to entrance him into an almost zombie-like state. Granted, she'd only done this twice before in her life, but she'd never had the man respond *at all,* let alone in a full sentence. Two, in Jace's case. "How... how do you—"

"Know what you're doing?" He hunkered down beside her and she pulled the edges of her shirt—*his* shirt—closer together. "Yeah, that's where it gets complicated." He traced a finger along her scales.

She gulped—and not because of what his touch did to her; this was solely surprise that he had even a glimmer of a clue, let alone this... coherency. "Compli... complicated?"

Jace dropped his head and shook it, his sigh as loud as the boom of thunder moving offshore.

Well, at least one tempest was dissipating. *This* one, however, was just ratcheting up.

"Come on, let's get you out of the rain."

"I don't mind the rain." Yeah, because *that* was the issue at the moment.

"I'd rather have this discussion indoors, then. If you don't mind."

Sure, why not, except... "Um, Jace, in case it's escaped your notice..." She flicked her tail as sarcastically as she'd said the words, "I can't just *walk* into the hut right now."

"Well, I carried you in last night; I can do it again."

Yeah, but last night she'd had legs.

And he didn't seem at all surprised that she didn't now.

Which surprised *her*.

Actually, it shocked her. She'd never seen a Human *not* freak out when meeting a Mer in full-on scales.

"Here, let me pick you up."

"No. Wait." She shoo-ed him back. She didn't need him touching her and confusing her even more. "The rain is good for—"

"Desalinization, right. I forgot."

Forgot? He for*got*? What did he mean he *forgot*? How did he even *know*?

She narrowed her eyes. "Who are you? A Cousteau?" That family—and only a select few in it—knew the truth, thanks to an alliance The Council had made with the patriarch decades ago. "No wonder you didn't want to tell me your name."

"I'm not a Cousteau." He exhaled and ran a hand through his hair. "Damn. I really didn't want this to come out."

"*What* to come out? What's going on? Why aren't you surprised to see my tail? How did you know about the song? And what did you *forget* about desalinization? What's going on, Jace?"

Jace plunked his butt onto the sand beside her. No concocted story would work with Mariana. She was too observant. Too smart. She wouldn't buy anything less than the truth because there was, literally, no story he could make up that would be anywhere near believable.

He exhaled again. "I…" He shook his head. "I need

to tell you something, but you have to promise to keep it a secret. It's life-or-death kind of stuff."

"You mean more than *this*?" She flopped her tail a couple of times, hard enough to flick sand over both of them. "I'm not making any promises until I know what you're going to tell me."

Jace nodded. "Fair." He ran a hand over his chin. "My name isn't Jace—"

"*What*?! You… You… You and I…" She flung her hands in the direction of the hut. "And you *lied* to me about your name?"

"No… That is… Yes, my name *is* Jace, but it's short for… Jason."

She cocked her head. "And? You're not the one of Argonaut fame, right?"

"No. Not *that* Jason."

"Okay, then what's the…" Her mouth dropped open. "Oh. My. Gods."

She got it in two.

"Jason… *Pontus*? But… But… *How*? I thought you were dead. We *all* thought you were dead. Including your brother—"

"Exactly. And that's the way it needs to stay. If Thaumus finds out I'm *not* dead, he's going to want to make me that way."

"Wait. You're Jason Pontus and you've been, what? Hiding out on this island for however many millennia to keep your brother from finding you? If you've been alive this long, you must have somehow gained Immortality."

He winced. He really didn't want this to come out; it wasn't all his story to tell. But Mariana would see through anything else he tried to come up with, especially since his brain hadn't been firing on all cylinders from the moment he'd seen her here. Gods, he should have just walked away and not let her know he'd been here, but seeing her like this… She was just so gorgeous that the words had been out of his mouth before he'd thought it through.

He raked a hand through his hair. "I, uh, didn't get *full* Immortality, just longevity and no illnesses. It's kind of a provisional sort of thing; I can still be killed. And, trust me, my brother would love nothing more."

"Why?" She shifted and water droplets glittered on her scales. "I have to admit my recollection of history is tucked away in the far corners of my mind, so can you enlighten me?"

He wasn't surprised. Most Mers didn't want to remember Thaumus' rule. It hadn't been a banner time period for Merkind because Thaumus hadn't exactly been the best caretaker of his people and the oceans. One big party was all his brother had cared about. Hedonism and bacchanalia—to the point that even Bacchus had been disgusted.

"Thaumus thinks I sold him out to the gods."

"Why does he think that?"

"Because… you know. Your family came to power after the gods stripped him of his."

"And he blames you for that?"

Jace shrugged. It's what was in the history slates; he knew because he'd made sure of it. "Yeah. He thinks I tattled to the gods."

"And did you?"

"No. No reason to. My brother did a good enough job making it obvious what a crappy job he was doing; I didn't need to. *No one* needed to."

"So, then, how *did* you get your Immortality?"

Here was where it got tricky. "Mmmmm. It's… not exactly my tale to tell."

"Wait. What?" She flicked some sand his way with her flukes. "You're giving me half-answers to what's now going to be the biggest mystery in our world? What do you mean it's not your tale to tell? Whose is it?"

Jace winced. "I really can't tell you that—"

She leaned onto a hip, finger wagging at him. "Don't pull that with me, Jace. You're going to tell me and you're going to tell me now. Or I'm getting right back into the water and letting The Oceanic Council know *exactly* what I've just learned."

She would, too. Mariana was all about Merkind and their way of life. If a deposed ruler's "spare heir" was still hanging around The Seven Seas and The Council wasn't monitoring him, that was a problem. Which was why he'd stayed under their radar all these *selinos*.

"Okay. But seriously, Mariana, this doesn't affect just me."

"Who else *is* there?" She flung a hand in the air. "You got the goddess, Pele, stashed away somewhere no one knows about?"

He winced. Damn, she'd nailed it on the first try this time.

"Oh. My. Gods. You do! How?" Mariana gripped his wrist. "I thought her sister killed her?"

"That's what you're supposed to think. That's what *everyone* is supposed to think."

"But… why?"

"It's complicated."

"I'm all ears."

"And tail." He smirked. It was a gorgeous tail.

She yanked his wrist and tossed her chin. "Eyes up here, buddy."

Right. Back to breaking a goddess' trust and spilling his guts to someone who could do something about it.

Something he might not like.

Something Pele *definitely* wouldn't.

And something that would change his world—and hers—as they knew it if she did.

He had to make sure she didn't. "Look, Mariana. This goes back eons. Way before your time."

"Stop stalling."

He wasn't going to get out of this. "Okay. Here goes." He crossed his legs under him and turned his wrist so that he ended up holding her hand.

Amazingly, she let him.

He linked his fingers with hers. "You know the story of how Nāmaka, the sea goddess, caught her husband, Aukele, cheating with her sister, Pele?"

"Classics 101. Continue."

"Right. Well, Pele wasn't exactly cheating with Aukele—"

"They were caught in bed together, Jace. *In flagrante delicto* I believe is the phrase."

"Well, yes, that's true, but it wasn't what it seemed."

She arched an eyebrow. "Oh, and last night wasn't either?"

He had to chuckle at that. "Last night was exactly what it was—"

"Except it wasn't, was it? You knew all along what I am, didn't you?" Her fingers tightened. "Ohmygods—do you know *who* I am?"

He winced again. "Yeah."

She threw his hand away. "Really? You seduced me under false pretenses? Why? So you could get your kicks out of saying that you'd slept with a member of the royal family?"

"Uh, *I'm* a member of the royal family, if you recall."

"*Former* royal family. One no one wants to lay any claim to or have anything to do with."

That hurt. "You, too?"

"Huh?"

"Do *you* want nothing to do with me now that you know who I am?"

Her shoulders drooped—that'd taken the wind out of her sails. But then she straightened up and smoothed her scales. "I… didn't say that."

"Okay, then. Don't go reading anything more into last night. It was what it was and we both knew it and enjoyed it. Who we are doesn't come into play. You're a beautiful woman and I wanted to be with you."

She nibbled her lip.

Hmmm, maybe he'd gotten through to her. Maybe Princess Mariana Tritone was as Human—er, Mer—as the rest of them, and flattery wasn't necessarily a bad thing.

Especially when it was the truth.

"So, do you want to hear the rest of the story?"

She exhaled then nodded. "Carry on."

"Spoken like a true princess."

"Which I am."

"I know."

"I know you know."

"Mariana, let me get on with the story."

She crossed her arms. "Go ahead."

It was his turn to bite his lip—so he wouldn't smile at her. Not only was she stunningly gorgeous, but she was utterly adorable when her curiosity won out over her regality.

"What Nāmaka saw was her husband *trying* to cheat with Pele. What she didn't realize was that Pele had set the whole thing up to prove to Nāmaka what Aukele was like. There'd been rumors, but Nāmaka had ignored them.

Insisted they weren't true. That, actually, was what had started the fights between them—all of Pele's volcanos erupting under the sea to become The Hawaiian Islands while Nāmaka kept trying to stop them with the waves she controls. It'd been a constant nightmare for Pele. She'd only been trying to show her sister the truth, but Nāmaka wouldn't hear it. Instead, she tried to kill her. You know, the old *don't kill the messenger* thing? Yeah, well, Nāmaka didn't subscribe to that current of thought. So, Pele finally decided that, if that's the way her sister wanted it, she'd go along with the program."

"On purpose?"

"On the *surface*. Appearance-wise only. She set up the scene, Nāmaka misinterpreted it, attacked Pele, and left her for dead. But Pele isn't dead; she's alive and living in one of her volcanos."

"But where does your Immortality come in?"

"Yeah. That. So…" He exhaled. He was getting in deeper by the minute. "Only Zeus knows about Pele being alive. I don't believe he's even told Hera. He's the one who gave me Immortality for saving Pele's life when Nāmaka almost killed her."

"*Almost*?"

"Well, it was pretty touch-and-go, but I was able to save her at the last minute."

"How? How does one save a goddess? Shouldn't she have been able to save herself?"

Damn it, the woman was too smart for his own good.

He sighed. It was time to fully come clean. With this much info, Mariana could do a lot of damage to both his and Pele's life, so, what was that saying—in for a drachma, in for a lepta? If she had all the information, maybe she'd see why he'd done what he'd done. "Pele is the goddess of volcanoes and fire. She can breathe in the most noxious fumes and survive. Her lungs can't be singed, but—"

"She can't breathe under water." Mariana finished for him, that famous brain of hers firing on all cylinders. "You didn't…"

He shrugged. "I did. I had no choice."

"You turned a goddess into a water-breather? That, like, breaks almost every rule there is."

"I know."

"And Zeus still gave you Immortality?"

"I know, right?" Maybe it was because both he and Pele had done nothing to deserve the wrath of murderous siblings and Zeus felt bad for them? Who knew; he was just glad that Zeus had seen fit to reward him, or Thaumus really would have been the death of him—if just for having a mortal life span.

Mariana leaned back and planted her palms on the sand behind her. "Wow. I don't know what to say."

"Say nothing. To anyone. You see why it's not just my story to tell? Pele's survived all these *selinos* in secret. If you out me, you'll out her, not to mention Zeus. We all didn't do what we did to have it be for nothing. I mean, the islands are a lot calmer—"

"But she still sets off volcanoes."

"Nope, that's not her. Well, mostly it's not her. It's usually the tectonic plates shifting. Modern science has been able to explain the phenomena in our world, enabling her to stay hidden. Trust me, it was a huge relief to both of us when scientists finally understood the mechanics behind what used to only be attributed to the gods. It's kept everyone—even her sister—in the dark." He cocked his head. "So… what are you going to do with this information, Mariana?"

She exhaled. "Nothing at the moment. I have to think this through."

"There's nothing *to* think through. You can't tell anyone or you'll affect all of our lives."

"I see that." She nibbled her lip again, and he could see the wheels spinning in her head. "What I don't see is…" She tossed her hair over her shoulder and looked him square on. "You offered to help me with the statue, but if I finish it and it gets noticed… that's going to cause problems for you, isn't it? Your island is going to get noticed."

He winced. "Yeah."

"So… why bother to offer to help me? I mean, it's not just you at stake, right? If people start coming here—Humans or Mers—you'll have to leave or risk discovery."

"Well… yeah."

She cocked her head, her eyes narrowing. "This doesn't make sense, Jace. Helping me is the very last thing you should be doing."

"Well, originally, that hadn't been the plan."

She raised her eyebrows. "Oh? What was the plan?"

The revelations kept getting tougher. And he'd thought telling her who he was would be the hardest one…

He pulled his knees up and wrapped his arms around them. "I'd hoped to scare you off the island."

She cocked her head. "By giving me three orgasms?"

"Four."

"Ah, right. Four." They chuckled. "Not exactly the scariest thing, Jace."

"I… know. I hadn't planned for that to happen." He put up a hand when she opened her mouth. "Not that I'm complaining—far from it. Trust me, I was wrestling with the decision the minute I saw you. But… I'd been hoping to just come on strong—strong enough for you to want to get away from me, but then you jumped right in and—"

"Oh, so it's *my* fault we slept together?" She smacked his arm.

"No, that's not what I was saying—"

"Because, if I remember correctly, you weren't exactly pushing me away—"

"Well, you weren't either—"

"I know—"

He didn't know who moved first, but, somehow, they were suddenly in each other's arms, kissing like there was no tomorrow.

Which there might not be if any of his and Pele's story got out.

He yanked his mouth from hers. "Seriously, Mariana, you can't finish that sculpture."

"Oh my gods—were you trying to kiss me into agreeing with you?" She shoved him away. "Wait. Was that what last night was about?"

Her mouth fell open and he had to hide the flush of guilt because, yeah, it'd started out like that, but somewhere along the way, it'd gotten very real. He touched her hand but she backed away.

"Of all the despicable—"

"No, that's not what I was doing. Can you hang on a moment, woman?" He raked both hands through his hair. "Look, I like kissing you. And you obviously like kissing me. Last night was about us. It was a moment—a lot of moments—and they were all real. Last night had nothing to do with… *this*. Me. Pele. Your sculpture." He'd swear on that to his dying day because the minute he'd gotten her in his arms, all thoughts except her had fled. But now… now they'd come back with full force. "But we *do* have a problem, Mariana, and we need to figure something out."

She opened her mouth, then closed it. Those wheels were spinning again. Gods love an intelligent woman. And so did—

No. The *gods* did. The. Gods. He needed to remember that distinction.

She blew out a breath. "Okay, you're right. Last night was what it was, I get that. But this…" Her lips tightened. "We need to find you another island. The sculpture is too far along for me to have to start over. I'd need another rock of the correct proportions, I'd need to be where no one knows who I am to finish it, and I'd need the location to be out of normal Human shipping lanes. This island is perfect for what I need."

"What about what I need?"

She chewed on her lip. "That's a problem."

"It is."

"But I'm sure we can come up with a solution that works for both of us."

"Really? Like what? We share custody of the island? This isn't a divorce, Mariana."

"That's taking it a bit far, don't you think?"

"Do I? No, I don't. I, too, need an island that's off the beaten path. One that Mers would have to make a concerted effort to get to—not to mention, Humans. One with a climate that's conducive to staying off grid, which removes all Arctic and Antarctic ones from the list of possibilities. I have to make sure there's not much avian traffic because I have to be out of sight when they come around so I don't have to pop in and out of caves and huts every six minutes. And then there's the sea traffic.

Whales come by here on occasion, but I can hear them from leagues away, so I make sure to stay landed 'til they pass. I found this place a long time ago and it checks all the boxes. The most important being that, so far, no Humans or Mers have decided to set up a colony here. And given the way Humans have taken over the planet in the last century or two, I'm not so sure I'd be *able* to find another one that has all those characteristics."

"Well, there has to be some way we can both get what we want."

"I don't understand why you can't build something else instead of a mountain. Why does it have to be a Moai? And here?"

"*Build* something?" She poked his bicep. "*Build* it? I don't *build* things, Jace, I *create* them. I find the soul of the stone and I bring it out. "

He shifted out of poke range. "And so you… what? Just happened to be swimming by this out-of-the-way island and saw the big chunk of lava and thought, 'Why, hey. I bet there's a Moai buried under there that I need to bring out'? Pardon me if I don't believe it was that serendipitous."

Mariana exhaled. "Well, okay, no, it wasn't exactly like that. I did intend to create a new Moai, so I knew I needed a big enough mountain. And I needed a deserted island. I checked out some oceanic maps and found this place."

"Exactly. So why can't you do the same thing for some other place. Then I could keep living my peaceful—" *solitary* "—existence and you'd still get your statue." Interestingly, that *solitary* part bothered him. Which annoyed him. He hadn't been bothered about it until she'd shown up. Now, here he was, trying to bend over backward for some woman who'd invaded his space.

Except… she wasn't *some* woman. She was Mariana.

The woman who'd turned his world upside down in such a short time it'd be laughable if only it… wasn't…

"It's not that easy, Jace. Like you said, with the way Humans traverse the globe, there aren't a lot of options. Not to mention, the time factor. Conch is going to be here in less than ten days. That doesn't leave me a lot of time to start over."

"*Helmut* Conch? He's coming *here*?" The art critic. That made sense, but when he'd heard her say she needed validation, he hadn't realized she'd intended to bring the famous art critic to his island. And in less than ten days, no less. Shit. He couldn't find a new place and relocate all his stuff that quickly. "This has to do with the clam sculpture, doesn't it?"

She looked away. "You know about that?"

He felt like he'd just flicked a dogfish. "I do." He wished he could take it back but his life—and Pele's— were at stake here. "What happened?"

She shook her head, her drying hair cascading down her back. "Conch didn't like it."

"I heard it fell over." Really hated bringing it all up, but if they wanted to find a solution, they had to look at every angle.

"It did, but that wasn't it. It was… after."

"After?"

"After he'd eviscerated it in his column." She ran a hand through her hair. "After he'd eviscerated… me."

He swiveled to face her, then crossed his legs under him. "What do you mean he eviscerated *you*? He didn't like a piece you did and panned it; that's what art critics do. Isn't that part of the job?"

She cleared her throat, but didn't look at him. "I could take criticism of my work; I'm not that fragile. But when he came after me personally—and I quote, 'Ms. Tritone seems to feel that we serfs of the realm should bow to the largesse of a royal who deigns to present us with a wholly unremarkable recreation of a daily item so common in our lives, though, perhaps, not hers. After all, why should a member of the royal family ever need the services off the backs of clams when they live off the backs of the rest of us?'" She shook her head. "There's more, but you get the gist."

"Wow. Sounds like Conch has issues beyond art."

She glanced at him out of the corner of her eye. "Ya think?"

"So why do you think him seeing *this* statue will change his mind?"

She straightened up and faced him. "Because no Mer has ever created something this large outside of the sea. I have to, as the saying goes, go big or go home— and that's *literal* in my case. If I can't prove to him that I do have the talent and the insight to find what's hidden and reveal it for others' eyes—not to mention the drive and dedication to do so—then I might as well just give up. No one will ever see me as anything more than how he's portrayed me—a royal playing in the sand." She dug a finger into the sand between them. "But I am an *artist*." Then did it again. "I'm *not* resting on my royal laurels." And again. "I work hard, dammit, and I deserve to be judged on the merits of my work, not on his prejudice against the ruling family." Now she pounded the sand with her fist. "After all, it's not as if I could control which family I was born into, but I sure as Hades can control my career. Except…" She exhaled. "I can't. Not with him panning my work and my reputation without even giving me a chance." She shook her head and blinked rapidly.

Were there tears in her eyes? He had zero defense against a woman's tears.

Gods, there had to be a way for both of them to get what they wanted.

"Okay, what if…" He had his own wheels spinning. "What if… you finish it and Conch shows up and gives you the review you deserve and then, after he leaves…" He winced as the idea gelled. She wasn't going to like this; he knew it before he even said the words, but what, really, were their options? "What if we, you know… destroy it?" When she gasped, he jumped in to fill the space with his reasoning before she could tell him what he could do with his idea. "He'll have seen it; he'll write about it; you'll get the recognition you deserve, and I'll get to keep my home."

"*Destroy* it? You want me to *destroy* it?" She flung her arms. "I can't destroy it, not something I created. That would be like… like…" She flung her arms again, which sent her hair cascading all over the place. "It'd be like saying it's not good enough—that *I'm* not good enough. This statue is *me,* Jace. It's what's inside of me. I can't just destroy it—that'll destroy *me.*"

Her eyes flashing, her chest heaving with almost hyperventilating breaths… There was obviously a lot more riding on this piece than he'd realized—or, possibly, even *she* realized.

But what he *did* realize was that she was at Conch's mercy as much as he was at Thaumus' and all of it, frankly, sucked. She didn't deserve to have to justify her existence to another being or have it be defined by that being's standards. He, personally, understood what a pain in the tail that really was.

They both had a lot at stake because finishing this statue and getting Conch's endorsement was as important to her as him keeping his existence secret from his brother was to him. So how to resolve both issues?

Maybe… if he could help her get what she wanted, then she would see that what he wanted mattered just as much and she'd agree to destroy it.

Except… The transactional nature of that thought bothered him. Because, without Thaumus hanging over his head, he would never even think about suggesting she destroy her art. Especially after she'd just told him what it meant to her.

Damn Thaumus.

Which… actually…

Jace straightened his spine. Yes, *damn* Thaumus. Jace was tired of living his life in the shadows to avoid his brother. Hadn't he done enough of that? Did he really want an eternity of doing that because that's what his Immortality had granted him—

Wait. *Had* Immortality been a blessing from Zeus or… a punishment?

Well, *that* put a whole new spin on things.

But the thing was, he hadn't saved Pele to get Immortality or any reward; he'd done it because it'd been the right thing to do.

And the right thing to do now was help Mariana reach her goal. He'd figure his own problem out later. She was right; it was a lot easier for him to move his home than for her to move a mountain. "Okay, Mariana, how about this? How about I help you get this ready for Conch—"

"You can't *help* me, Jace. It's not a like a paint-by-numbers. I can't tell you to go carve out a cheek—"

"No, but you could tell me how much rock to remove to get to the right depth so you can then finish that area. Smooth it out or whatever you do. I can do the heavy lifting. Get you lunch, water, whatever, so you can concentrate on your art. You know, help you."

She side-eyed him. "I'm not going to destroy it."

"I understand."

"Then why are you helping me?"

Because she really needed Conch's validation and that broke his heart?

Yeah, he couldn't say that to her. That'd be revealing too much of her vulnerability which would do what to her concentration?

"Let's just say that we're at an impasse, okay? You came here to carve the thing and Conch is headed this way, ergo, it needs to be finished. It's not like I can stop what's already been put in motion." Not without coming across as a selfish prick and involving a lot more beings, which would open him and Pele up to even more risk. No, this was the best of a bad situation. At least one of them would get something from it.

And she *would* get what she wanted from this; of that he had no doubt. Because Mariana *was* talented. He may not be an art connoisseur, but he could recognize talent, and what she was carving on that mountainside was good. So, if he had to give up his home and find a new place, at least it was for a good cause.

Oh who was he kidding? He wasn't doing this for a *cause*; he was doing it for Mariana. And that worried him more than his brother finding out he was alive because, after spending so many millennia alone, he realized that losing Mariana was going to be harder than losing the security of his island.

So he was going to do whatever he could to help her out, the consequences—or his future—be damned.

Chapter Sixteen

Surprisingly, for all the distraction that watching Jace in action created—with his flexing muscles and contracting abs and some really attention-grabbing movements in his glutes when his shorts slid down a few inches—he actually *was* a big help. It sucked that he wanted her to destroy it—she wasn't stupid; she knew what he was hoping for, but, for now, she was just thankful he wasn't pushing the issue.

Because, honestly? She was considering it. What if… what if, though she was putting forth her best effort, Conch *didn't* like it? What if his vendetta or issue or jealousy or whatever it was that had him writing such a horrid piece about her last project was still here and he couldn't see beyond who she was to her actual art, and his next review became her last foray into the art world? Then it wouldn't matter what she did with the statue.

Then… she actually wouldn't mind destroying it.

Her chisel slipped, slicing merely a thin sliver of rock—thank the gods. Easily enough to smooth over, but her thoughts and her nerves were going to take a lot more work.

So, she had to get her mind back on her work and let Jace and his dilemma wait until later.

She was glad he'd offered to help. He'd helped her get up the rockface once her tail had morphed back into legs because his more experienced ones were better equipped for climbing. He could carry her tools much easier (and looked damn good in that toolbelt), and he was more than willing to do the heavy grunt work of chipping away at layers of the tuff to get her to the depth that she needed for the *Elvis muscle*. She shook her head at the term for the muscle that lifts the lip and dilates the nostril—that Human was so famous that Human pop culture was *popping up* on Mer anatomy lessons. What was her world coming to?

"You ready to break for dinner yet, Princess?" Jace yelled from what they'd taken to calling base camp.

With both their Mer secrets out in the open, they no longer had to pretend to be Human. Which also meant Mariana no longer had to worry about rationing the gods' oil. She could go in the water whenever she needed to without worrying about losing her legs permanently. And Jace had been able to pull out a stash of things he'd hidden from her; among them had been part of today's lunch—kippers he'd had brining in an old pirates' rum barrel, and eggs. She hadn't had kippers in a long time. They'd tasted delicious—which might have had something to do with the residual rum, but she wasn't complaining. She was just thankful that Tahiti hadn't been around to see the eggs. Jace hadn't told her what avian they'd come from and she hadn't asked; sometimes it was good to *not* have all the answers. She'd just enjoyed the treat. But the treat she was *really* looking forward to would be sleeping in her own skin—er, scales—tonight.

Was Jace planning to sleep with her?

Mariana almost dropped her chisel. Now that she knew he was Mer, and he knew *she* was Mer, there were some very interesting implications for tonight…

"Mariana?" he called up a little louder. "You're doing it again."

She cleared her throat. "Doing what?"

"That spacing-out thing I'm not fond of when I'm talking to you."

Ha! Wouldn't he like to know *just* what she'd been *spacing-out* about? "I'm not spacing-out, Jace. I'm thinking. I have a lot going on in here." She tapped her head. That was her story and she was sticking to it.

"Well, do you *think* you're ready for dinner? I've been chopping up all this fruit, and I caught a dorado."

"How'd you catch that without fins on your appendages? Those things are fast."

"Hey, I might not have a tail, but that doesn't mean I don't have fins."

"Ah. Human ones, right?"

"Yup. Humans are good for some things."

"Except for taking over the world," she muttered. Jace wouldn't have to stick to this island if he had other choices. And she could have found a different island.

"What?" he called up.

She waved a hand. "Nothing. Never mind. I'll be right down." Their situation was what it was and anything else would be dealt with *after*.

She climbed down, foot after foot, fingers and toes finding purchase in the rock. She'd be glad for the day when all of this was over and done, and she was back in her world, never having to think about toes again.

"Very nice." Jace clapped as her feet touched the sand.

Except she'd never see Jace's toes—or the rest of him—again then. After all, he was a legend in her world and that's what he'd have to stay if he was going to remain alive in his.

She flung her head to get the hair out of her eyes—and got an eyeful of what he'd gotten an eyeful of.

The shirt had crept up her back. He was getting a full-on show of her glutes.

Well, she *had* seen his, so turnabout was fair play, right?

Still, she tugged the shirt back into place. They didn't need any sexual tension during dinner. She needed sustenance. Of the *food* kind.

Any other kind could come later.

And she'd worry about never seeing Jace again later as well.

"Dinner smells delicious. Do you always cook on land?" She crossed her arms in case any of the three leftover buttons had come loose on the way down. She wasn't about to check while he was watching her.

"Have to." He crooked his arm, inviting her to slip hers through it. "No magma vents nearby. Plus, I tend to stay out of the water as much as possible. The fewer beings who see me for who I am, the better."

She slid her arm in his. "So you tend to eat the ones who do?"

He winced. "Hey, there's that *wrong place, wrong time* saying for a reason. And a guy's gotta eat." He led her to a round table he'd said he'd salvaged from a pirate ship, along with its matching chairs, then held one out for her to sit.

She looked back over her shoulder as she did so. "You're a regular Swiss Family Robinson sort of guy, aren't you?"

He took the seat to her right. "More like Robinson Crusoe, I'd like to think. But how do you know about them? Those are Human stories." He handed her an opened nut of coconut water.

"Angel. My sister. She's been fascinated by Humans her whole life and salvages whatever she can find. The books weren't in the best shape, but she used to keep them on land. My parents never discouraged her treasure-hunting as she called it, so whenever we couldn't find her, we'd check either the closest island or the nearest shipwreck." She saluted him with her drink. "Thankfully, she married a Human so she can get her answers first-hand."

"Your parents seem pretty open-minded with three of their offspring marrying Humans."

Mariana shrugged, then set her drink down. "They want us to be happy." She got that, but she still didn't get why her siblings had chosen *Humans*.

Not that that had stopped her from wanting Jace when she'd thought he was Human. Maybe there wasn't as much difference between their races as she thought. Maybe it was just a matter of geography—

"Hello?" Jace waved his drink in her face. "You blanked out again."

"Jace, I do not *blank out*. I'm thinking. I don't know why you expect me to fall at your feet and worship you for your god-like face and body to the exclusion of all else, but I actually have a few brain cells in here and I don't want to turn them off to pander to your ego."

"Wow." He almost dropped his coconut as he set it

on the table. "Where did that come from? I was just asking for simple courtesy of staying in a conversation with me, not undying worship."

She exhaled as she slumped back in the chair. "I'm… sorry. I don't know… where that came from. I'm not usually so rude."

"Well, maybe it's the stress getting to you. You have a lot riding on this statue."

She did. And she was tired of carrying that stress. And she was *really* tired of having to prove herself threefold. First, for being female; second, for being a member of the royal family; and, third… Third, for just being her. Sure, she might have all those accolades from school and scholarships and whatnot, but the reality was, she had major Imposter Syndrome. She *didn't* always know what she was doing. She *wasn't* always sure of the answers, and she *didn't* always know if she was doing the right thing.

Like now, for instance. Was continuing with this sculpture really the best thing? Or should she just forget about it and leave Jace to his peaceful existence? Should she just forget she ever met him and learned his story, and go back to her life as it was and find something else to do with it? Hanging her sense of self-worth on a chunk of lava and a disgruntled gastropod didn't seem like the best plan right now. After all, she was struggling along in her existence just like everyone else on the planet, and to have Conch condemn her for her birthright—something she had no control over—she was just… just… so over it.

Because she *was* talented. And it had nothing to do with being a member of the royal family. She'd studied the masters, she'd practiced her craft, she'd developed her own style.

Conch *had* to see that.

Gods, how it pissed her off that she needed him, that pompous, arrogant, swim-bladder.

What gave *him* the right to be the definitive know-it-all in their world? Why were *his* thoughts on a piece what counted? Why did *he* have to bless everything anyone did and why did she have to prove *herself* as much as she had to to prove her art had merit? What was it about Conch that he was so insecure that he had to lord this one thing over everyone else—

Wait. *Insecure…*?

Conch's bluster and snootiness were… insecurity?

She'd seen him snivel up to the greats of their world, Fordestra and Inkolini, the Mer world equivalent to Humans' Botticelli and Michelangelo. She'd watched him preen on the stairs of the AMoMA in Atlantis for the annual gala that all Merkind glitterati showed up for. It was so sickening how up-and-coming artists would prawn at his foot for even a glimmer of his interest.

Mariana had stayed far away.

And, perhaps, that was the problem. Perhaps she hadn't groveled enough.

Or, rather, at all.

Well, she wasn't going to. She was going to make it on her talent alone, not on who she was or who she knew or who, gods-forbid, she sucked up to. His ego was not her problem.

Yeah, you've got your own to worry about.

She winced and picked at the fish. Damn subconscious, always pushing her to face that fact.

Oh, it wasn't her ego in an *I-want-to-be-famous* sort of way, but more of *who-am-I-and-what's-my-purpose*? She'd been struggling with that her entire life. Everyone had always assumed that she knew who and what she was and where she was going because she'd had such success in school. But school was over; who was she supposed to be now?

"Are you done?" Jace's waved his thingamabob of dorado her way.

"I'm sorry, what?" She raked her hair back.

"I asked if you're done. You know…" He pointed at her head and the fish flopped onto the table. "Thinking whatever thoughts you were thinking. You do realize, right, that you might just be overthinking things a little? Not everything needs a full breakdown of pros and cons."

"I…" Wait. Was he right? *Was* she overthinking things?

"Sometimes, you just have to go with the flow, Mariana." He picked up his fish and popped it into his mouth. "Sometimes, life just happens, regardless of what we try to plan for. Case in point." He circled the utensil between them.

"Well, that's just foolish. How will you get anywhere if you don't have a plan to follow?" She'd never *not* had a plan. And just because she was annoyed at Conch's power over her future didn't mean she was going to abandon her plan now.

He nudged a piece of her dorado toward her. "Where do you want to go?"

She speared the fish. "That's easy—to the top of the art world."

"Why?"

"Why?" Her thingamabob stopped just before her lips. "What kind of question is that? Why wouldn't I? What's the point of doing something only for mediocrity?" She'd never half-tailed anything in her life and she wasn't about to start now.

"Maybe for the joy of it?"

She rolled her eyes as she popped the fish into her mouth. "There will be enough joy once Conch gives me a good review."

"So you're waiting for someone else to decide how you live your life? What's the point of living if you don't, ya know, live?"

She washed the fish down with another swig of coconut water—had he added something to it? Pineapple maybe? "Uh… hello? Pot? Kettle? Aren't you living yours because of your brother? Every day, wake up, eat, maybe swim, eat again, go to sleep?" She speared another piece of dorado. He'd definitely put pineapple on the fish. It was good.

"You make it sound monotonous."

She swallowed. "Isn't it?"

"No."

"Really? What do you have to look forward to, Jace? What joy do you find, if you're so 'for the joy of it'?"

It was his turn to slump back in his seat. "Hey, I'll take lazing on a beach any day to having to run from my brother for the rest of my life."

"But isn't that what you're doing? Running from him even if you're staying still on this island? Is that *really* what you want to do with your life? What about having a purpose?" She jabbed another piece of fish into her mouth. The guy sure could cook. He would make someone a very lucky wife someday—

Nope, not going to go there. Marriage wasn't a goal; it was part of the journey… and *only* if she found someone compatible.

He was pretty compatible *last night…*

Shut. Up.

"Uh, Princess?" He leaned onto his elbows. "In case it's escaped that vaunted memory of yours, I've already fulfilled my purpose. I saved a goddess' life, remember?"

His lips closed over his next bite of dorado in a way that had her having a hard time *not* remembering last night.

She shook her head—as much at herself as at him. "So now you're just resting on your laurels for the rest of your existence? Do you get up each morning and think, 'Well, I saved Pele so my life is complete'?" She shuffled some fish around on her banana leaf. "Sounds to me like you're just counting off days. Marking time. What's the point of living, Jace, if you don't actually, *ya know*, live?"

Jace shut his trap and stared at her.

Damn. The woman didn't pull any punches. What *was* his purpose in life? What did he do with this Immortality Zeus had gifted—or cursed—him with besides eat, sleep, repeat?

He hadn't done much, actually.

He dropped his spork, then leaned back in his chair. Again. Well… shit.

"Jace?"

He raked a hand through his hair. "Yeah, okay, but if I hadn't just stayed here and *rested on my laurels,* as you put it, who would be helping you? Who'd feed you and move rock for you?"

She shrugged. "I was prepared to do that myself."

"And now you don't have to." See? He had a purpose. He leaned forward. "So, Princess, my purpose right now is to help you. And when I'm done doing that, I'll find someone else to help. So *that's* my purpose." He sat back and crossed his arms. "Satisfied?"

She cocked her head and waves of her hair fell over her shoulder.

Well, he surely wasn't satisfied. Not with *memories* of what her hair had felt like falling all over him.

Damn. His fingers itched to smooth it back into place. And then keep on going—

"It doesn't matter if I'm satisfied with your life choices Jace; it matters if *you* are." She tapped the table top. "Are you? Satisfied, I mean?"

He would be if they could just finish dinner and then maybe… *satisfy* both of them—quite satisfactorily—and end this conversation. It'd gone down a deep and angsty trench he didn't want to go down. He didn't want to examine his history with his brother to figure out why he was fine with staying out of sight. He didn't want to examine his life choices too closely because *he'd* made them. The one good thing he'd done—maybe the *only* good thing he'd done—had been to save Pele. Unfortunately, only Zeus and Pele knew about it—well, and now Mariana. But he didn't need public accolades; he'd saved the goddess because it'd been the first thing to pop into his mind to do when he'd seen her drowning. It hadn't been a conscious decision—something he'd had any control over—he'd just done it on instinct.

If he *had* thought about it, he probably *wouldn't* have done it because it was against the law, and then where would he be?

Yeah, this conversation was beyond heavy. Damn, he didn't want to consider any of this. He was just Hades-bent on staying alive and the rest… whatever. At least he'd gotten her out of her own head and she was talking to him.

Maybe *that* was his purpose.

Yeah, he'd go with that.

For now.

"Hello?" She waved her hand in his face. "Now who's the one *blanking out*?"

"I think we need some rum." He definitely did. All this soul-searching wasn't good for the soul if one didn't like what they found.

He went to the pile of things he'd brought from the hut and pulled out the bottle. He'd debated before packing it, but thank the gods he had. He could finish the rest himself and *blank out* until morning so he wouldn't have to think about what all they'd just said.

"You know, I was fine living here on my island all alone before you showed up." He plunked the rum bottle onto the table between them.

She arched an eyebrow. "And now you're not fine? You want to leave? That would solve my problem."

"That's not what I meant." He poured a healthy amount into his coconut. Or maybe it was an unhealthy amount. He didn't care.

"What *did* you mean?"

"Why? What's it matter to you, Mariana?" He held the bottle out to her.

She shook her head. "You're right. It doesn't. It's just a way for me to get out of my own head."

He almost dropped the bottle. Look at him—he'd figured her out and she was admitting it. "Oh really?"

She rolled the coconut between her palms, a little bit of liquid sloshing out over the top. "Yes, really. I've been asking myself the same questions and feel like…" She rolled it some more as she looked out to see where the sun was just dipping below the horizon. "I'm really tired of trying to figure out where I stand in the universe."

"Then why bother? Why not…" He stood up and held out his hand because she was in danger of heading down that angsty trench again, "…just figure out where you stand right now?"

She glanced at it then met his gaze. "What's this?"

"Let's go for a swim. I've found that being in our natural environment tends to put things in perspective."

Chapter Seventeen

The moment she hit the water, her scales returned.

And he'd thought they'd been beautiful on the sand? Nothing compared to the way the moonlight glittered over them, twinkling each one like a tiny star beneath the sea.

Jace dove in behind her, feeling the flutter of her flukes on his fingertips before she outdistanced him in an instant. Legs—even with Human swim fins—could never keep up.

A metaphor for his entire life.

Jace shook his head. He wasn't going to go there. He had enough to forget about, what with all they'd said on the beach, for him to want to go any deeper. Well, mentally. Physically?

He headed for the reef.

"Jace! Yo, Jace, buddy!" Merc's shriek bounced off the coral, reaching him before the crab did.

"'Sup, Merc?" He scooped the guy off one of the very few mounds of serpentine cup coral.

"Uh, you know there's a Mer in the water with you? The princess, to be exact?"

"Yeah...?"

"Well, aren'tcha, ya know, just a little bit concerned that she's gonna tell on you?"

"No, Merc, it's okay. She knows what's going on. Matter of fact, I'm going to help her with her project so she can finish up."

"What the—*what*? I thought you didn't want her to be here or finish that big ol' carving because the place is gonna be overrun with tourists and stuff."

"Long story, but we're working on that part."

Merc swiveled his eye stalk after Mariana's departing tail. "Well, I hope you know what you're doing, but I gotta say, she's not being too discreet. I mean, I thought the purpose of the frigatebirds was to keep strangers away."

Crappy, he forgot to tell her about the frigatebirds. "Uh, Merc, I gotta go. Will you be okay if I put you down now?"

Merc's eye swiveled around again. "Yeah, I'm off-island only a few hundred feet and the coast is clear; I oughta be there by morning."

"Let the waves carry you; you don't have any seabirds to worry about getting you."

"Oh, right. I forgot about that. Sheesh, this is gonna be fun—I love carapace-surfing, but I haven't been able to do it in quite a while. See ya!"

Jace tossed him into the next whitewash that came overhead. Wouldn't hurt to give the guy a leg up on the situation. Even if he did have ten of them.

"Hey, Mariana, wait up! There's something I forgot to tell you."

She did the most graceful figure-eight right in front of him, ending up facing him.

That figure-eight didn't hold a candle to her face. Gods, the woman was gorgeous.

"What'd you forget to tell me?" Her hair fanned out behind her on the waves and his fingers itched to stream through the strands.

"Uh, you might not want to swim out much further."

"Why not?"

"I posted some sentries out here."

"You did?" She laughed.

"Not sure what's so funny about that. It helps to have advance warning when you don't want to be found."

"I know. I posted some sentries here, too."

"What kind—wait. Let me guess. Albatross?"

"Yup. You?"

"Frigatebirds."

"Did they report me to you? Is that why you returned to the island?"

"Actually, no. I give them time off when I'm not here. I only reinstated them on my way back. Didn't your albatrosses tell you about them?"

"No. I told them to bother me only if there's a direct threat."

"So I'm not a direct threat?" He swam up and pulled her into his arms, his legs sliding against her scales.

"That remains to be seen." She cocked an eyebrow.

He wasn't really in a mood to joke about this. "Yeah, but I'm concerned that they didn't see me. Not much in the way of spying."

"How did you make your approach? At the surface or down deep?"

He nodded once. "Ah, right. I came in through an underground cave."

"So they *couldn't* have seen you. And what cave?"

"You haven't found the cave?"

"I haven't been looking. My focus, in case you've forgotten, is the *surface* of your island."

"Good point. Well, yes, there's a cave. I can come and go quickly, easily, and, most of all, hidden. A quick getaway in the event I ever need it."

"*Have* you ever needed it? I mean, there are a few shipwrecks around here so I'm sure you've had Humans showing up on occasion."

He shrugged. "Pirates, mostly. I had fun with them."

"Fun?"

He chuckled. "I swear, I don't know how the lot of them were ever successful in their endeavors, though I guess the ones I met on the island *weren't* since their boats had sunk. You should have seen them when they saw me emerge from the sea—looked like they'd seen a ghost."

"Or a Mer." She flicked his nose. "I *know* you know that you're not supposed to let Humans know about us."

"Yeah, but I figured, who were they gonna tell? The last ship went down a century ago, so it's not like they'd had any prayer of being rescued. No satellites or GPS or airplanes back then. Plus, even if they *did* mention me, people would just think they'd been hallucinating. The risk was worth the reward."

"Reward?"

"It…" He shrugged and dropped his arms. "Gave me someone to talk to."

"Oh, Jace." She put a hand to his cheek.

Jace captured it—he couldn't *not* capture it. The last time anyone had touched him—*him*, Jason Pontus, not Jace Pacifica, worldwide playboy—had been far too long ago.

He slid her fingers to his lips.

She watched him.

"Have you…" He kissed her palm. "Had enough?"

She gulped. "Enough?" Her violet eyes widened.

He slid his lips to the inside of her wrist.

Her pulse hammered there.

Good.

"Enough… swimming?" He trailed his lips up the soft skin of her arm to her elbow.

"Swimming?"

He smiled against the bend in her elbow. "Want to…" He kissed his way up to her shoulder.

She tilted her head to the side.

"Do something…" he kissed her collar bone, "… else?"

Her pulse thundered beneath his tongue as he tasted the slick skin of her neck.

"Else?" The word came out on a groan.

That was enough for him. Jace scooped her into his arms just as his lips touched hers.

And he lost himself to the kiss.

~~~

Up above, Sonny the frigatebird was making one last lazy circle on the ocean breeze before heading in for a well-earned rest after his tenth twenty-four-hour stint this moon-cycle. Hanging out in the skies was boring as fuck since he didn't have a clue what he was supposed to be looking out for— "Just anything out of the ordinary" was what he'd been ordered to report.

Did vanishing dinner count as *out of the ordinary*? The damn Marauders—the previous shift—had dive-bombed most of the schools out of the area. Those flying fish might have mush-for-brains (he knew; he'd eaten enough of them), but they weren't stupid. A couple dozen daily air raids and they took off for deeper waters, leaving
~~~

him and the rest of the Raiders crew with slim pickin's. He needed to talk to the captain to see if he could switch crews or patrol a new area for the next shift so he could actually *eat* something. He might get a bump in pay for the near-island patrol, but his muscles were achin' from lack of sustenance. A guy couldn't live on the private water acreage he was going to be granted in payment for this assignment if he couldn't hunt it when he was hungry and workin'. Sheesh. This shit was for the bir—*other* birds. Besides, his allotted acreage wasn't that far away, and with all the bait fish high-tailing it out of the area, what was he going to be left with?

He'd promised Sunny they could start a family when this job was over. But without enough shoals in his allotment, he wouldn't have enough to keep the two of them fed, let alone a third, fourth, and fifth hungry bill to fill.

He needed more. The chances of him getting it, though…

Sonny shook his shoulders, ruffling his feathers. Captain Kam had made it more than clear that they only had limited resources to divvy up, and what he was getting was *all* he would get. He was gonna need a side-hustle because he couldn't go back to swiping other birds' catch. He'd almost lost Sunny for doing that—she had such a stick up her gullet about the shame involved in not being able to catch enough. Never mind that it kept him away from home for longer periods of time; she was so proud of him when he returned with freshly-caught bounty that she'd crow about it to her friends.

That was Sunny, always needin' to one-up her girlfriends.

But at least she kept coming back to him each season. Not many of his kind did, but Sunny… she was his world and he was just glad she liked being in his.

Which was why he always made his life sound better than it was—he didn't know if she'd still want him if she knew his life consisted of working endless night shifts and having to scavenge for food.

He shook his head again and dove toward the water. Maybe there was a wayward squid on the surface to check out the moon since it was such a nice night—

Hello. What was that?

Or, rather, *who* was that?

Sonny beat his wings twice to stop his descent. His eyesight was good enough to catch the sparkle of scales and the long green hair streaming around the definitively Mer body.

There hadn't been a Mer around here in ages. Not that he'd ever heard, actually. Too remote. Nothing out here but the deserted island and a small shallow reef.

What was she doing here?

And more importantly, what was that *Human* doing swimming with her?

There was going to be all kinds of Hades to pay when The Oceanic Council heard about this. Humans could *not* learn about Mers.

But... Humans also couldn't breathe underwater like Mers and that guy had been under long enough without air—

Had she turned him?

Oh, boy, was *she* gonna be in trouble. Humans learning about Mers was *nothing* compared to Mers turning a Human into a water-breather. Yeah, this was definitely something out of the ordinary.

Sonny shifted his tail to turn leeward. He had to get back to report this. Maybe he'd even get a reward. Or, at the very least, a snack.

Chapter Eighteen

"How have you kept the marine world around the island from knowing who you are?"

Jace readjusted the arm he had beneath Mariana's neck as she linked her fingers with his, and stared up at the pink tendrils of light streaking across the morning sky. "You know about the cave and you've seen the hut." He rubbed a few strands of her hair across his lips with his other hand, the sand cool beneath his back.

That was the *only* part of him that was cool.

They hadn't needed to make a fire last night when they'd returned to the beach.

She snuggled against him and Jace could stay here for the rest of his life.

"Sure, but the sea isn't empty around here and you can't hunt everyone who sees you."

"True. But most are just passing by. It's not the issue you might think. And then, there are the few who call the island home who either *do* know who I am or know that I don't want to be seen. They help keep a lookout."

"One of them wouldn't happen to be a marine iguana, would it?" She became inordinately interested in his fingers on hers.

"Ah, you've seen Hermán?"

She bobbed her head. "Uh, yeah."

"Problem?"

"No. No problem." She nudged him with her hip. "Who else?"

"Who else is here?" He brushed some hair off her cheek, gazing into her eyes. The sunrise couldn't even hope to compare. "Well, there are several morays whose electricity short-circuited from a nasty lightning strike, a consortium of octopi who'd gotten tangled in fishing nets and damaged several tentacles who came here to recover and never left, plus assorted fish and birds damaged in one way or another who typically hang out in the lagoon on the southern side. And then there's my friend, Merc. He's a crab with one eyestalk. He'd have a tough time of it if he were with the general population of the sea because he's a little lopsided when he scuttles, and his peripheral vision is for shit. There's even a bunch of koi that somehow managed to get here who live in the river. We all work together to ensure our survival."

"And your anonymity."

"Exactly. Win-win. There's safety in numbers, even if some of those numbers are natural enemies. It's amazing how necessity makes the strangest bedfellows."

"Oh, is that what this is?" She rolled into him. "Strange bedfellows by necessity?"

"Princess, it's *definitely* by necessity, but there's nothing strange about it."

"So, that's it? You all live in harmony? One big happy family?"

"Well, let's just say that we live and let live."

"Until you need dinner."

Ouch. "Uh, yeah, that."

"But you can't monitor the ocean floor twenty-four/seven. What if someone shows up unannounced? How do you handle that?"

"Well, Pele helps out some. If too many schools are heading this way, she'll create a fissure in the sea floor to steer them off course. And since there's very little coral around here, there isn't enough feeder fish for the bigger predators, so they don't bother making the trip. And then there are the frigatebirds."

"But how does Pele know to get involved if no one's supposed to know she's alive to tell her?"

He shrugged. "Kam—he's the captain of the frigatebirds in this area who knows my secret; it's been in his family for generations—flies to the big island and prays to her at the mouth of the crater. Or that's what he tells his flock to explain his absence. In reality, she's listening to the reverberations of his words as they bounce off the volcanic walls. She then ejects a few small lava rocks with a code on them we developed eons ago, and he drops them down to me on his way back so I can decode them."

"What if this Kam guy gets the message to her wrong?"

"Well, it's not a perfect system, but we've been lucky so far. And every so often, I'll go visit her. Too risky for more contact if we don't want to be found out. Especially now, with Humans crawling all over that island with their hiking and the stupid helicopter tours, I have to be really careful about visiting. Can you imagine what they'd say to see me standing at the lip of the crater?

Or her trailing a fiery path of lava down the mountain to visit with me at the sea's edge? Humans have made our lives much harder."

"And lonelier, it sounds."

Jace looked away. He didn't want to think about the loneliness. Oh, he consoled himself with dalliances here and there with Humans, but the reality was, he *was* lonely. It sucked to be by himself, *selino* after *selino*, not able to be who he was with anyone other than the occasional one-eye-stalked crab or a frigatebird, both of whose existence was a blink of an eye in his, which meant he had to keep reinventing the friendship wheel with a new friend he *hoped* he could trust with his secret.

"It's actually really nice to be able to be myself with you. To not have to hide who I am."

She clasped his hand. "I'm glad. I can't imagine what it must be like having to hide from everyone."

"And let's hope you never will."

She glanced up at the mountain. "Well, that remains to be seen because if Conch doesn't like this, I don't think I'll ever be able to show my face again."

"You could always stay here."

"Huh?"

"Think about it, Mariana. I have Immortality and so can you. We could both just stay here and not have to face anyone again."

"I'd get lonely."

"You wound me, m'lady."

"Oh, please. I didn't wound anything. Your ego is more than intact."

The thing was… was it? Oh, sure, he knew what he looked like to the females of the planet. He knew he could bring them pleasure. He knew that Zeus, at least, valued him enough to grant him Immortality, and he knew he and Pele had a mutual admiration society going. But… that's all he had.

He'd been able to keep himself alive, but to what end? Just endless millennia of swimming through life with no purpose? Where was the value in that? What contribution did he make to the world?

Sure, some would argue that saving Pele's life was enough, and maybe it was, but… He sighed. He didn't know anymore. Before he'd seen Mariana's tail, she'd been just another beautiful woman to him. One it'd be no hardship to seduce to get her off his island so he could live in peace, but still, just a distraction. But, now… Who she was changed everything. Because, *now*, she wasn't just a wayward female to spend some agreeable time with and then forget. She was someone who knew his world. Who lived in it. Who had a life and dreams and plans and goals. She had a purpose.

He… did not. She was right; he *was* just marking time until… Until… what? The *end* of Time?

He didn't want to live like that.

Hades, that wasn't even living; it was existing.

He wanted to *live*. He wanted his life back, not this shallow existence on a deserted island away from his world.

Well, unless Mariana wanted to stay with him.

Think about it? Think about staying here on this island? With him? Forever? What was there to think about? She wasn't about to give up the life she was building, not for *any*one. Not Conch, not her family, and definitely not some playboy legend who certainly knew his way around a woman's body. That wasn't an innate skill; the guy had been around the Seven Seas long enough to perfect that knowledge.

And if last night was anything to go by—and the night before that—well, that knowledge was definitely perfect.

She shook her head. She was an adult, for gods' sakes. A good lay did not a future make.

But her sculpture… that *did* make a future. *Her* future. And she needed to make it happen.

And, besides, she'd only get Immortality when she married; the rules were funny like that. It wasn't as if Jace had just proposed to her.

And it wasn't even a thought she wanted to entertain. She had a career to create, not a family home. That could come later. If at all. Besides, the art would be her legacy—she'd decided that long before she'd met him. The sculpture—and her reputation—could outlive her. That was the whole point. That had always been the whole point. After all, she wasn't exactly overjoyed at the patriarchal idea of a royal female's Immortality being dependent on marriage. Of all the archaic practices…

And she was going down an avenue she had zero reason to go down at this moment in time when she had much more pressing matters to get to.

She slapped him on the stomach. "Okay, Casanova, fun's over. Time to get to work. This mountain isn't going to carve itself."

He groaned and rolled as she stood up, reaching for her ankle. "Come back to bed, Princess. The sun's barely up."

He, however, was bare *and* up.

Mariana shivered. It'd be all too easy to lie back down on the sand and let Nature take over.

But she was more than her base instincts. He was a living, breathing, sentient being, and she had a mountain to carve.

"Come on, Jace. Hold that thought until tonight."

"I'd rather you hold it…" he grumbled as he exhaled and climbed to his feet. "Fine, fine. Your wish is my command, Your Highness. Do with me what you want." He arched an eyebrow. "Or, rather, do with me what *I* want."

She rolled her eyes. "Do you ever think about anything other than sex?"

"Normally, yes. But with you around… Honey, I don't seem to be able to think of anything *else*."

Sad thing was, she was coming to feel the same thing.

And that scared her for her future in a way that any bad review from Conch couldn't.

~~~

"No, you did *not* see a Human with the Mer. That's impossible." Captain Kam ruffled his feathers so hard, Sonny thought the guy was going to molt.

"I know what I saw, sir. The guy was hanging out under the water and didn't break the surface. Matter of fact, it looked like they were doing a little more than swimming… and she wasn't complaining."

"It did *not* happen."

Sonny cocked his head. It most certainly *had* happened, and nothing the captain said was going to convince him otherwise. He knew what he'd seen.
~~~

Or… *did* he? Maybe there was more to the situation that what he thought. After all, the captain was going all-in on trying to convince him he hadn't seen that Human. *Trick of the moonlight on the waves. School of herring glittering in the light. A lost beluga.*

Bullsharkshit. It'd been a Human. Sonny didn't know why the captain was denying it—or why that denial was more important than the fact that there'd been a Mer in these waters. After all, Humans shouldn't be a big deal; there were enough boat wrecks on any given week, but a Mer? And one so close to a Human? Unless the guy *had* wrecked and the Mer was leading him to his death… But then the captain wouldn't be so adamant about the Human not being here and would be focusing on the Mer.

Something fishy was going on.

"You will keep your bill shut and repeat this folly to no one else, is that understood?" Captain Kam puffed out his big, red gular throat sac like he was the only one who had one.

Granted, Sonny's was smaller since lesser frigatebirds were called that for a reason—and who'd come up with those designations anyway? Talk about degrading.

As was the captain's tone. Sonny might not have the sac size the captain had, but he had the same brains and eyesight. He knew what'd he seen.

But for some reason, he wasn't supposed to have seen it.

Why?

"I'm waiting." The captain clacked his bill.

"Yes, sir." The words came out automatically, but Sonny had zero intention of honoring them. His brain was buzzing with all sorts of possibilities.

"Your allotment depends on your silence, soldier."

"I understand, sir." No-he-fucking-did-not.

But he would…

"Good." The captain did another bill-clack for good measure. "You're dismissed. Enjoy your R&R."

"Aye-aye, Captain." Sonny saluted his commander, then executed a one-eighty and headed out the opening of the outcropping.

Only to leap atop it and put his ear to the opening.

"Damn it." The captain ruffled his wings as he appeared in the doorway. "All you'd had to do, Jace, was stay on the island. That was *it*. *That* was the plan. Stay on the island or in the shallows and no one will be the wiser, but you decided to swim off-island? What the fuck for? And trailing a Mer? Are you on a freaking suicide mission? I swear to all the gods, Jason Pontus, I'm going to peck you to death myself when I find you." A rock skittered out of the office and bounced down the outcropping as the captain took flight.

Sonny jumped off the overhang and swooped to the backside of the outcropping, trying to pick his bottom bill up with his feathers at the same time. Neither was successful. *Jason Pontus*? But that guy was… dead. A legend.

Wasn't he?

Apparently not if the captain was cursing him out and now going after him.

Jason Pontus was alive…

And obviously living on that island.

Which explained all the security and need-to-know conversations and strict latitudinal and longitudinal grids they'd had to abide by. Not to mention, the Mer female.

Sonny rubbed the tips of his wings together.

Apparently, he *wasn't* going to need a side-hustle. Not now.

Not now that he knew something important. Something earth-shattering. *And* knew just the person who would reward him handsomely for this information.

He turned away from the barracks of nests used for surveillance respites. He wasn't about to sleep with this opportunity at wing.

He cracked his neck, stamped his feet, then ruffled his feathers, imbuing new energy into them. He had a long flight to make during his scheduled R&R—one he wasn't planning to return from.

"Sunny, honey, better get to pickin' out all the pretty colored shells you want. You're about to be able to afford the prettiest nest Thaumus' reward can get us."

Chapter Nineteen

Mariana's days passed in a flurry of activity, her nights in hours of passion.

She couldn't resist a small smile as she touched up the statue's cheekbone. All that nightly exercise ought to tire her out during the day, but the opposite was true. She had more energy and focus than before, so the work just seemed to flow from her shoulders, through her arms, down to her fingers, to infuse the very essence of the sculpture into her tools. She'd never worked so effortlessly before. Had never had a piece flow so easily from her chisel. It was as if someone or something was guiding her hand—

Kind of like Jace had done last night when they'd—

"Uh, Mares?"

"Tahiti?" Mariana grabbed the statue's nostril to keep from falling off. The bird's habit of stealth flying wasn't the surprise Mariana needed right now. "When did you get back?"

"Just now, and, boy, are my wings tired."

Mariana rolled her eyes.

"So, um… Mares?" Tahiti tapped her on the shoulder with a talon, her wings beating the air so hard, Mariana's hair blew into her face.

"What?" she gritted around the chisel in her mouth as she brushed some dust off the curve of the nostril.

"You know the lips are off, right?"

Mariana spat out the chisel. "What do you mean, *off*?"

Tahiti flapped ferociously to stay relatively in one place, then turned her beak to the side and narrowed an eye. "I mean, it's been a while since I've been to Easter Island, but I could swear those guys have really thin lips that are almost just a line with a big-ass chin. This one doesn't. And it's not as grumpy-lookin' as those others."

"What? That's not possible. I studied those statues in depth." She stared up at the upper lip. "Can you get my notes, please, Tahiti?"

"No."

"No?" Mariana swung her head around so fast she almost lost her grip on the lava. "What do you mean *no*? They're just down there in my sack." She'd woven seaweed together to create a sack so she'd be able to bring the slate tablets with her with the measurements she'd painstakingly planned out.

"Hey, look, hon, you know I'd do whatever I can for you, but I put my talon down at loopin' a sack of stone around my neck. That's only going to keep me grounded. And I'm not *about* to ruin this manicure by draggin' that sack and myself up this rock—if that's even possible. My wings are strong enough for air currents but notsomuch against stone. Not to mention, ya know, the whole tired thing?"

Mariana exhaled. She couldn't argue with the logic. She also couldn't argue with what Tahiti was seeing unless she saw it for herself.

She slid the chisel and brush into the work belt on her waist, then climbed down.

What the heck was the bird talking about? It's not like Tahiti knew anything about art or the artistic process. She was good company and handy for retrieving dropped items from atop the mountain, but as a critic… Well, Mariana wasn't basing her career on Tahiti's opinion.

Except… Damn, the bird was right. The lips and chin *were* off. They weren't anything like the Moai statues' mouth and jawline. They were more like—

Oh, Hades.

She'd carved freaking Jason Pontus' face onto this statue.

First, his nose. Now… this.

Gods damn him. Why'd he have to fill her nights so completely that he was obviously filling her days that same way? *And* filling her mind with him to the point that it came out naturally in her artwork.

She was going to be ruined.

Worse—she'd carved the one thing she'd sworn she'd never choose over her art. A person. Into the very thing meant to outlive her.

And *he* was going to be outed because if anyone knew Jason Pontus, they would know *exactly* who this was.

Her life savings was gone, she was out of time and resources—especially available rock face—to salvage it, and Conch was on his way. What in Hades was she supposed to do?

"See? Was I right or was I right?" Tahiti puffed out

her yellow chest feathers as she drifted onto a pile of the sheared-off lava rock that was taller than Mariana.

She'd carved a lot of rock.

"I mean, I gotta tell ya, I'm no art critic, but I know what's good when I see it. And this statue is good. It doesn't look like what you started out makin', but, hey, you could say it's your own interpretation, right? Artists say that they look at something and create it the way they see it. Look at that Picasso dude. He musta been chewin' on some wacky seaweed when he did that big wall painting in Spain that people call art—and what I call a Human five-year-old's crayon drawing, but… whatever." She shrugged her blue shoulders. "Maybe I'm not such a good critic after all. I mean, thousands of Humans go stare at that piece and it just makes me want to laugh. But I'm not laughing at yours, Mariana. Sure, the mouth is different, but there's somethin', ohIdon'tknow, *different* about this one. Dare I say, even… attractive? Those other ones… Meh. Notsomuch. I mean, I know they're supposed to represent dead relatives, but they all look alike, minus those little hats some of them have—"

"Pukao."

"*Gesundheit.*"

"No, I meant those hats are called pukao, not hats."

"Sardine/herring, same difference." Tahiti swiped one of her broad wings toward the lava. "What I'm saying is, you've got something here. It's the same, but not. Recognizable but different. You'll get people talkin', and isn't that what you want?"

It had been. Now…

Mariana rolled her neck to get the kinks out. She could despair that she'd failed in her desire to bring a Moai to this island *or* she could look at it through Tahiti's eyes.

This *was* something different. It was recognizable, yet… wasn't.

It wasn't as if Conch—even if he recognized the face—would look at this and think, *Oh, she must have used the real Jason Pontus as her muse so that means he's not dead.*

So, no, it wouldn't *out* Jace. At least there'd be that small consolation when Conch laid into her for messing up a Moai.

"You know…" Tahiti cocked her head and looked down her beak at the statue, then closed the eye on this side of her head. "It looks kinda familiar." The bird took off from her perch to fly eye-level with the carving. "Well, hot diggity dogfish! Now I know why it looks so familiar." She slapped her wings against her thigh then dive-bombed back down to Mariana, putting the brakes on mere inches in front of her face. "You carved Lover-boy."

Mariana refused to say a word. Bad enough she'd actually *done* it; she didn't want to have to own it.

"Someone got a lil' ol' crushy-poo, hmmm?" Tahiti tickled her feathers against Mariana's shoulder. "Can't say as I blame you—guy's pretty hot. Well, for a Human. But how's this gonna affect that old fart, Conch? I'm guessing he's gonna have to meet your muse then—"

"No."

"No? Why not?" Tahiti motioned for Mariana to stretch out her arm, then landed on it. "Once Conch sees just how much it looks like the dude, he's gonna *have to* give you five stars, or however his sort measures talent. I mean, *day-um*, Mares, you hit the nail on the head with this one."

But Tahiti only knew this because she'd seen Jace. She knew what he looked like, but, thankfully, didn't know *who* he was. And the bird had no reason to suspect that he was who he was because the history slates had him listed as dead—though they did note that his body had never been found; it was presumed he'd died in a flow of fiery lava. Therefore, Tahiti couldn't have a clue and neither would Conch.

"Uh, you know…" Tahiti scratched the top of her head with a wing tip, then flapped up into the air. "Now that I look at this…" She zipped from one cheek to the next, going up and down the length of the face. Even alighted onto an eyebrow, turning upside down to peer into its eye.

She then soared out about twenty feet, turned and hovered as best a macaw could, rotating her head from side-to-side, checking out the statue from different angles. Then she flew to the other side and repeated it. "You know, your Lover-boy looks an awful lot like a sculpture I saw in Athens, well, minus the beard. Humans have said it's of Poseidon, but it's not."

Mariana grimaced. She knew exactly which bronze Tahiti was talking about. The Oceanic Council had been trying to find a way to recover that thing from Humans for centuries. Not because it was a statue of Poseidon—because it wasn't. And not because it was a Mer statue—though it was—but because… it was of an event in their history Humans knew nothing about—a depiction of Thaumus' younger brother during their epic fight.

Which everyone in her world thought Thaumus had won.

Including Thaumus.

"Your boy-toy is Jason Pontus, isn't he?"

Mariana exhaled a breath she hadn't even been aware she'd been holding. "Tahiti—"

"I knew it!" Tahiti squawked as loudly as Mariana

had ever heard her. 'Ohmygods, Jason Pontus is alive? Well, this is gonna stir up some shit."

"Tahiti, you can't tell anyone."

"Oh, sweetie, I'm not gonna have to. One look at this thing—" she flicked her head toward the rockface—"and I won't have to say a word. If Conch is the art know-it-all he likes to think he is, the secret's gonna be out."

"But it can't be."

"Then I don't know what you're gonna do, Mares, 'cause this thing is a dead ringer for that guy."

"I know." She winced again. How could she have been so absorbed in the act of creating that she missed *what* she was creating? "But… but I could have been inspired by that sculpture."

"Oh, sure, you coulda. But one look at the guy hangin' with you and the story's out."

"Which is why Conch can't see him."

"True, but what about the frigatebirds? You know there're tons of them around here, right? All off-island and hangin' around the same area—which is odd, b-t-dubs. Never heard of a flock stickin' to certain grid markers, but whatever. Unless… Do they know he's here?"

"They know Jace Pacifica is here, not Jason Pontus. Only the captain knows the truth."

"Oh, honey, if one frigatebird knows the truth, they all do. Those things like to gossip. They can't keep their beaks shut."

"Well, Jace has been here a long time and I've never heard of him being alive, so I'm guessing they don't know—and you can't tell them, Tahiti."

"Moi?" Again with her blue feather tips to her yellow breast feathers in a dramatic pose. "Me spilling the beans is the *least* of your worries, honestly. You've got less than five days to turn Lover-boy here back into a Moai before Conch gets here."

That was a huge problem. Time notwithstanding, she'd shorn off too much of "Jace's" jawline to turn it into the square, bulky one of a Moai.

She was going to have to suck it up and let Conch think the Grecian piece was her inspiration.

She unbuckled the belt and threw it to the ground in disgust. Maybe it's what she deserved. After all, if she couldn't focus enough to carve what she'd set out to do—when the stakes were her entire *career*, not to mention Jace's *life*—then she didn't deserve to be called an artist.

"Whoa whoa whoa whoa whoa." Tahiti flew to the belt and lifted it with her talons. "Oomph, this thing is heavy." She set it onto a pile of slough lava. "You can't give up now. It might not be what you'd planned, but you have to finish it. Conch's gonna be here; he needs to see *some*thing. If he doesn't, you're going to have a huge problem."

Mariana picked up the chisel, sighing. She'd been so worried Conch wouldn't recognize her talent with this statue; now she was worried he'd recognize something all right—Jace.

And there wasn't a damn thing she could do about it. She just hoped Jace didn't see himself in it—

"What in Hades did you do, Mariana?" he said from behind her.

Too late.

"That's... *me*."

Chapter Twenty

Mariana spun around and held out her hand. "Jace, I can explain—"

"Don't. Just destroy it." He sucked in a breath, not caring what—who—it looked like; it just needed to be gone.

"What?! No."

"You have to. Now." He grabbed the stitch in his side.

"Look, Jace, Conch isn't going to know—"

"I'm not talking about Conch. There's a Human. Heading here." He bent over and sucked in a few more gulps of air. "That's what I came to tell you." He looked up. "We have to destroy it."

"But Conch—"

"Is the least of our worries. If the Human sees this—"

"But Humans never come here. You said so."

"Yeah, well I also said there are fewer places to hide these days because of Humans' desire for world dominance. Case in point with this guy." He poked his thumb back behind him to the shoreline. "He's got a huge yacht beyond the shallows. He's putting a tender into the water as we speak. I tore through the hut to get rid of signs of our existence. We don't have long before he finds this, Mariana." He reached for her toolbelt and—

Saw the macaw was looking at him. Appraising him.

She even rubbed her chin with a talon. "It really *is* you."

Oh, Hades. Not this. Not now. "Look, bird, I'll explain later. That's another story for another time. Right now, I need that chisel. I have to do what I can."

The bird wrapped her talons around the tool. "Name's Tahiti, Ja…*son*." She cocked her head and looked at the carving. "Yeah, Mares," she said, nodding to Mariana, "you nailed it. And *him* apparently." Her head bobbled as she cackled.

He was finding nothing about this funny. "Look, we don't have time for this. Those Humans are going to be here soon. This has to go."

Mariana stormed over to the toolbelt and yanked it off the ground.

The bird went squawking.

Good riddance.

"You're *not* touching my sculpture, Jace. I am *not* destroying it. We will discuss this *after* Conch sees it. I'm not even considering it until then. You don't understand, this is my career."

"And you don't understand—this is my life. Where there's one Human, there are more. This guy's not lost; a boat that big… He's got to have enough supplies to hang out a while. And once one of those people with him starts posting photos of this on their internet, it'll all be over. Conch's not going to be able to step his one foot onto this island to see it because Humans will be all over the place. I'll have lost my sanctuary and you won't get what you want. You'll just have to convince Conch with something else."

"Okay, well, maybe I can cover it up or something." She looked at the pile of rocks she'd chipped away. "I could put some of this back—"

He wanted to yank out every hair on his head in frustration. "There's no time, Mariana. Matter of fact, maybe I should have Kam fly over to ask Pele to light up this old volcano. It's the quickest way to destroy it *and* get that Human and his cohorts out of the area."

"A volcanic eruption? You can't—*she* can't."

"Sure, she can. And then, when the lava cools, you can start over."

"It'll be too late."

"I'm sorry to say this, Mariana, but it's already too late. We have to destroy it."

"Hold on, you two. Wait a minute." The bird swooped down onto the pile of discarded rock and pointed a couple of blue wing feathers at him. "What you talkin' 'bout, Pontus? *Pele*? Are you saying she's alive and living 'round here, too? What? You two got somethin' goin' on? If so, how's she gonna feel when she finds out you were bumpin' nasties with my girl, Mares, here? As I recall, infidelity hasn't exactly been ol' Pele's friend."

Shit shit shit shit. He'd forgotten about the bird. And now she knew about Pele. Godsdammit. "Look, bir— Tahiti." He raked a hand through his hair yet again. At this rate, he'd be bald by the next lunar cycle. "Can we table all of this for now? The important thing is to get rid of this thing so the Humans won't see it."

The bird flung her wing feathers in his face. "No, the

important thing is for Mare to make her mark in the art world. I don't know what you got stuck in your craw about these Humans, but they won't be staying. Not with a big fancy boat like that. I've found that Humans who have those things only stay on sand for about as long as it takes to crack open a bottle of bubbly, take some photos, and then they're off."

"Exactly. And those photos *are* the problem." He exhaled, then turned to Mariana. He didn't have time to deal with the bird. "Look, I'll help you, I promise. We'll work night and day to get a new one finished, but this one has to go."

"I can't Jace. Conch is on his way. There's not enough time."

"The immediate threat is these Humans, Mariana. Can't you see—"

"Hey! Lover-boy!" The bird flew in his face. Literally. Her talons grabbed his lips.

He shut up real quick. Those things could do serious damage if she tightened.

He was listening.

"You both seem to forget something." She released his lips, settled back onto the pile of rock, then swung her blue head between them. "Oh, come on—you can't tell me you can't think of *any* other way to keep the Humans from finding this thing?"

They stared at the bird…

…who rolled her eyes. "Oh boy, are you two pitiful." She whistled, then swept her wing tips over her head, smoothing the crown feathers down. "You. Have. An. Entire. Ocean. Of. Sea. Creatures. To. Do. Your. Royal. Bidding." Each word was punctuated by a jab of that long blue wing feather. "Royalty *squared*—who's gonna refuse you? Have a couple of whales rock that boat. I hear there's a pod in the Strait of Gibraltar havin' a *grand* ol' time these days doin' just that. Bet a few on this side of the world wouldn't mind some of that action, get my drift?" She cocked her head, blinking at them.

"I don't want whales to know I'm here," they said at the same time.

The bird sighed and dropped her shoulders, shaking her head. "I swear, you two have your priorities screwed up. *And* your information. Those birds you have circlin'?" She twirled her wing feathers skyward. "They haven't gone unnoticed. There's chatter under the sea. Folks are thinkin' some bigwig's on vacation or something. So they know somethin's up. Use that. Take advantage of it." She spread both of her wings, under-feathers up. "No? No one? Beluga? Nothing?"

She tossed her wings into the air. "Okay, lemme spell it out for ya. You." She pointed at Jace. "If they even know you're here, they obviously don't know *who* you are, so you're not bigwiggy enough to merit all this security. That leaves you, Mares." She pointed at Mariana with her other wing. "I know you're all 'I need privacy' and all, but let's face it, girl, Conch knows you're here and that you want to show him something, so how much longer do you think that's gonna be a secret? Logic says we need to let all the rest of the whales know you're here, and that this needs to be kept on the Q.T. It'll make 'em feel important. Never hurts to stroke an ego." She arched an eyebrow at him. "I said *ego*, Lover-boy. Don't get all excited."

If what the bird was saying hadn't been making sense, he'd dropkick her off the island, but she actually had a point… "Continue."

"Oh, why thank you, Your Highness." Tahiti did an exaggerated bow, complete with a rolling wing in front of her.

He didn't have time for this.

"Anyhoo, as I was sayin', let's tell 'em to go have some fun. Nothing too wild—no need for blood in the water—but a bunch of bumps and nudges ought to do the trick. 'Specially for the Humans in that dinghy thing. That'll *really* rock their world. Whaddya say?"

Damn. It made sense. Even the part about outing Mariana. "Not bad, bird."

The bird darted up and put her beak to his nose. "It's *Tahiti* and I'll thank you to remember it, *Lover-boy*. Got it?" She nibbled his bottom lip.

He got it.

He nodded, then looked at Mariana. "What do you say?"

She exhaled. "It ought to work. I mean, I figured Conch wasn't going to head all the way here without telling someone who he was going to see."

"He probably told a lot of people, Mares. I mean, after all, this is *you* we're talkin' 'bout. You're not exactly Conch's favorite Mer."

Now he wanted to punt *Conch* off the island. But not until after the guy had delivered his verdict on Mariana's work.

Which looked like it was going to live to see another day.

Chapter Twenty-One

"Well, Tahiti, that was a great idea." Mariana high-fived the bird as they all sat atop the sculpture, watching the Humans' tender motor back to the yacht, two pilot whales nudging it along into the sunset.

Well, a little more than *nudging* it. Those girls didn't know their own strength.

Jace didn't really care. Those Humans had almost caused him a major problem.

"Um, you might want to fly out there and let them know they can stop now," Mariana said, shaking her glorious hair down her back before leaning back onto her hands.

Tahiti looked over her shoulder. "Party pooper. They're havin' fun. It won't hurt to shake those Humans up a little more. Make 'em think twice about flingin' their sense of entitlement all over the place, ya know? There're other beings on this planet besides them."

Jace brushed his fingers over Mariana's—he couldn't

not do that. Today had been close. *Too* close for his liking. If the Humans had seen them or her sculpture, his sanctuary would be gone. He'd have to find somewhere else.

And so would she.

He wasn't ready for this idyll between them to end.

Does it have to?

He sat up.

Did it?

He almost smacked himself. Of *course* it had to end. Once she'd finished the sculpture and Conch had gotten a look at it, she'd… what? Do what artists did—go on to have art shows and publicity tours, then go back to her art studio in Atlantis to create some more. Go back to her family—all of whom could *not* know that he was alive.

Well, crab. This was the only chance they were going to have to be together, wasn't it? Unless she took a holiday and headed out here at some point in the future, hoping to ditch any entourage or paparazzi along the way, but what sort of life was that for either of them, her being out in the public eye, him hiding in the shallows?

"Oh, look!" Tahiti pointed to something out on the horizon—feathers weren't exactly the best thing to point with. "Those two are headed for the swim deck."

Jace got to his feet in time to see two sleek, gray heads aim for the back of the yacht. "No, they shouldn't. They can't go near the propeller or they could get injured. We need to warn them." He wasn't about to have their injuries on his conscience.

"Jace." Mariana wrapped her fingers around his calf. "You can't go out there. The Humans will see you. Isn't that why we asked the whales to do this in the first place?"

Right. Damn. He had to stay here.

Tahiti however…

He looked at her.

So did Mariana.

Tahiti stared back.

"Tahiti?" Mariana said.

Tahiti blew out a long, put-upon breath and unfolded her wings. "Okay, okay. Geez, you two are no fun." With a flap, she was airborne.

Jace sat down, then nudged Mariana's shoulder with his own. "We're no fun, huh?"

She smiled back. "I can think of lots of fun things we like to do."

So could he, but first things first. "Hey." He brushed some strands of hair off her shoulder. He'd rather dive into that glorious tangle, but… this wasn't the time. He put his hands in his lap. "I'm sorry for the 'let's destroy it' thing earlier, but when I saw that tender being lowered, I knew we didn't have a lot of time *or* options."

"I get it, Jace. I understand. But… *Pele*? Volcanoes? That's a bit extreme, isn't it?"

He glanced away. "It was. I'm sorry. But it was the only thing I could come up with. I'm glad it didn't come to that. Even if you *did* turn it into me. Care to explain that?" He was *very* interested to hear this.

It was her turn to glance away. "Yeah, here's the thing. I didn't even notice I was doing it. I was in such a groove, you know? I was just working with my tools and the tuff, and I just *felt* it. I closed my eyes and the shape just happened. Tahiti's the one who noticed."

"But how did she know it was me?"

She explained about the Greek artwork. *Figured.* That thing was the bane of his existence. He'd tried to steal it more than once, but Humans had big issues with someone touching their "cultural artifacts." Too bad the same didn't hold true between countries, but, hey, that wasn't his fight to have.

"I mean, don't get me wrong. I'm flattered that you were thinking of me so much, but it's too good of a likeness. Even if Conch doesn't recognize me, Thaumus will."

"But I thought the gods excommunicated him; how's he going to know?"

He circled a finger skyward. "You said Tahiti recognized it from the statue. A lot of those birds are very well-traveled. There's now precedent." Which was yet one more argument for destroying the thing. He almost wished Tahiti hadn't come up with the whale idea, but then Mariana would have been devastated.

What did it say about him that he was more concerned over her feelings than his own life?

Especially since he wasn't going to be able to have her in his life once Conch gave her his blessing.

"You make a good point. We have to make sure no one else sees this until after Conch does."

"And… what? Just hope for the best? Not exactly how I like to live my life, but I'll check in with Kam and reiterate how important it is that no one knows I'm here because, if I know my brother, he's not exactly living the life of a monkfish. He's got minions. And those sycophants will do anything to stay in his good graces."

~~~

Tahiti returned from her whale-recognizance mission only to have to do a security run. She hadn't been happy, but there'd been no other option to get word to Kam quickly.
~~~

Which, given the way his Chief of Security was gaping at him at their rendezvous spot by the lagoon, might not have been the best way to introduce the subject.

"Are you out of your mind, Jace?" Kam's gular sac was inflating with every word he uttered. "You went swimming *on the surface*? And with a *Mer,* no less?"

"How do you know that?"

"Oh, great, I see you're not denying it. Just great." Kam jumped from frond to frond in the tree he'd landed in, which wasn't exactly the easiest thing for a greater frigatebird to do given his size. It spoke to his level of annoyance that he was doing so. "One of my men saw you and I had to convince him that he did *not* see you. Lucky for us, he's not the sharpest feather quill of the flock. But, seriously, Jace? A Mer? Do you *like* to live dangerously? And you swam with her? How'd that happen? Mers aren't supposed to let Humans know about them, and, to her, you're a Human."

Jace didn't say anything.

"She *does* think you're a Human, right?" He jammed his beak toward Jace, almost hitting him on the chin.

"Well…"

"Son of a barnacle! What if she recognized you?"

"She did."

"*What*?" The bird screeched so loud, he—and a coconut—fell out of the tree.

The nut clipped Jace's ankle.

Damn, that hurt.

"*She. Knows. Who. You. Are*?!" The bird's wings were going a mile a minute to keep himself from hitting the ground, fluffing sand all over the place, and his gular sac was turning so red it was almost purple. "Why'd you hire us, then, if you're going to do exactly what you should *not* do?" He landed on the sand, shaking his head so hard that his beak rattled. "I swear to the gods, I don't know which is worse—my thick-headed guard or my thick-headed client. I can't guarantee anything now, you know. You've shot our whole protocol to Hades. I told the guard that he didn't see what he'd said he'd seen and that this whole mission is top secret so he's not to tell anyone, but anything's possible. That's why I specifically said to *not* go off-grid. To stay exactly where we'd talked about, so I could have those areas covered, but now you go and… and…" The gular sac was turning blue, which couldn't be good. Lack of oxygen, probably.

Jace clamped the bird's beak shut. Talk about a huge breach in protocol, but since he'd already committed one, what was another? "Kam, calm down. She's not going to say anything."

The bird yanked his beak free. "I swear to the gods, if I had a hat, I'd throw it on the ground and stomp all over it and you know how much I'm not built to do that, Jace."

It was time to put the guy out of his misery. "Kam, hang on. It's not as bad as you think."

"Not as bad?" The bird sighed again, then settled his wings over his back, twitching his neck until the gular lined up where it was supposed to go. "What could be worse than a *Mer* knowing you're a supposedly *dead* prince of historical proportions?"

"She's not going to say anything. She has too much at stake."

"Oh, sure—her anonymity in the Mer world because once she breaks this story, she's going to be famous." The bird was back to flinging his wings all over the place—so much for the moment of calm. "You are *such* a sucker for a pretty face, Jace. I swear to the gods. For once—*once*—" he hit his forehead with a few feathers, then flung his wing tip into the air— "could you have just kept it in your shorts already? You've bedded half the planet; couldn't you have just left this one alone?"

"She's not going to say anything."

"Uh huh." Kam did something with his wings that made it look like he put them on his hips.

Jace didn't know frigatebirds *had* hips. "She's not, Kam."

"Oh really? And how do you know this?"

"Because she's Mariana Tritone."

For once, the Chief of Security was at a loss for words.

"She's *who*?"

Well, not for very long.

"You let the princess of the current ruling family know you're alive?! Why in the blue skies would you ever do that?! Have you lost your mind?!"

That was a lot of yelling and wing-flinging for a normally rational and stoic security professional.

Jace started to say something, then shut his mouth and shook his head, rethinking his explanation. Kam didn't need the specifics right now; that'd take too long. Besides, the guy worked for *him*, not the other way around. "Look, Kam, it's a long story, but know that it's okay. She's not going to out me and I'm not going to out her."

Kam stopped mid-spin, his wings in the air like a ballerina Jace had seen in an opera house in Venice once. *"Out her*? What do you mean?"

Jace relented and gave him the highlights of Mariana's situation. "There? See? We both have something to lose if anyone finds out what's going on here."

Kam whirled around in a slow pirouette that Jace was sure the bird hadn't intended to look graceful, but actually, did. "Oh. okay. That makes me feel somewhat better. But couldn't you have clued me in to all this? I might have handled my guard differently."

"I didn't know he was watching."

"Jace," Kam settled his wings onto his back, clicking his beak before assuming his usual manner of competent authority, "in your position, you have to expect someone to *always* be watching."

"Noted. I'll be more careful." He held out a hand to shake Kam's wing. "Besides, can't you just assign that guard to a far outpost where he won't run in to anyone?"

The bird returned the gesture and they shook limbs. "I could, but he was due for some R&R. I couldn't take that away from him; he deserves it. I'll reassign him when he's back on duty."

"Thanks. I appreciate it."

"You'd better. This goes above and beyond our usual contract."

"I'll be sure you're well compensated."

"The money isn't what concerns me. My reputation's on the line here. My business. If word somehow gets out, it won't matter how much you pay me. I'll have lost all credibility, and, in the security business, that's the most important asset anyone has."

Great. Now it wasn't just *his* ass…et on the line.

They all had a lot to lose.

Jace sucked in a deep breath. They needed Conch to show up and get this over with before anyone else was the wiser.

Chapter Twenty-Two

Mr. Sangiovani to see you, sire." The marlin that'd greeted Sonny at the entrance to the cavern waggled its sword for him to enter the reception room of the lair Thaumus had been relegated to by the gods.

He hopped in, hating that he had to, but the gods hadn't designed his noble species for walking. Nor swimming, so he was very thankful there was a walkway above the waterline. He just hoped he was out of here before the tide came in.

Something he should have thought to check before he'd flown here.

He ducked under a low area in the ceiling, trying to keep his feathers from getting wet. If he had to make a quick getaway, he wanted to be able to.

Once his eyes adjusted to the darker interior, he looked around. The harpoon, fish hook, and other fishing nightmares on the walls were, um, intimidating, but as far as non-royal residences went, it wasn't bad. Sand floor, some rocks to sit on, a few more above the waterline held bottles of what he'd guess were kelp wine and a few clamshells of what were probably snacks, the refracted daylight turning the water a pretty shade of blue. A bit damp for his tastes, but probably right on the mark for what a deposed Mer king would like.

Though Thaumus didn't look like he was enjoying anything at the moment.

"Why are you wasting my time, bird?" He couldn't sound more bored if he tried.

Sonny was re-thinking this decision. Maybe he should have weighed the pros and cons a little bit more before heading here. At the very least, he should have checked the tide schedule, but pulling all-nighters to get here after a shift of all-nighters didn't necessarily make for clear-headed decisions.

He glanced behind him. For some reason, there were an awful lot of scylla serrata crabs hanging by the opening he'd been escorted through, pincers raised.

Okay, he wasn't going out that way.

He looked around the cavern. The only other way out was down. Through the water. Which would be the death of him.

So… he had no choice. He was here to sell the information he had. He just hoped Thaumus was in a mood to buy it.

"Bird, you have about three seconds before my patience is done. I was told you had information I'd be interested in. Let's hear it."

"Well, yes, Sire, that's true, I do. I was, uh…" He glanced back at those scyllas—had even more lined up in the opening? "That is, I uh…"

He cleared his throat, which made his gular sac

shake. He hated that his nervousness was so obvious, but one didn't just show up at a deposed king's cell all, "Hey, guess what, buddy? You're in jail for something you didn't do," and expect smooth sailing.

He slicked his gular down with a wing, then raised his head. "I've learned something I think Your Highness will find very… rewarding." He hoped he was getting his point across.

"You think to *blackmail* me?" Thaumus hefted his considerable bulk toward him, rising a good three feet out of the water—and his scale line wasn't even close to being visible. This guy had to be huge.

Sonny was feeling smaller by the minute.

Yeah, this hadn't been his best thought-out plan.

"No, Sire, not blackmail. Never." He should probably bow, right?

He tried that—problem was, there wasn't any place to bow *to* except into the water.

He shook his head, flinging water everywhere.

"What do you know, bird?"

"It's Sonny, Sire. Sonny Sangiovani."

Thaumus glared at him.

"Right. Um, that is…" Sonny hopped from one ineffectual foot to the other, his claws scraping the rock.

"I've seen enough. Pluck him." Thaumus frittered his fingers then rested against the rock again.

The scyllas were on the move, their pincers clacking like an offkey death march.

"No! Wait! Sire! I have news of your brother!" Sonny inched forward on his precarious perch.

Thaumus held up his hand.

The pincers paused.

"Jason? You have information on *Jason*? Perhaps

you haven't heard, my fine feathered fricassee, but there's nothing *to* hear about Jason since I *killed him*." He smiled and it was truly terrible.

Somewhere since his reign ended, the ex-king had gotten his teeth filed into sharp points like a great white's.

Sonny gulped and his gular shivered. He *really* should have thought this through. "Er, yes, um, Sire, but, you see… The thing is…" Sonny didn't know that telling this guy that he'd failed to kill his brother was in his own best interest.

Thaumus waved a hand and the pincer-clicking picked up. Got louder.

Closer.

"Your-brother's-alive-and-living-in-the-North-Pacific!" Sonny shouted, then hunched over, wiggling sideways to make himself as small a target as possible, trying to keep his tailfeathers as far from those pincers as possible.

"Halt!" Thaumus held up his hand, then zipped toward him, his obviously powerful tail frothing the water behind him.

A resulting wave splashed across Sonny's perch, soaking his lower feathers.

At this point, drowning would be preferable to those pincers. And Thaumus' spiky teeth.

The pincers stopped pincing.

"Look at me, bird."

Sonny looked up, his shoulders still hunched.

"Why do you say this?"

Sonny shook his head to get his beak to work. "I… um… heard my boss talking to himself about your brother. It was as if he was actually talking *to* your brother, saying all Jason had had to do was stay on the island, but, no, he couldn't even do that. And then I saw him. Your brother. Swimming in the water." He was going to leave out the female. He didn't need *two* deaths on his conscience. Besides, there was no guarantee she'd even still be in the area. And it wasn't like she hadn't been doing anything she shouldn't have—well, once he'd figured out that the guy she'd been swimming—and doing other things—with wasn't a Human.

Thaumus moved closer and strummed his fingers on the perch right under Sonny's breast feathers. "Which island?"

Here it was—the moment of truth. Did he sell out Jason for his own gain?

Thaumus poked one of Sonny's feathers. Right below his heart. "Bird?"

Forget gain; he was selling Jason out for his own life. "It's on the Mid-Ocean Ridge, northwest of Hawaii. Small. Uninhabited."

"Not according to you it's not if my brother is living there." Thaumus leaned in. "And I'm guessing you want to be paid for this information, hmmm?"

Sonny cocked his head. Blinked. Cocked it again. "Well, if you find it valuable, I wouldn't be opposed to a… um… *reward*?"

"Oh, you'll get your reward." He grabbed him by the gular. "Don't ever try to bribe me again, got it?"

Sonny nodded. A lot.

"And don't ever try to con me."

"But it's not a—"

Thaumus squeezed the gular tighter.

Dark spots swam before Sonny's eyes. He was never going to be able to give Sunny that nest she so wanted, was he?

"You *will* give me the coordinates and *if* this pans out—and I mean *if*—*then* I'll consider a… reward. Are we clear?"

Sonny used what little air he had left to cheep out a, "Yes, Sire."

Thaumus released his gular, almost flinging him away in the process. "Aella, see to it our guest has hospitable accommodations while he remains with us until I can confirm his information."

"Yes, Sire." A large brown sea eagle stooped to enter the cavern. She was huge. Double his size. Maybe triple. And that beak and those talons…

She glanced at him, hooding her yellow eyes in disdain. "Follow me."

Yeah, Sonny wasn't going anywhere without permission.

What had he done? All for a few pretty shells for his mate? He was about to destroy a man's life for *that*?

Gods, he *really* hadn't thought this through.

Chapter Twenty-Three

Thaumus hooked his chariot to the two marlins waiting in the courtyard. He couldn't believe he had to travel this way, but the gods had taken away his ability to use magic and had posted sentries at all travel portals. He'd tried bribing a few, but the gods had already promised them double what he'd offered if they turned him in.

They all had.

Greedy bastards.

"You have a shift changed lined up, right?" one of the fish asked him.

"Don't worry about it." Disrespectful. In his day, no one would have ever dared question him like that.

But it wasn't his day any longer, was it? All thanks to his pain-in-the-tail brother. Who should have died.

The fucker had always lived a charmed life. Granted, as a second son he hadn't been born to Immortality and he did have legs, but the gods had gifted Jason with a face and body Mer females went crazy over.

The guy could charm a snail out of its shell and get any female he wanted who would never even glance at Thaumus—even *with* the throne to offer said female.

The fact that they'd *always* chosen Jason over him had made him lose hope in finding a suitable queen.

Not that the Mer world even used that term—nor *king*—anymore anyway. Another repercussion of Jason turning on him. The current ruler went by the moniker, *High Councilman*, which implied a government by committee, no longer the autonomy he'd enjoyed.

He'd scared the gods with his power.

Thaumus had to smile at that. The gods had been frightened of him. Imagine that.

As a result, they'd yanked his magic and his power, and left him this stupid corner of just one of the oceans he'd once ruled. If he hadn't had Immortality by birth, they probably would have taken that from him, too.

Well, he still had it and he wasn't going anywhere. Except to Jason's haven to pay back his brother for taking away his birthright.

That ray's spine he'd jammed into Jason's heart should have made this unnecessary. He'd left his brother for dead, certain of it.

The gods must have stepped in after he'd left.

And now, obviously, they'd given Jason Immortality since he was still alive. All these centuries when Thaumus had thought him dead, he'd been swimming around the oceans, living a charmed life.

So what was Thaumus going to do? He obviously couldn't kill him now, but after what Jason had done to him, his brother deserved to lose the life he had.

And Thaumus was all about delivering that justice.

~~~

Jace didn't know what he'd done to deserve this time with Mariana. Sure, she spent most of that time attached to a rock, but he actually enjoyed her straddling his face—even if it was only vicariously. It certainly sent his imagination soaring. And, whew, his imagination didn't hold back.

Nor did he when she finally climbed down off that rock, and he had the time to *show* her exactly *what* he'd been imagining.

"Jace, stop it." She batted away the feather he was tickling the back of her neck with as she sluiced the pool water over her arms.

"Stop what?" He moved it behind her ear.

"That!" She flung her hair, the strands stippling across his chest.

He loved her hair.

He flicked the feather against her throat.

She brushed it away. "Come, on. I need to get all this dust and debris off."

He tossed the feather aside, took her chin and turned her to face him. He wanted her undivided attention. "I can help you do that."

She bit her lip, but not before he saw the beginning of a smile. "Then we'll never get dinner."

"Some things are more important than dinner."

"Really?" She cocked her head. "And what, pray tell, is more important than providing us sustenance?"

"It depends on what you consider sustenance." He put his lips where the feather had just been. "And I, for one," he inhaled her scent, "find that I need *you* far more than I need food."
~~~

Her breath caught in her throat.

He knew because he felt it happen against his tongue.

Why…

Oh, gods. What he'd said. He needed her.

…

His breathing stopped, too.

He didn't know for how long, but they both knelt there, at the water's edge, each one not breathing, but also… not moving apart. As if… waiting for the other one to do something. Say something. Make a move.

Fuck it. He'd been alone for eons and here she was. The one person who could match him in wit, intelligence, bloodline… *and* having a secret.

He pulled back and looked at her.

Her violet eyes stared through him as if she was trying to see into his very soul.

He hoped she could because he wasn't quite sure what to say.

He loved her. That, he knew. But… how did she feel about him? Should he risk it? Was this just an island fling? A vacation romance? She had her world and the one place on this planet that he did *not* belong was in that world.

"Jace…?"

He didn't know what to say. So he said nothing.

But he did show her.

He gripped the back of her head beneath that glorious fall of hair and pulled her up against him and kissed both of them senseless.

Here, like this… *this* was how they worked best. This was where they could say the things they couldn't give voice to. Where he could show her how much she meant to him without crossing that boundary of real life. Because their real lives couldn't mesh. Couldn't work.

But here, as long as she was here, everything worked. *They* worked.

He kissed his way down her face to her neck. The scent of her perspiration called to him, as it did every day when she was finished on the rock.

The image of her straddling the rock swelled up before him and Jace knew this was another lost chance to tell her how he was feeling.

But it was better this way. Better to not say it. Better to show it. So that she'd know but they could still both be able to walk away.

Because they would. They'd have to.

Conch was coming to make her a star and *he* had to fade into the dusk. He could never stand by her side.

He laid her down on the sand, his tongue tracing her delicate yet oh-so-strong collarbone, down to the valley between her breasts. His shirt had lost so many buttons it could barely be called a covering, but she insisted on wearing it. And he insisted on letting her.

He flicked the last button loose with his teeth.

Her breath hitched—at some point she'd started breathing again and he guessed he had too, though he couldn't remember taking that breath.

She gripped his head and pulled him back up to her, claiming his lips with her own.

No words could express the feelings between them the way their bodies could.

"Cop out!" his subconscious yelled at him, but Jace was beyond caring. He wasn't going to rationalize this. Not now. Not here.

Here, now, he was going to enjoy this time with Mariana. The time for rationalizations would come later.

Chapter Twenty-Four

"There." Mariana made one more sweep with her brush over the divot of Jace's upper lip.

The one made out of rock, that was.

"It's finished." She climbed down the un-carved rock beside it.

"You're sure?" Tahiti tittered from a nearby tree.

"I am." Mariana ran to the spot beneath Tahiti's tree to get a head-on view. Yes, she was done. Finally.

"Okay, as long as you're sure."

"Is there a problem with it, Tahiti?" She cocked her head, studying the angles and curves. No, she hadn't missed anything. It was all in proportion. She'd added the obsidian-and-coral eyes, even though it wasn't a Moai anymore because she'd put a lot of work into them and there was the time thing. But it was still a giant bust of a person; Conch couldn't take issue with it. Especially since it looked *just* like Jace—well, minus his gorgeous aquamarine eyes—not that she'd be pointing that out to the art critic.

Tahiti hopped onto another frond. "Good thing ol'

Lover-boy didn't take a chisel to it, or get Pele to do his dirty work. Sheesh, I can't believe she's alive, too. Who'd-a-thunk it?"

There were a lot of things happening that Mariana couldn't have conceived of.

Jace—Jason—being the preeminent one.

He'd been a myth. A part of their collective past. History. But now… here… he was part of her reality and—dare she say it—her future?

Mariana shook her head. She was dreaming. He couldn't be part of her future, not with where she hoped her career would take her. He had to stay hidden, and once Conch gave his blessing, anonymity wasn't going to be anything Mariana would have any experience with. At least, that'd been the hope.

Now…?

She exhaled. It still *was* the hope. This was her dream, what she'd put all this effort out for.

If she was going to make it in the art world, her work had to be seen—*she* would have to be seen, so she couldn't be with someone who couldn't be part of her world. That was the very definition of a relationship. Her brothers and Angel had made it work, but with Jace's need for secrecy and her trajectory into the art world, there simply was no workaround.

She was just going to have to have this statue as a memory of him. Her own little secret. Well, hers and Tahiti's, and the frigatebird's…

Ugh, this was getting complicated.

She clenched her fists. It shouldn't be, dammit. It was just supposed to be her putting her heart and soul into this one project to make all her dreams come true, but now, her heart seemed to be elsewhere—

Wait. What?

Her knees buckled, then her butt hit the sand.

Stupid knees. No wonder Mers didn't have them; they gave out at the silliest things.

Except… Jace wasn't silly. He was…

Uh oh. This wasn't good. Her heart *couldn't* be involved. She had a career to put into high gear. She couldn't be thinking about a guy—especially one who didn't want to be on the world stage. This wasn't the right time in her life. She could do that later—once she was known for her work and not her family name. Except…

Time was no longer on her side.

Not without marriage. Without it, she'd have a mortal life span. With it…

She looked out at the sea. Wave after wave rolled onto the shore, as they'd done for millennia. As they would continue to do…

Just like she could… with Jace.

That actually had win/win all over it. She could have Jace, she could wait out Conch's lifespan and hope his successor didn't have his myopathy when it came to the royal family.

Except…

That wasn't how she wanted to earn her reputation. She certainly didn't want it to be contingent on Jace—he'd forever wonder if she was with him *just* for Immortality. And, frankly, so would she.

No, her art *had* to stand on its own, which was why getting Conch's recognition for her talent meant so much—precisely *because* he didn't like her. Because he actively wanted her to fail. Her art had to stand on its own two feet—or volcanic rock, as it were.

She looked up at the sculpture again. It was good—

better than good; it was perfect. She'd gotten everything just right, and the fact that she cared for the subject might just be what made it so perfect. If something was made through the eyes of love, then—

Wait. What? *Love?*

"You okay down there, Mares?" Tahiti shook a palm frond at her. "Lookin' a little green around the gills."

"No gills, Tahiti." Mariana scrambled to her feet and brushed the sand from her bottom and the fog from her brain. She needed to get over herself and focus on her career—the one thing that was hers and hers alone, up to her to make or break it. Love—or whatever this was— could come later.

"I know you don't have gills, Mares. Just a figure of speech. Since when did you start gettin' all literal?"

"Sorry. Didn't mean to snap at you. But I have a lot more work to do. Any chance you want to lend a hand getting rid of some of this debris?"

Tahiti raised her eyebrows, then waggled one of her talons at her. "Did you not hear me about the manicure? I had to wait over a fortnight for Magda to fit me in for a good filing, and you want me to *haul rocks*? Sorry, babe, but no can do. Maybe you ought to get Mr. Big-and-Muscly to help you out. Where is he anyway?"

"He went to see a bird about security."

"That ought to be an interestin' conversation seein' as how you've both pretty much given up the laying low thing, but what do I know?" Tahiti ruffled her feathers, then took to the air. "If you ask me, Mares, I say just give up this whole secrecy thing, tell the world he's alive, and go live your happily-ever-after. Even if you think you have forever, why wait to begin it? You never know when life's gonna throw you a curve ball. Look at his brother, for instance. Bet that guy thought he'd be rulin' these seas for eons to come. Ya just never know, Mares. Ya never know what's over the next wave…"

~~~

Sonny glanced around at the desolate peak they'd put him on—and then at his guardian circling high above. It'd been more days than he wanted to think of with that old eagle-eye flying around. He wasn't going anywhere.

At least she'd brought him lunch today, and the lone scraggly tree *did* offer some comfort from the sun since he couldn't fly to let the breeze cool beneath his wings. The fallen fronds even offered some comfort for his poor feet on the craggy rock, but, *fish!* what he wouldn't do to be home in his nest with Sunny.

She had to be wondering where he was. What'd happened to him.

Maybe it was better she didn't know.

No, that wouldn't be fair to her. After all, she'd promised to give up the polyamory his flock delighted in, no longer changing partners each breeding season. She'd said she thought it was sweet that Sonny only wanted her and, after some of the mates she'd had, Sonny was the perfect one for her.

But he knew if he didn't get her those pretty shells she wanted, Sunny's mind could change in an instant.

No, he needed to let her know that he was coming home to her. And, hopefully, with everything she'd ever wanted. But, to do that, he'd need to get off this rock.

He glanced skyward. The old bat, er, eagle, was just
~~~

floating around on the thermals, as if she wasn't holding his life in her talons.

Sad part was, it was his own fault. He shoulda thought this whole whistleblower thing through more thoroughly. Telling Thaumus no longer seemed to be in his best interests because, when it came down to it, sitting around on a rock, waiting for the deposed ruler to decide his fate, proved he wasn't some big superhero but more of a home-birdie who just wanted to be by his mate's side.

Well, if that was ever gonna happen, he was gonna have to make it happen. What was that old saying? He'd gotten himself into this mess; it was up to him to get himself out of it.

He looked around. Not a boat in sight he could fly to—the old bird upstairs wouldn't dare approach a human vessel. Those humans were annoying and destroying the seas, but they did put the fear of gods into marine life. But he'd risk it if they were around because anything was better than sitting here, waiting to see if Thaumus would consider feeding him again. After all, the guy wasn't exactly known for his charity, and Sonny had already served his purpose.

Well, his purpose to *Thaumus*. What would *Jason* Pontus do if he knew that his brother knew he was alive?

Sonny scratched his chin. This would be a tricky wriggle, given that *he* was the one who'd spilled the beans about Jason being alive in the first place, but warning the guy had to have *some* sort of good repercussions, right?

He grimaced. He'd definitely gotten himself between a rock and a, er… He looked around. Between a rock and a *watery* place, but still… He couldn't just stand here and starve to death waiting for Thaumus to decide he wasn't worth the effort of being kept alive. He had to do *something*. He'd rather die trying than die *not* trying.

That settled it.

He scanned the horizon. No ships, no whales, and not a friendly bird in the sky. That left him the sea. But since he couldn't dive—frigatebird feathers weren't designed for it—he had to check the shallows.

Glancing at the eagle once more—she wasn't paying him a lick of attention, but that would change if he took flight—Sonny side-stepped ever so slowly down the rock to the water's edge.

Not even a fry swimming around. Stupid fish; didn't they realize how safe this inlet was to birth babies?

He blew out a breath, then glanced upward again. She was beginning the north-south run of the grid over this island, so he'd head west to the other side.

After what seemed like hours but was probably only about fifteen minutes of shuffling, he finally got lucky. There, in the shallows was a squid. Not the giant kind that would be able to take his message back quickly, but one squid was better than no squid since this one squid was *all* there was in the shallows.

Sonny tapped a toe in the water. "Uh, hey. Excuse me." He swished the water toward the cephalopod.

It opened its eye. "Huh?"

"I said, 'Excuse me.'"

"Oh, I know what you said, and I figure if you were going to eat me, you wouldn't have been so polite about it, so, while I know what you said, I don't know *why* you said it."

"Well, I didn't want to startle you out of your, er, nap."

The squid blinked. "And, yet, you did." It rippled its tentacles to latch on to a few smaller rocks—probably as slingshots if Sonny got too close. "But I'm awake now, so what do you want?"

What he wanted was to slurp that thing up for lunch, but he wouldn't. Gods, it sucked being at this creature's mercy.

But he *was* at its mercy, so he'd better be nice to it—him? her? Who knew with cephalopods; it wasn't as if he could just look under its hood to tell.

Ew. That wasn't an image he wanted to dwell on.

"Uh… I was wondering…" He coughed to put a nicer tone into his voice. "…if you wouldn't mind getting a message to my wife, Sunny. She's on Kure. Nest number forty-five. It's on the leeward side." Where any frigatebird with an ounce of sense would build.

"No way, dude." The squid dragged the stones toward its center. "I don't wanna end up as her lunch."

"I promise you, she's not going to eat you."

"Uh huh. This from a guy desperate to save his own neck. I don't think so."

"Please. I'll give you anything."

The squid's eye blinked at him. "Doesn't look like you got anything *to* give."

"I'll get it for you after I'm outta here. The royal family will pay a big reward."

"The royal family?" The squid rolled over and the other eye blinked at him. "What's the royal family got to do with this?"

Sonny ruffled his feathers. "There's gonna be some trouble. Thaumus is gonna go after one of their own." Not really what he needed the guy to know, but he had to show him how important it was for Sunny to know he was okay, so if he had to dangle the lure of a royal award, he was gonna do it.

"Do you really think I'm that simple-minded?" The squid waved all eight tentacles. "The dude can't hurt a dragonfly let alone a member of the royal family since the gods took his magic."

"But they didn't take his physical power. He can still swim and mangle things—people—with his hands. Plus, he's got a nasty assortment of hooks and other fishing junk at his disposal."

A tentacle tapped the water, ripping it. "Right. Which makes it suicidal for me to do anything to piss him off."

"But you'll be saving a member of the royal family. Surely *their* gratitude is a bigger draw than not pissing off Thaumus?"

"Do you *know* the dude? Like, seriously, he's not someone whose bad side you want to get on." The squid's eye glanced at the eagle in the sky. "Though, I guess you already know that."

"Ya think?" Sonny gritted out, wanting to skip the damn cephalopod over the waves, but that would alert Aella that he was having this conversation and he couldn't fucking believe his life had come down to a squid. "What if I…" He couldn't believe he was about to say this. "What if I guarantee you and your family safety within my allotment once I get out of here, in addition to whatever the royal family decides as your reward? You'll have a safe place in the ocean, which, really, you can't beat. I know your kind has a long migration and you probably have to be on your toes, er, suckers, the entire way. This way, you'll know you have a safe haven to regroup and regain your strength. Come on, what do you say?"

The squid stroked his mantle. "Just where is this allotment?"

Sonny gave him the coordinates.

The squid's eye opened even wider. "That's a sweet location."

For squid migration, maybe, but, frankly, Sonny was going to be utterly grateful for it in a whole new way if he made it out of here alive to get it. "So you'll do it?"

"Not so fast." His two arms came up to stroke the area of where a chin would be if squid had chins. "My whole squad, right?

"All of 'em. Even your mother-in-law."

The squid blinked. "Well, let's not be *too* generous."

Sonny cracked the first smile he'd felt since Thaumus had imprisoned him. "I get it, dude, but, remember, happy wife, happy life."

The squid nodded. "True that." He held out a tentacle—er, six. "Okay, it's a deal."

"Great. All you gotta do is tell my wife that I'm okay and I'll be home just as soon as I can."

"The royal family's gonna give a reward for *that*? I don't think so, dude. Not unless your wife's a Mer?"

Sonny counted to eight—one for each of his toes. "To get to my wife, you'll need to swim by the island where Princess Mariana is and let her know that Thaumus knows his brother is alive and he's coming after him."

"Princess Mariana? Thaumus' broth—*whoa*. Thaumus is going after his *brother*?" The squid propped his mantle up on his two arms. "I thought Thaumus killed him eons ago."

Sonny summarized the situation as succinctly as he could while trying to impart the importance of getting this information out asap.

"I still don't see why you're counting on a reward from the royals—they'll be happy if Thaumus kills his brother. No challenges to their throne."

"Because…" Sonny stamped a semi-webbed foot. "Princess Mariana is with him on his island, and if Thaumus shows up screaming bloody murder, she could get hurt, and they are *not* going to like that one bit. So, you tell them, which will save her, and the royals will be happy and give you a reward. Kills three birds with one stone, as it were."

"You actually use that saying? What are you, a sadist?" The squid shook his mantle. "But, whatever. You do make a decent point. Rod *would* be kinda pissed if his sister gets hurt." He puffed out a spot of ink. "Okay, fine. I'll warn them." He shook his mantle. "Fish, I can't believe he's still alive. I heard he wasn't a bad guy in his time. Wonder what he's been doing all this time."

Hiding from his brother, and Sonny didn't blame him. He should have thought about *that* before he came here to turn the guy in.

But… what was done was done. He just had to handle the fallout. "And then you'll get a message to Sunny? I don't want her to worry about me."

The squid eyed him up and down. "I don't know what she sees in you, dude, because you're a sorry-looking specimen of a frigatebird, but I guess there's no accounting for taste."

Sonny bit back that this dude would probably *taste* really good, but only because he had to get the word out. But he had zero intention of honoring the bargain he'd just made with— "Hey, what's your name? Need to know who to protect with my allotment."

"Name's Quetzal. And you are?"

"Sonny."

"And your wife's name is Sunny?"

"Yeah. Kinda predestined, wouldn't'cha say?"

The squid shrugged all ten appendages. "Or the gods were just having a laugh at your expense." He spun around. "Catch you on the waves, dude. You'll be seeing me."

Oh he'd catch him on the waves, all right…

Sonny nodded as Quetzal propulsion-ed out of the shallows. Joke about sweet Sunny's name, would he? That *dude* was in for a bit of a surprise when he showed up at the allotment—*no* one insulted his wife and got away with it.

But him? He *had* to get away.

And, a few hours later, when he glanced at the frothing water where the entrance to Thaumus' cave was and saw the rising tide of fearsome marine life emerging, all decked out for battle, he hoped his chance had come and could get away from this rock before all Hades broke loose.

Chapter Twenty-Five

Mariana paced the sand. She'd opted for legs for this meeting because she wanted to be above Conch's level when he arrived. She wanted to show him what she'd endured to bring this art piece to life.

"Relax, everything's going to go swimmingly," Jace said as he walked out of the mangroves.

"How do you know?" she asked, biting her nail. "You don't know him. He takes great pleasure in humiliating me."

"You can't be humiliated if you don't value his opinion. It's good; you know it's good."

"But the rest of the world *does* value his opinion, so I need to as well, therefore, yes, he *can* humiliate me. He's done it on one occasion already, if you recall." A spectacularly monumental occasion. One she'd had a hard time living down. Sure, it hadn't been her fault the inebriated guy had fallen into the sculpture, but she could have secured it to the base better so it should have been able to withstand drunken shenanigans.

Maybe she had been a little too big for her scales, thinking her work could stand on its own.

Ouch, the irony was painful.

She looked up at the side of the mountain. No one could say this one didn't stand on its own—figuratively *and* literally. Jace was right, it *was* good. It was so lifelike she was actually more impressed with herself than if she'd managed to merely copy someone else's Moai.

But she couldn't allow herself to be impressed—pride went before the fall. She'd had firsthand experience with that already. She needed to let Conch see her talent, see how she'd captured the reality of a fellow being. How the sculpture's eyes seemed to shine with intelligence and warmth. How the mouth curved in just the tiniest bit of a smile. How his skin shone, seemed to beam in the sun—

"He ought to be here in about fifteen minutes." Tahiti's pronouncement cut in to her thoughts as the bird landed on the palm above her head.

Quarter of an hour. Not much time to put off reality.

She looked at Jace.

Fifteen minutes before her life was going to change and Jace would no longer be a part of it. Whatever Conch decided, it would make the news. Either she was going to be a success or a spectacular failure. Her name would be everywhere.

And Jace could be nowhere.

She moved closer to him and slid an arm around his waist.

His arm came around her shoulders, then he kissed the top of her head. "It'll be fine. It's amazing. *You're* amazing. Conch will see that. And then all your dreams will come true."

But… would they?

Standing here, the sunrise bathing his face—the rock one—in muted golds and yellows, the quiet sound of the surf harmonizing with the whisper of palm fronds in the sea breeze, the warm sand beneath her feet, his even warmer body beside hers… wasn't this a dream, too?

She didn't know anymore. She honestly didn't know which she wanted more—her career or this quiet peacefulness with Jace by her side.

She rested her head on his shoulder. How had it come to this? How had she not seen it coming? Why had she never listened to her siblings when they'd explained that being with their spouse was worth whatever sacrifice they'd had to make because the reward was bigger than whatever they'd thought they were losing?

Well, it didn't matter now what she wanted. Everything was in motion, on its own path, converging like the tides with the lunar cycle, and there really was nothing she could do to stop it.

"T-minus twelve and counting," Tahiti squawked. "He's making better time with the advance guard we sent out. Molokalani is a quick little tropicbird that's for sure. Probably trying to garner some brownie points for a raise next review period."

Mariana didn't know whether to be grateful or angry that time was rushing toward her as fast as Conch was.

Well, there was nothing to be done about it. Like the tides, Conch was going to hit the beach whether she wanted him to or not.

"Jace," she flattened her palm on Jace's abs. "You shouldn't be here."

"I know. I—

"JACCCCCCCCE!" A frigatebird came dive-bombing from the sky behind Jace, its wings stopping it mere inches from the ground, the fierce pounding pinging sand onto Mariana's legs.

Jace spun around. "Kam? What's wrong?"

The bird dropped onto the sand, his gular sack wheezing in and out so fast, he looked like an accordion. "Thaumus…" He gulped and the sack rippled like a pelican swallowing a fish. "Thaumus…" He gulped again. "He… knows…"

"He what?" She and Jace said it at the same time, their knees giving out, putting them eye-level with the bird.

The frigatebird gulped again, nodding. "He's headed this way. A whole contingent…" The bird took a deep breath, the sack inflating like a bagpipe. "Marlins, swordfish, great whites, a flotilla of pincers… they're on their way and not being quiet about it. One of my scouts caught them about seven leagues east of here. He's coming for you."

"But how does he even know about me?"

The frigatebird cursed in about six different languages. "The sentry I mentioned? The one I gave R&R to?" He shook his head and another dozen languages of curses followed. "He hasn't come back and his last known flight path was in the direction Thaumus is coming from. You do the math."

"Son of a M—" Jace stormed to his feet and raked a hand through his hair. "This is *not* what I need right now."

"Right *now*? How about *ever*?" The frigatebird paced right beside him. "I cannot believe one of my avians—" The squawk he uttered was probably the foulest language a fowl could utter. And Mariana agreed with him. "We gotta get you somewhere safe."

Mariana nodded. "I can get my brother to send an army. I'm sure he will when I explain—"

Jace stopped. "No."

"No?" she and the bird said at the same time.

"No." Jace shook his head. "I'm done running. I want my life back, and Thaumus is not stealing one more *selino* of it, let alone any more of the centuries I've had to hide. I'm going to confront him."

"No!" This time it was a chorus of three screeching at him.

"Jace, you can't." Mariana grabbed his arm. "I can't lose you."

He put a hand over hers. "Who says you're going to?"

"Look, Jace, sir…" The frigatebird bowed. "This is my screw-up. I'll fix it. We are not putting your life in danger any more than it already is. I can't allow that."

"And last I checked, I outrank you, Kam. Because I hired you." Jace brushed a strand of hair off Mariana's face. "Look, this is the worst possible time for my brother to show up. We can't have a confrontation when your art critic is here. You deal with him and make your career goals happen. This isn't your fight. I'll lead Thaumus away and deal with him as I should have centuries ago."

"Jace, my art isn't important compared to your life. You can't face him alone—Kam said he's got an entire battalion with him."

"What about Pele?" Tahiti's question stopped everyone in their tracks.

"Pele?" Kam's eyebrow arched. "Are we involving a supposedly secret goddess now? Just how much truth are we opening up here, and does anyone want to consider what Zeus is going to say when we out his other big secret? Besides, Pele is the goddess of volcanoes and fire and lightning; Nāmaka would be who we'd need to ask since she runs the seas in these parts."

Tahiti uttered the same curse. "Oh, great. The sister who thinks her sister is dead at her own hand—you think she's gonna side with *Jace* when she finds out what's been going on? She'd probably hop on board Thaumus' train since they have the same motivation, don'tcha think?"

"Exactly." Kam grunted. "So that idea's out. The last thing she'll want to do is help Jace for a cause she's not going to care about when she finds out what he did."

That was true, but… Pele *would* have a vested interest in saving Jace's life specifically *because* of what he'd done for her.

Mariana tapped her lip. There had to be some way to stop Thaumus and protect Jace.

"Not to be a rebellion-pooper," Tahiti landed on Mariana's shoulder, "but Conch's gonna be here in about eight minutes. We gotta make some decisions, folks."

"Well, I've made mine," Jace said. "I'm going to head north and lead Thaumus away. You keep your meeting with Conch, sweetheart, and make all your dreams come true."

"Jace, you can't do this on your own—"

"I'll do whatever I have to to keep you safe, Mariana."

"I'm perfectly capable of taking care of myself, Jace." He did *not* get to play knight-in-shining-scales when it came to her making decisions about her own life. *And* his now that she wanted to be in it.

"Except you don't have Immortality yet—unless you forgot to tell me you got married somewhere in the past?"

"Of course I didn't forget to tell you—because there's nothing to tell."

"So, you aren't married?"

"Would I have slept with you if I was?"

"Well, I'd like to think I'm that irresistible—"

She punched him in the arm.

"Ow. That hurt."

"Yeah, well you leaving is going to hurt more."

He dropped his chin to look at her from under his brow, and cupped her cheek. "Sweetheart, please, let me do this. We'll figure something out once I lead Thaumus away. It's the only way I can protect you because I wouldn't put it past him to kidnap a royal princess as a bargaining chip for his restoration to the throne."

Sadly, that scenario hadn't been out of the realm of possibilities for a royal in the past, but ever since her father had taken over, there'd been no issue. Still, if his brother was willing to risk it, who knew what would happen... "But where will you go?"

"Hey, I have a few tricks up my sleeve."

"You're not wearing sleeves."

"That's because you've got my shirt on, sweetheart."

"Don't try to charm me, Jace. This is serious."

"And so am I. I need to protect you from my brother, and the best way I can is to get off this island. Trust me, I'll be back."

"Spoken like a true superhero." She coated her words in sarcasm instead of fear because, just like she didn't want anyone telling her what to do with her life, she couldn't tell him what to do with his.

But it didn't mean she had to like it.

"Not a hero, sweetheart. Just a man who doesn't want to see you get hurt or give up your dreams." He dropped a quick kiss onto the tip of her nose then strode toward the water, diving into it like the stupid superhero he said he wasn't, leading the bad guy away from her.

Yeah, well, she wasn't going to let Conch dictate her destiny any more than she was going to let Jace and his stupid insecure brother decide it for her. Three could play at their game. She just had to figure out which hand to play...

Chapter Twenty-Six

So what is the actual plan, Jace?" Kam huffed when Jace popped his head out of the ocean to survey the area. "No disrespect, but your legs aren't a match for the flippered and tailed contingent your brother has. They're going to be here sooner than you know it."

"I'm counting on it, Kam—ah, there." He angled a little more to the northeast, opting for a freestyle stroke on the surface to keep his target in sight.

"Where?" Kam thermal-ed up a few feet and looked in the direction Jace was heading. "That? You're heading to that tiny atoll?"

"That tiny atoll has almost no land mass but plenty of shallow reef—

"…which the sharks can't penetrate. Got it." Kam swooped back down to just above crest-height.

"Yeah, so if Thaumus wants to come after me, he's going to have to do it on his own."

"You're forgetting the pincers he's got with him."

"That's where you and your men come in. Lunch is on me."

The bird managed a salute, his perpetually smiling beak widening its smile. "I'll put a call out." With that, the frigatebird banked to the right and zoomed westward to bring in more troops.

This had better work.

Jace dove back beneath the waves to surveil the area. He needed to make it to that atoll before any of Thaumus' advance guard reached him. It wasn't ideal, but there weren't a lot of spots in this neck of the oceans for him to be able to confront Thaumus on semi-level conditions. At least, this way, he could mitigate the guards around Thaumus, and the frigatebirds were more than up to the task of picking off the pincers one-by-one while he put his plan into action.

He navigated the sharp coral protecting the small spot of land above the waterline, knowing Thaumus would have a much tougher time. Good. His brother's bulky tail, which had always been such a pride-and-joy to Thaumus—for whom size *did* matter and who believed that bigger was always better—would be the perfect hindrance in attacking Jace. The guy's self-proclaimed—and self-deluded—*masterpiece* would be his downfall; so often the case with those wanting power. There was some poetic justice in that.

The atoll was about a-soccer-pitch in length of exposed coral and sand. A bit rough on the soles of his feet, but that would translate to scale damage for his brother.

He found a mound of driftwood and Human garbage—the only time he was glad for the migrating islands of plastic polluting the ocean—and parked himself in front of it to protect his back. He hadn't wanted this confrontation, but he was going to make sure it happened on *his* terms.

He didn't have long to wait.

"You're actually fucking alive."

As a brotherly greeting, it wasn't the warmest. But it was definitely heartfelt; disgust oozed through every syllable.

Jace didn't rise to the bait. Thaumus had always used insults to try to get under his scales-which—too bad for Thaumus—Jace didn't have. His brother could never see the irony. Then again, a lot got lost on the guy.

Thaumus dragged his bulk up onto the sand. "How the fuck did you survive?"

"Nice to see you, too, brother." Jace drummed his fingers on a broken crab shell—just as the first wave of scylla floated onto the sand. "I'd call back your contingent if I were you." He waved a finger toward the crabs.

"Why?" Thaumus' smile was grotesque—the guy had had his teeth filed. "Think you're going to be able to pick them all off before they do some damage to your... *feet*." There could not be more disdain in Thaumus' voice if he tried.

Except when Jace said, "No, but *they* will," and pointed behind Thaumus.

The sky was filled with frigatebirds.

Every single crab on the beach turned carapace and scuttled back into the sea.

Thaumus scowled. "Think you've got it all figured out, do you?"

"No, Thaumus, I don't. I'll never have you figured out. Why you'd believe I—your brother—would rat you out to the gods is beyond me. I've thought about it for all these centuries and I still can't come up with a reason why you think I would do that."

"Oh, come now, Jason, the throne is enough incentive for fratricide."

"Well, you'd know, wouldn't you? I mean, you did

try to kill me." He emphasized *try* just to show Thaumus that he hadn't succeeded.

"How did you survive? That ray spine in your heart should have done the trick. I jabbed you with it myself."

"Oh I know you did." Jace rubbed the spot where there should have been a scar, but Zeus had kindly removed that reminder as well. Too bad the god hadn't been able to do anything about the one in his brain. He would always remember that moment when he'd looked up to see his brother stab him to death.

"So how *did* you survive it?" Thaumus undulated his tail, pushing himself farther up the beach.

Just what Jace wanted him to do. He needed his brother out of the water. He was still working on how he'd keep him out for the allotted time to make his tail disappear since he couldn't kill him. But destroying his spirit by turning his tail into legs for eternity would be a fate worse than death to Thaumus. He just had to keep his brother talking until he could figure something out. "It doesn't matter how I survived; what matters is that I did. No thanks to you. Why, Thaumus? Why would you believe I would do something like that to you?"

"Because you wanted my throne. Who wouldn't?" He shrugged. "Well, you're not going to get it, little brother, and, this time, I'm going to make sure of it." Thaumus undulated closer.

Damn, the guy was faster on land than Jace had thought he'd be. Maybe having this pile of flotsam and jetsam behind himself wasn't such a good idea after all.

He rose to his feet.

"Where do you think you're going?" Thaumus rose up on his tail, taller than a bull walrus in full lekking mode. "My men have the island surrounded and, sorry, bro, but Aethos ain't gonna show up to save your tail—

'cause you don't have one." Thaumus chuckled at the stupid joke he'd been repeating for *selinos*. It still wasn't funny and still made him look like a juvenile wrasse.

"Just getting some refreshments. Looks like we're going to be here a while."

Thaumus did a full-on belly laugh. "Oh Jason. You still think you're smarter than me." With a flick of his tail, he lunged toward Jace.

Jace took off running. Legs were faster on land than a tail, but damn if Thaumus wasn't faster than he'd like. Especially because there wasn't much land left for him to run on.

This wasn't looking good.

It looked even worse when, suddenly, the water just offshore started frothing and—

"Did you really think I'd come alone, little brother?" Thaumus called after him, his laugh rolling across the water like a wave while a woman rose from the sea in front of him.

A woman whose lower part didn't end in legs.

Nor a tail.

It was…

Oh, Hades.

A whirlpool.

Charybdis had entered the fray—and sucked Jace into her swirling mass, pulling him under with deadly churning water.

Somewhere above the churning, Thaumus was smiling. Jace would have bet his life on it... which he might actually have done.

Small comfort, all things considered. But at least Mariana was safe—and right now, drowning in Charybdis' death spiral, he'd take it.

Chapter Twenty-Seven

So what's the plan, Mares? Are you gonna blow off the blowhard heading *this* way for the hot hunk who's heading *that-a-way*?"

The idea was so tempting. But what Jace had said rang true—they couldn't out Zeus' secrets, so she had to stay and meet up with Conch because, if she didn't, the mollusk would definitely use that against her. *Especially* once he got a look at her sculpture—in about five minutes—and that was not the kind of notoriety she'd been angling for.

"No, Tahiti. Jace is right. I have to get this meeting over with, but then I'll figure something out."

"Yeah, well you aren't going to have long to wait. Will you look at that blowhard?" Tahiti nodded to the east. "And I don't mean the one spouting that spume in the air. It's the one riding on the palanquin on its back I'm talkin' about." Tahiti flapped so strongly she almost helicoptered straight up. "Stupid idiot probably coulda been here quicker if he didn't need all the pomp and circumstance he's got with him. I bet he's got a bigger entourage than Jace's brother."

Mariana shielded her eyes with a hand to see what Tahiti was talking about.

The bird, if anything, had underestimated Conch's flamboyance.

He'd somehow managed to convince a sperm whale to not only bring him here, but to do so in style. There was a fully-constructed bamboo canopy on the whale's back, resplendent in rippling fuchsia silk, and a bed of what looked to be seagrass before it. Conch's opalescent-like shell gleamed in the mix of sunlight and spume spray—the gastropod was known for his love of spa treatments—and he had more silk ribbons flying from his pointed horns that Mariana knew had been manicured into spiral spikes for her ill-fated hotel grand opening debut. He had a coterie of scarlet ibis on the whale's back, an affectation that would have made Mariana roll her eyes if the stakes weren't so high. The coup de grâce, though, was his signature stunt—he had the whale *trumpet* his arrival after the spray dissipated. It was a sound sperm whales were known for and, therefore, the reason Conch employed them. He was his own best audience.

"Is this guy for real?" Tahiti muttered as an ibis finagled the gastropod onto its back then flew it to shore.

"Sssshhhh, Tahiti. I need this to go well."

"Well, if it doesn't go well, don't you worry; I plan to have him for lunch."

"You don't eat conch."

"There's always a first time."

Mariana hid her smile. It was nice when friends had your back.

Which she planned to do for Jace if she could just get Conch off this island and come up with a plan…

The ibis sauntered up to her in a surprisingly regal manner for its short legs, but then, ibis were known to be quite graceful. But if he were going for a red-carpet-like entrance, he should have found some dark pink flamingoes.

The bird lowered its head and Conch slid along its neck, then, using his operculum, lurched onto the bird's crown.

It didn't make him any taller than her thighs, yet his, "Ms. Tritone," was emitted in a tone that made him sound much larger than he was.

An affectation Conch was known for.

"Sir." She'd never been able to address him with the *Maestro* he preferred. That was more than a little aggrandizing and wholly unwarranted in her opinion. *Sir* wasn't much better, but at least it was considered polite, and she could meet him at his game if that's what he needed to make himself feel important. She wasn't going to get into a pissing contest on formality; she needed him to be in a conciliatory mood to have a prayer of a legitimate, unbiased review of her work. A *quick* legitimate, unbiased view of her work.

"Well? I don't have long. Where is it?" His eyestalks glanced around in different directions, a mannerism that always made Mariana uncomfortable—she never knew when he was looking at her or what else he was seeing. She figured he did this on purpose for that very reason.

"There, sir."

Conch's left eyestalk followed her pointing finger to the side of the volcano.

The sun was hitting Jace's profile perfectly.

The gods had to be helping her, that was the only reason she could see for such perfect timing. It couldn't have worked out better if she'd planned it.

"Hmmmm." The sound whistled from the lip of his shell, another sound he was well known for. Conch never committed himself at first glance. There was always a period of observation, some moving around to view the piece from different angles, then some contemplation in silence before rendering his verdict.

Sure enough, the ibis turned away from her and headed back down the beach.

"Go after him," Tahiti muttered as Conch and his escort gracefully stalked away.

"I'm not going to grovel."

"Oh, c'mon, Mare, play the game. He's here, so make the best of it. You give a little, he'll give a little… We know the piece is good, and he knows it, too, but you gotta give some to get some. Especially with your history with the guy."

Mariana didn't like playing games. She didn't like this back-and-forth. Either the piece was worthy of note or it wasn't; her kowtowing shouldn't make it better.

But he'd come here; she at least owed him something for that. Besides, he was only here for a short while—thankfully—since his kind weren't really adapted for breathing air. That was working for her plan to get him off quickly.

Sighing, she followed after him to help this along.

"You'll notice, sir," she said when she reached him, "that the proportions are on point, and the skin seems to glow in the sunlight."

He didn't look up at her. "Property of the stone."

Really? she wanted to say. Since when did cooled lava glow? It wasn't as if there were any luminous properties in tuff; it took a skilled artisan to carve angles to catch the sunlight to make it appear so. And Conch knew it.

She didn't call him on it, though she desperately wanted to.

And she hated that she felt desperate.

Though… what was her desperation for? Twenty-five minutes ago, it would have been for his approval. Now… Now, she just wanted him to leave.

She stumbled. How priorities could change when the situation was life-or-death…

"Not very original," was his next comment. "The Artemisian bronze *has* inspired others before, though the lack of a beard is a… choice."

At least she wasn't going to have to try to convince him that's what her piece was based on, so she didn't bother replying. Anything to hurry this along.

"The dimensions are interesting, I'll grant you."

That was a huge concession—Mariana sucked in a breath as quietly as she could. No use letting on that she recognized the import of his statement.

The ibis headed to the right as both of Conch's eyestalks focused on the sculpture—which meant he wasn't watching her for her reaction. He was actually looking full-on at her art.

Dare she hope?

She did dare, and she did hope—for the next-freaking-ten-minutes that Conch had the ibis guide him around the beach, covering every viewing angle possible short of eye-to-eye contact. Couldn't he hurry it up?

And then the bird took off, Conch still atop its head.

"That's some serious stunt flying right there, that is," Tahiti said. "One wrong lean by Conch and it'll be his last. That operculum can only suction onto feathers for so long, and his shell is almost as big as the poor bird's head."

He better *not* fall off until he rendered his opinion.

She hadn't put all this work in—and Jace's safety at risk—for Conch to die on her before giving his benediction. Or his condemnation. At this moment, did she really care?

The ibis flapped into the sky, raising and lowering Conch to study every part of the face, gliding from side-to-side then up-and-down as if he were mapping a grid.

She should probably be thankful he was taking his time and actually studying her work rather than condemning it from the get-go, but all this time was taking her away from coming up with a plan to save Jace.

Conch needed to hurry up. Either he recognized that she had talent and wasn't resting on her laurels, or he didn't, but he needed to make that decision *now*. Everything was riding on this moment—not only her reputation but possibly Jace's life.

Finally, after what seemed like hours, the ibis coasted back to the beach.

Mariana's stomach leapt to her throat. The moment of truth.

And, hopefully, departure.

Now if only the damn ibis would hurry the Hades back up the beach—

"Go on down to him," Tahiti whispered, having some discretion. For once.

If she could, so could Mariana.

She started jogging.

"Interesting piece," was Conch's first statement when she reached him. "As interesting as the fact that you chose to do this with your legs instead of a tail."

Mariana employed the discretion she was barely hanging on to by deciding not to point out that a tail would be useless for climbing the rockface.

"Does your brother know you're doing this?" Conch's two eye stalks focused on her.

"My brother has no idea I'm doing any of this." Because he would have put a stop to it, something both she and Conch knew.

"Curious." The eye stalks swung back to the sculpture. "There is talent there."

A compliment. She took a breath.

"Finally."

Then swallowed it. He just *had* to get the insult in, didn't he?

He tapped his eye stalks together, then swung them her way again. "Well done. Excellent composition, perfect proportions, good use of light and shadow… you have promise with this, Mariana."

Promise? *PROMISE*? Mariana wanted to rip those stupid eye stalks out of his cephalic mass and feed them to the nearest octopus. She had *way* more than *promise*. This sculpture was exceptional and he knew it. And he knew *she* knew he knew it.

He was playing tuna with her, the pompous wrasse…

She took a breath. It actually *was* exceptional and he actually didn't have to say it because just acknowledging that she had *promise* was enough of an admission from him—and they both knew that, too.

But the thing was—and his pompous answer made her finally realize—*she* knew it was good. And she knew *he* knew it was good, and, suddenly, with his stupid ego-trip power-play and Jace's imminent danger, it actually *didn't* matter what he thought. He was just trying to get a reaction out of her, for her to defend herself—to beg him to give her the cachet his endorsement provided—so *he* could feel better about *him*self.

In that, he was not unlike her.

All of a sudden, she realized… *she* didn't need his opinion. *And* she didn't want it—well, no, that wasn't true. She *did* want it, but she was not going to subjugate herself to get it. Either he saw her for the artist she was, without his ego getting in the way, or…

Or what? *What* was she going to do without his endorsement?

She tapped her toes. She actually didn't need his endorsement. She *knew* she was talented, and this sculpture was testament to that—for anyone to see. And, if no one did, well, *she* saw it. *She* knew it.

All her life, she'd gotten the accolades: best student, leader of this, captain of that, highest grades, fixing things for her siblings… It'd all been public. Everyone telling her of her accomplishments and being praised by them— by *others*… yet never feeling worthy within herself. Always wondering if the compliments and the grades and the votes and awards were all because of who her family was.

But now… *now*… she finally believed she was what she'd thought and hoped she was. That she *did* have the talent, and it had *nothing* to do with being royal. That she *wasn't* resting on those laurels or the family name. She *was* talented, and if Conch couldn't get his own ego out of the way to acknowledge it, that was a *him* problem, not hers.

She was finally free of trying to meet others' expectations because… because she'd met her own.

She took a deep breath and straightened shoulders that she hadn't realized had been hunched until just this moment—a posture of humility and subjugation that she wasn't proud of and did not need.

She took another breath, this time, raising her chin. "Thank you, Helmut—" she would address him as a peer from now on, no more groveling— "for traveling all this way. I appreciate your acknowledgment of my talent, and I hope you have a safe journey back."

Conch's eye stalks studied her up-and-down at the same time, then they came together—actually, they *banged* together—in surprise…

Good.

She was done begging.

If he wanted to be on her side for where she knew her career was headed, Helmut Conch could lurch there on his own.

He glanced back at the sculpture. Longer this time.

His shell rose then fell as if *he* took a deep breath. "Yes, well…" The shell shuddered and a wave of water flowed from it. "You have done justice to the original and I shall give full accolades in *The Atlantian Review* next month. I'm sure you'll have a buyer in no time, though how you plan to move this piece is, thankfully, not something I must worry about. I bid you good day and look forward to your next show." His lone foot tapped the ibis' head, then the bird executed a full one-eighty-military turn—surprising with those spindly legs—then stalked to the water's edge and took off back toward the waiting whale offshore.

Mariana watched him leave, a sense of calm stealing over her like she'd never felt.

Well, for just a moment; then real life and real danger intruded. Time to figure out a way to help Jace.

"You wanna tell me what just happened?" Tahiti flew beside her. "I mean, he was all, 'I am the Great and Powerful Conch of Art' and you were all meek-and-mild, and then, suddenly, boom! You come outta nowhere with this 'Thanks for nuthin, you blowhard' and the guy practically starts genuflecting to you. What just happened?"

Mariana shrugged. "What just happened was… I realized I don't need him."

"Uh… ya kinda *do*? Isn't that what all this has been about?" Tahiti's wings skimmed her forehead as she dodged a leafy hornmouth's spines sticking out of the sand. "I mean, that review ain't gonna write itself, Mares."

"I know, Tahiti, and I will be glad to have the public endorsement, but… really, I don't need it. Not anymore."

"Not anymore? What does that mean? What the heck has changed in the past fifteen minutes that I didn't see? I swear to the gods, it's like you've become this thing I don't even recognize. What? You get some real action and all of a sudden, the sun's brighter, the moon is shinier, and songs are singing on the breeze? What happened to my practical, I'm-gonna-take-the-world-by-storm Princess Mariana Tritone?"

What, indeed… "She became Mariana. *Just…* Mariana."

"Huh?" The bird bumped into her back then fell to the sand. "What in Polly's cracker does *that* mean?"

"It means…" Mariana brushed some sand off Tahiti's crown. "It means, I finally know who I am."

Tahiti rolled her head, eyes, shoulders, and left talon so hard, she fell over. "Well, I'm glad that means something to *you* but me?" The bird spit out a beakful of sand. "Does this mean I need to find another travel buddy? Are you done gallivanting around the Seven Seas in search of inspiration from now on? Are you going to just stay here and stare at that—" she tossed her head toward the sculpture— "for the rest of your life?"

"No, Tahiti, I'm not. I'm finally going to go after what I really want."

"Well, kickin' ol' Reviewer Guy off the island isn't really gonna help you, Mares."

It wouldn't if her art career was the only thing she wanted, but… it wasn't.

She wanted Jace. And if that meant that this sculpture was a danger to him, to outing him, well, it'd served its purpose—and that wasn't about getting Conch's approval. It was finally realizing that she'd never needed it to begin with.

And as soon as Jace returned, she'd tell him so.

If he returned…

Which soon became apparent was in jeopardy of happening when Kam showed up completely out of breath and possibly missing a few tail feathers that'd been blown out in his haste to return to her to tell her the devastating news… that Thaumus had won their battle and Jace was now his prisoner at the bottom of the very trench she'd been named for.

The irony was a little too horrific to contemplate, but it was enough to tell her exactly what she needed to do to save him.

She dove into the ocean and set off to save his tail…

… and her heart.

Chapter Twenty-Eight

Mariana gave her sailfish taxi a fast shove to send it on its way before she headed into the cave's entrance, hidden behind a thick lava pillar that she suspected had been Zeus-made because of its girth. Having worked with this substrate on many projects, she understood the properties and the shape this one had… it was definitely not natural.

She had to be in the right place.

She swam into the opening—only to be met with a terrorizing sight. A dozen anglerfishes' gaping maws were illuminated by their glowing lights, a veritable barrier of death.

"Who goes there?" one of the fish boomed.

Yeah, she was definitely in the right place. Only a goddess would be able to not only employ anglerfish, but get all of these ladies to coexist peacefully in this passageway without killing each other.

Though the poor guys attached to each of their sides weren't having as much luck.

"I am Mariana Tritone. *Princess* Mariana Tritone." The first time she'd willingly used her title for the power it wielded.

The angler fish didn't budge.

Wow, talk about putting her in her place...

"I'd like to see your mistress." Best not to use Pele's name in case they weren't sure who exactly they were guarding. Pele wouldn't still be in hiding if everyone knew of her existence. Having just learned that even Kam's most trusted birds could be turned by their own ambition, discretion wasn't optional.

"We don't have no stinking mistress. Be on yer way."

Mariana huffed out a pint of seawater. "We all know that you are working for someone and I want to see her. Now." She pulled her shoulders back, lifted her chin, and put on the best haughty look she could muster—and lied through her teeth, "By order of the royal family." Her brother would never sanction this visit nor what she was about to propose. Rod was all about bringing peace and tranquility to the oceans, where everyone could live in harmony. Angel was all about trying to effect a working relationship with the Humans to bring about peace above the waves as well, and, now, here Mariana was, about to destroy all that peace in one single request, but it was the only way she could see to save Jace.

"Begone," the angler said more forcefully, this time spitting out bits of her dinner.

Ew.

And disrespectful.

"I am Mariana Tritone, daughter of Fisher Tritone and sister to the High Councilman, Rod Tritone. I demand you announce me. Speak to your mistress; she will order you to let me pass. Now."

The anglers' lights bounced off the walls of the cavern as they looked at each other. Mariana was highly impressed at their coordination and cooperation because these fish were, by nature, loners, and didn't play well with others. Pele must either be paying them well or have enough dirt on each one to ensure their silence. Either way, they needed to get over their blind loyalty and get her an audience.

"Tell her it has to do with Jace Pacifica."

One of the fish broke away from the school, its lure fading as it disappeared into the cavern. The others remained, their lights dimming slightly. She wondered how long they would stay illuminated. Not that she couldn't see in the dark, but she would be at a disadvantage in comparison to these deep-sea dwellers for whom darkness was a constant state of being. All this light gave her the upper hand, though their razor-sharp teeth counteracted that dominance. Not to mention the sheer number of them. Like a feeding frenzy of piranha, these ladies could do serious damage if they cared to work in tandem.

She was counting on their solitary natures to keep that from happening.

After a few minutes, the anglerfish returned and passed a message up to the front.

The school parted like the Red Sea (though without all the wind), allowing Mariana to pass.

Keeping her head held high—but her eyes darting side-to-side in the event of an attack—she headed further into the passageway.

Around a bend, the passageway opened into a beautiful large room lit by at least three magma wells that Mariana could see. Its ceiling soared fifty feet straight up.

Around the twenty-five-foot level, a balcony was carved out of alabaster, colorful butterflyfish swimming among it, with a set of double doors of epic proportions rising behind it.

Those doors opened.

A young woman appeared, her red muumuu flowing over the railing as she swam above it, long black hair streaming around her, and a small white dog doggy-paddling behind her. The yellow *lau wiliwili* fish ringing her head like a jeweled crown followed her all the way down, then circled the top of the throne she sat upon.

The little dog floated onto her lap.

"Hello, Mariana." The woman's—Pele's—voice was as soft and melodic as an *ohe hano ihu* flute.

"You know who I am?"

"Doesn't everyone in the oceans?" She stroked the dog's back.

Mariana sighed at the curse of being royal, which was how Conch was able to make or break her—*had* been able to. Now… she just didn't care.

Which was why she was here. "Do you also know that Jace is in danger?"

The goddess' hand stilled above the dog's head. "That… I do not. Please explain."

Mariana gave the goddess a quick rundown.

"And you are here, why? Surely, you do not wish for me to intervene? Jason would not approve, as he is alive because of what he did for my protection. To reveal myself would undo his sacrifice." She set the dog at her feet.

"Well, I'm pretty sure he didn't sacrifice his freedom only to pay with his life." She took a step forward. "Is that what you want?"

"Of course not." Pele rose. "But you must understand that the world suffered greatly because of the fight between my sister and I. Whole continents—including your very own Atlantis—disappeared because of Nāmaka's anger. We cannot perpetrate any more upheaval on the Earth; it is already in a far-too-delicate a state."

"But if Thaumus finds out about you, the truth *will* come out. And it'll be too late for Jace by then."

"Jason will never reveal my existence."

"Explain how I know then."

Pele, instead of looking angry as Mariana would have expected upon finding out Jace had outed her, only smiled. She picked up the dog and tucked it under her arm. "It proves that he has great feelings for you. I cannot condemn him for those."

Normally, that would have made her smile, but Mariana wasn't into self-sacrifice for the sake of love. "Look, he saved you; it's your turn to save him. I'll do my best to keep your secret, but not at the cost of his life. I don't do Pyramus and Thisbe." The story of these star-crossed lovers was *not* a romance but a Greek tragedy, a point she'd made in her Greek lit senior thesis, and yet another reason she'd questioned her siblings about the sacrifices they'd made for love.

Now, she realized that love was its own reward. And if she couldn't convince Pele to intervene, Jace wasn't going to return as hers. He'd trusted her with this information about Pele; she needed to make sure that trust was warranted.

"I do not see how I can help him without giving away my existence."

"Well, I do." Thank the gods for Angel's endless

"lessons" on the merits of Human technology she'd suffered listening to. "Here's what you're going to do."

Once she'd laid out her plan, Pele cocked her head. "You want me to purposely unleash the power of a volcano? Do you understand the ramifications?"

Mariana nodded and crossed her arms, her flukes tapping the alabaster floor. "I'm expecting you to do right by Jace. Humans know that volcanic eruptions happen all the time scientifically, so it's not like someone is going to immediately think that you're alive. I mean, *have* you been responsible for all the eruptions since your supposed death?"

"Well, no, but—"

"Then this one is no different. Besides, it'll be in the Trench; it's not like the lava is going to hit land. We just need something to shake up the ocean floor."

"The resulting earthquake will certainly do that. As will the tsunami that will follow."

Exactly what she was counting on. "*About* that tsunami…"

Chapter Twenty-Nine

Jace kicked his way out of the churning waters, his eyes searching for any glimmer of light in the darkness around him. Oh he could see in the depths, but it took his eyes a while to get there without light. And there wasn't one flicker of it wherever he was.

He bumped into a wall. Well, that wasn't the way out.

He turned around, arms in front of him, moving forward cautiously.

And bumped into another.

He had a feeling the same thing would happen whichever way he turned. Where in Hades had Charybdis landed him? Where had Thaumus told her to? And what did his brother have planned?

He rubbed his eyes, hoping the bursts of light behind his eyelids would spark some sort of light generation so he could see where in Hades he was—which he thought might be true except it was way too cold for that place.

Which left one very unsettling possibility…

He waited for his eyes to adjust before moving

anywhere else. If he was where he thought he was, it wouldn't matter, but if he wasn't… he didn't want to take a wrong step.

Gradually, his eyes adjusted and he was able to see the walls. Solid sheets of rock, extending upward as far as he could see. He tried swimming up, but at about a hundred feet or so, he hit a titanium mesh barrier. Damn Humans and their sea junk; it was the only way his brother could have gotten hold of the perfect cage top. And that was what it was. Wedged into the rock, not a sliver of space for even an octopus to slither through.

His brother had created the perfect trap.

He peered through the bars. Not a glimmer of light to be found up there which could mean only one thing: he was trapped in the deepest part of the ocean. In the Mariana Trench.

The *Mariana* Trench. Of all the places in all the oceans in all the world, Thaumus had put him *here*. Even his brother's cruelty had a sense of humor.

And because all oceanic surveys of this Trench had been shut down after being sabotaged with ignition lines in an attempt on High Councilman Rod's life, no one would be checking this area any time soon. No one would find him for a very long time.

If ever.

Certainly not before his brother got here.

He was dead in the water.

He shouldn't have hidden from Thaumus the moment Zeus had given him Immortality. He should have swum straight to his brother's lair and reclaimed his life.

Instead, he'd chosen to hide in the shallows. Lurk in caves. Go off sonar. He'd subjugated his life for safety, but, as Mariana had asked him, where was the life in that? Life was to be lived, yet he'd chosen merely to exist. He hadn't formed any lasting relationships because he never knew who he could trust with his secret, and even those he *did* trust only lived a mortal lifespan. He was constantly alone… something he hadn't really even thought about until now. Until… Mariana.

If there was one thing his brief time with her had taught him, it was that an eternal existence didn't matter if he had to live it alone. What good was Immortality when he had no one to share it with?

He had to get out of here. Had to get back to her. To live—

Suddenly, the ground trembled beneath him. It heaved as if it was… breathing. Chunks of rock fell off the walls, fissures stretching through what remained.

Jace backed away, dodging the cascading boulders. The water heated and churned with a boneshaking roar, orange veins of light flickering among the cracks in the wall—and none of this had anything to do with Thaumus or Charybdis because neither one of them had this much power. The only one who did was…

Pele.

OhHadesno—the world was about to erupt around him.

And then… it did.

~~~

A wave hit Quetzal just as he surfaced to check his position, and he went tumbling arm-over-tentacle. Great. Now he was going to be all discombobulated and not know which end was up when he finally made it out of this churning undertow. He really hated tsunamis.
~~~

Just keep propelling… just keep propelling… His mantra since he'd started on this ridiculous journey, but a safety net for his squad on their annual migration was worth making the trek.

Still, what a flippin' nightmare…

It took a good ten minutes for him to corral all his appendages out of the knot the waves had tied them into and straighten out. Another three to make it back to the surface to regain his orientation, and another two seconds to dive down when he saw a contingent of frigatebirds overhead because that guy Sonny hadn't promised him safety from others of his kind. Still… that one in the front looked like the commander. Surely, he would abide by his subordinate's truce?

Quetzal peeked his mantle out of the water until his eyes cleared the surface. It might not be the smartest chance to take, but he wasn't going to make it to Princess Mariana before the wave hit no matter how hard he propelled.

He weighed the risks, using his arms as a scale. On one sucker, he had the risk of being eaten alive, on the other, safety for his family…

Quetzal spat out a mantle-ful of water. No risk no reward.

Here goes nuthin'…

~~~

Kam did a doubletake. There was a squid waving nine of its ten appendages at him? What the—! Did the guy have a death wish?

"Head to the island," he said to his VF of Ops. "I want to check something out." Something was eating at his gizzard because squid didn't flag down frigatebirds
~~~

for no reason. And since he'd already eaten, he wouldn't harm the guy because that would be murder and, under his rule, there was no justification for murder. The cephalopod was safe from him.

He dove down, pulling up just above crest height, far enough away to show the guy he wasn't a threat. "Something you need?"

"Uh, yeah." The squid side-eyed him. "I have to get a message to Princess Mariana from some guy named Sonny. Know him?"

Oh did he… And him, he'd like to murder—which *would* be justified. "I do. What's the message?"

The squid tapped a small whitecap with a tentacle. "How do I know you're going to give her the message?"

"How did you know I wouldn't eat you?"

The squid shrugged. "I, uh, didn't. I just kinda hoped you wouldn't."

"Same thing with the message, then, okay?" Kam sighed. "Look, I didn't eat you, I know who Sonny is, and I know where to find the princess. I'm actually trying to mitigate a disaster right now, so if you have information, rest assured, I will get it to where it needs to go. What's the message?"

The squid nodded, that tasty mantle dipping beneath the surface momentarily. "He says that Thaumus knows and is on his way to kill his brother. Make sense to you?"

"It does." No sense telling the guy this was already in motion—and that it was already too late. But Sonny had tried. That counted for something, even if the ledger between them wasn't anywhere *close* to being balanced by that effort. And Kam knew exactly where to find him. "Thanks. Now, do you need assistance getting where you're going?"

The squid other-side-eyed him. "You offerin' or are you eatin'?"

Kam shook his head. "Not me. Like I said, I'm in the thick of this mess. But there's an oarfish half a league away. I'll have him help you out." The oarfish had had the good sense to get out of the way before the earthquake hit, as oarfish were wont to do. And it wasn't exactly the best squid hunter in the seas. This guy deserved a break for trying to help Sonny and Jace out.

Sonny, on the other wing, was going to have to answer to a whole different set of standards.

"Normally, I'd pass, but with what's coming… Yeah, I'll take you up on that offer." His tentacle tapped his mantle in salute.

"Very well then. Hang on. I'll go round him up for you."

~~~

"Oh *skata* oh *skata* oh *skata*." Zeus raked a hand through His hair, seriously considering if He was going to rip it out. This was not good. Not. Good.

"What's that, *glykiá mou*?" Hera wiped Her hands on Her apron as She came out of the kitchen. "I've made some baklava—what's that?"

Zeus looked up from His iPad. Oh *skata* was right. "Uh, it's nothing, Dear."

"Pegasus's patootie it's nothing. I know that look. What did You do?"

Hades, He was in for it. "Um… Really. It's nothing—"

"Can it, babe. I know guilty when I see it. What. Did. You. Do?" Hera ripped the iPad from His hands. "Who's that?" She asked as Jace tumbled across the screen.
~~~

"Um… well, it's…"

"Spit it out, Zeus. I'm going to find out one way or another, and from the looks of this poor guy, he doesn't have the time it'll take for Me to ferret it out of You."

Hades, She was right. "It's Jason. Pontus." He winced, bracing Himself for a storm of epic proportions.

"Jason Pontus. I see."

Zeus opened one eye. She wasn't raging.

She was… smiling?

"Did you really think I didn't know?" She set the iPad onto the tabletop. "Fix this."

"Fix… it?"

"Of course. Send that poor boy into a Travel Chamber so he can get out of this mess. You owe him, after all."

"I… owe… him?"

"Oh, come now, Zeus. Did you really think My monthly Thursday spa day was at just *any* old spa?" She turned around and swished back toward the kitchen. "Pele has the most divine mud baths. Good for the complexion." She looked back over Her shoulder. "Fix it. You owe him."

Zeus' mouth fell open. She knew—and *had* known all along.

He shook his head, a small smile forming. He'd never understand women—and He'd created them. But He knew better than to go against His wife.

He looked back at the screen. Poor Jace. The guy really *had* been through it. Forget Immortality; it was time to give the guy what he really deserved.

He waved His hand and a Travel Chamber yawned open right for Jace to tumble through.

~~~

One minute, he was trying to swim for his life—but failing miserably—as the waves tossed him head over heels literally in Charybdis' death spiral, the next, he was floating in calm water near an island as if he'd just been transported through a Travel Chamber.

He hung suspended for a moment, waiting for his body to catch up with that information because there *weren't* any Travel Chambers near the Trench, but he wasn't about to look a gift horseshoe crab in the mouth.

He angled toward the surface to see—

Wow—he was… home. That was his island, there was… what was left of Mariana's sculpture, and there was Mariana on the beach, her tail flipping in the seafoam as if her life depended on it as she scoured the sea.

Or his did.

"Holy magma well, Mares!" Tahiti's screech split the air above him. "You did it! He's here!"

Mariana followed Tahiti's pointing feather, locked eyes with him, then dove into the surf, her tail getting her to him in half the time it took him to reach her, hitting him full force and sending them under in a tangle of limbs and hair and salt water and laughter that neither of them had breath for. He didn't mind; he had her, and she was real and warm and *here,* and that was all he needed.

They surfaced, laughing, gasping, touching.

So much touching…

"Jace." She cupped his face in both hands, her violet eyes searching his like she couldn't believe he was in front of her. "*Ohmygods*, you're really here. It worked."

"I'm *definitely* here." He kissed her with every ounce of his being, cherishing all that The Trench had
~~~

shown him he'd stood to lose. "Wait. *What* worked?" he managed to gasp when they came up for air—water—whatever. He didn't know if they were above the waves or below them and he just didn't care. He was with Mariana and that was all that mattered.

"Pele." She ran her fingers through his hair as she told him what she'd done. "Now you guys are even."

"There was never a tally, Mariana. I didn't help her to gain anything; it was the right thing to do."

"As was her saving you. Now all is right with the universe."

"Is it?" He glanced at the sculpture. The rock face above it was already fracturing, the tsunami's damage working its way up from the shoreline. He looked back at her. "Mariana, that's your career."

"I know."

"It's the reason you came to my island. Your—"

"I know. And it doesn't matter." She touched his cheek again, as if reassuring herself he was real. "Here's what I figured out up on that rock, Jace, while I was carving your face into it without even realizing it." She glanced up at the sculpture, then back at him. "I didn't need the sculpture for the sculpture's sake. I needed it to prove something—to myself, *not* to Conch. Not to anyone else. I needed to know that I'm an artist. That I can create something on my own, without trading in on my name or copying someone else's genius." She shook her head. "I'd started out with the Royal Atlantian Hotel disaster sitting on my shoulders, worried that I'd fail again. So, I decided that if I could recreate an already existing masterpiece—the Moai—that would prove I was good. But art isn't in the copying; it's in the creating. And once I stopped trying to re-do what someone else had already done and just *trusted* myself, it practically carved itself." She looked at him. "You inspired me, which is more than any accolade I could receive, more than any commission I can earn for a piece of artwork gracing someone's mantel. I know what I'm capable of now. I know I can trust myself."

And then, because her eyes lit up like the sun on the tips of the wave, he just had to kiss her. Again. He couldn't *not*. She was so beautiful in her certainty.

When he pulled back, it was to look at her properly. The green hair, the violet eyes, the salt water still on her skin… He'd spent millennia making sure no one could see him—not really—yet, here she was, seeing every hidden, exiled, lonely inch of him, and she'd walked into a volcano's mouth for him anyway.

"I need you to know something." His voice came out rougher than he intended. "I spent centuries making sure I wanted nothing. Needed nothing. No one. It was safer that way." He brushed his thumb across her cheek. "And then you dropped an anvil on my foot and changed everything."

Her laugh cracked in the middle.

"I love you, Mariana. And I'm guessing, since you sacrificed your art for me, you feel something for me, too?"

She put her hand on his chest where his heart beat strong and steady—with just the tiniest glitch of… hope.

"I do, Jace. And I almost lost you. The sculpture I can rebuild; but you… There's only one you."

As there would only ever be one *her* for him.

Epilogue

It hadn't changed as much as he'd thought it would.

Jace stood at the entrance to the royal palace in Atlantis, the magma wells turning the walls more golden than he remembered from his *selinos* here as Jason Pontus.

That seemed like so many lifetimes ago, but, really, it was one long time of waiting for… something. Something he hadn't even known he was missing.

Then she took his hand.

Mariana was what he'd been missing.

She squeezed his fingers. "Stop thinking so hard."

"I'm not thinking at all." He was remembering. And not a lot of it was good. Thaumus should never have been ruler.

"Good. That's the right approach with Rod." She swam forward, pulling him with her. "Just… don't mention the island. Or Thaumus. Or Pele. Or——"

"So I should say nothing."

"Probably safest. I'll handle my brother."

The throne room was nothing like he remembered. When Thaumus had ruled, the place had reeked of excess and neglect. Now it was… different. Ordered. Purposeful. Professional. The kind of place that suggested the person running it actually cared about the job.

Rod Tritone looked up from a slate he'd been reading and went very still. "Mariana." His voice was controlled. Hopefully that boded well—or at least ensured that they'd have a chance to present their case. "Would you like to explain why you've brought a dead man into my throne room?"

"He's not dead."

"Obviously." Rod set down the slate and folded his hands with the patience of someone who had spent considerable time learning patience—so unlike Thaumus. "Jason Pontus."

"It's Jace," Jace said, bowing. The moment called for formality.

Rod's mouth curved. Just slightly. "Jace. And I'm guessing there's a story." He held up a hand when Jace started to speak. "My question is this—are you someone we have to worry about?"

"Rod—" Mariana floated forward.

"No, Mariana. I need to hear what his plans are."

"Fair." Jace nodded. "Look, contrary to what my brother thought, I never wanted the throne. It's not who I am. And, after seeing what he did with it, well, it's in the right hands now. You have nothing to worry about from me. Hades, I just got my life back; I want to live it."

Rod cocked his head, his eyes narrowing.

Mariana slid her hand in his.

Jace squeezed it.

Rod glanced between them then nodded. "Very well. Welcome home."

Home… the word didn't quite resonate the way he'd hoped. Yes, he'd lived here, but it hadn't really felt like home then, and it still didn't. Still, at least now, he could come and go as he pleased.

"So, Rod, about what happen—"

"Hey, Jace! Get a load of this place!" Merc twirled in on his walking legs, claws raised, eyestalk swiveling so fast it was a wonder it stayed attached. "The crevices they got here! Perfect size and location! And the walls! They're gold! And the floors! I'm standing on *pearls*. I am actually *standing on pearls*! And did you see the kelp wine cellar? Forget about rum—they've got the biggest wine cellar I've ever seen with my own two eyes." He paused. "Well, one. Whatever. Point stands."

"Merc." Jace looked down at him. "You're here?"

"You betcha I am. Princess Mariana told me I could come so I rode a sea turtle on in. Well, three of them, actually. The first one got a bit tetchy around the Gulf Stream, though, so I had to—" He stopped. Swiveled his eyestalk between Jace and the throne. "Are we… are we in trouble?" he stage-whispered.

"Not yet," Rod said, and there was something in his voice that might, in another circumstance, have been amusement. "Mariana, Jace. Have a seat. Both of you." He glanced at Merc. "You, too."

Merc saluted with a pincer then promptly fell over in a dead faint.

As Jace and Mariana headed to the sea cucumber settee Rod indicated, Hermán and his… *lady friend* raised their tails.

"All packed for your trip?" Mariana asked them.

The iguanas indicated they were.

Jace shook his head; one more stop on their way home… wherever that was…

Once seated, Mariana told the story—most of it—while Rod listened with the stillness of someone filing everything away for later. Jace watched him and tried to get a read on whether he was about to be escorted to a cell or handed some kelp wine.

When she finished, Rod was quiet for a long moment, then said, "And Thaumus—"

"The tsunami—" Mariana began.

"Yes." Rod tapped the arm of his chair. "We've been monitoring him since the seismic event. He's alive—Immortality sees to that—but the earthquake stranded him on that atoll for considerably longer than two sunsets. He's not going anywhere quickly." The corner of Rod's mouth moved. Just slightly. "On foot."

Jace raised an eyebrow.

"He has legs now." This time, Rod *did* smile. "Permanently. And no idea what to do with them."

Jace couldn't help his chuckle. "That's—"

"Justice," Mariana's was a full-on laugh.

Rod inclined his head. "We'll keep watching." He signaled one of his sentries.

"And Charybdis?" Mariana asked.

Rod's expression shifted—not quite distaste, but close. "She has retreated. For now." He set his hands flat on the arms of his throne. "It seems she had been using Thaumus' ambitions as cover for her own. She thought to expand her reach beyond the Strait—leave her sister Scylla behind in Sicily and make the open seas her domain." He tapped his chair. "We reminded her what happens when sisters decide to upset the order of things between them. She was… persuaded that it was in her best interest to head back to Scylla. Where she belongs."

Between The Trench and his brother, this part of the

world's oceanic system didn't need any extra sea monsters. Good riddance.

"And Pele?" The words were out before Jace could stop them—three millennia of keeping her secret, and here he was, asking about her in a throne room.

Rod sat back. "That's not my story to tell without checking with her first."

Smart man. Pele had kept her secret for millennia; she deserved to decide who knew it and her plans. "Valid."

"And then there's this." Rod lifted the slate he'd been holding when they'd entered.

The Atlantian Current.

"Conch's review." He held it out to her. "It came this morning."

Mariana shook her head. "It doesn't matter. I don't need his validation. It was good; I know it was good. But after the tsunami…"

Rod raised an eyebrow. "Still, you might want to read it."

She pursed her lips then took it. She skimmed it while Jace held his breath.

One lone exhalation was her only reaction before she held it out to him without a word.

A work of singular vision and technical mastery… the artist has found in this remote and unlikely canvas something that speaks to the ancient and the immediate simultaneously… one does not stand before this face and think of craft. One thinks of truth. Of inspiration. Of promise.

Inspiration. Interesting choice of phrase. How much did the mollusk actually know and how much did he suspect? He, too, would bear watching.

It was the review she had wanted. The validation she deserved. But… she was right. After the tsunami, there was nothing left for anyone to see. She said she was fine with that… and he believed her. "Hmmm."

"'Hmmm'?" Mariana chuckled. "That's *all* you have to say? That's *your* face he's calling a work of singular vision."

"I've always thought it was."

Rod choked.

Merc fell over again.

Mariana rolled her eyes… and smiled.

Later, after Rod had asked more questions and received carefully considered answers, after Merc had been set up in what he declared to be the finest crevice he'd ever had the pleasure of occupying, after the palace had settled into its evening rhythms, Mariana found him at the edge of the palace gardens, where the coral topiaries gave way to open water, the mother-of-pearl shimmer of the abalone walls casting soft, pearlescent light across the shell-paved path behind him. He was staring out at the beauty he'd never thought to see again.

"You okay?" she floated beside him.

"I'm trying to remember the last time I was somewhere and didn't need an exit strategy." He sucked in a breath. "I can't."

"Well, you don't need one here."

"Not for danger's sake; I get that. But the thing is… I've been a second son my whole existence," he said. "No tail. No throne. No place that was mine by right." He turned to her. "But I'd like a place that's mine by *choice*."

She took one of his hands in hers. "You know… I didn't just invite you to the palace to talk to Rod, Jace. I invited you *home*. But it doesn't have to be the palace or Atlantis or even this hemisphere. I brought you to my family because they, to me, are home. And I'm hoping that *home* to you means anywhere I am—because wherever you are is home to me."

He closed his eyes as her words flowed over him. Home. He'd thought he'd had that on the island, but… it hadn't been. The physical location wasn't home; she was right about that.

He opened his eyes and found the answer to every question he'd ever had about what a family was supposed to be right there in her violet eyes. "Turns out, I've been homeless a very long time, Mariana. But now… you're right. I've finally found home." With that, he brought his other hand out from behind him and raised a golden actinia, its tentacles swaying in the soft current. "Will *you* be my home, Mariana? Forever and always, with volcanic eruptions, tsunamis, storms, roiling waves… all of it?"

She smiled as she nudged his hip. "Of course I will." She slipped the sea anemone onto her ear, the suction keeping it there for all their tomorrows. "But let's hope there's some smooth sailing in there as well."

"Where would the adventure be in that?" He leaned in, meeting her halfway. It was not a kiss of passion, but one of promise. A promise of forever.

When it ended, she rested her forehead against his. "You know… I'm going to talk to Hera about your tail."

"Don't."

"Jace—"

"I mean it." He lifted her chin. "I never wanted the tail. Never wanted the throne or the title or any of it. Thaumus could have had all of it with my blessing." He dropped a quick kiss on her nose. "The only thing I've ever wanted that I didn't have—that I didn't even know I was missing—was this."

"Well, you get *this*," she returned the nose kiss, "but I'm still going to talk to Hera."

He laughed and just shook his head. He had a feeling this was a battle he couldn't win, so he wasn't even going to try. "Far be it from me to try to talk you out of anything. I learned my lesson with your sculpture."

"Yes, you did. Good." She nudged him with her hip. "C'mon, I'll race ya to…" her violet eyes sparkled as she dove into the open water, "a place we can call our own."

After the Rocks

Olympus

See?" Hera swatted Him with the palm frond. "*That's* what we're missing. That. Right there. That playfulness. The teasing. The… passion." Tears filled Her eyes. "Where did it go, Zeus? We had it once. Don't You miss it?"

Zeus put down the iPad. "You're right, *psychí mou.* I have let the pressures of Our worlds get in the way of what's important. *Us.*" He slid His arms around Her.

"I know You have a lot of work to do. We gods have many responsibilities, but couldn't We… sometimes… couldn't We just forget who they all know We are and just be Us?"

"I'd love that, Hera, but, You see, there's a problem with that."

"A… problem?"

She looked up at Him from under Her lashes and it was all He could do to keep His eyes from twinkling; She always said they were a dead giveaway when He was teasing Her. But He wasn't *really* teasing Her. Regardless of the mythological tales mortals loved to tell about His, er, prowess, He loved Hera too much to make light of Her feelings. If there was one thing Hera *had to* know, it was that She would always make Him smile. Even when hitting Him with palm fronds or yelling at Him to put His tablet down and come to dinner. Because Hera was everything to Him.

"Yes, you see, the problem is that… that *is* who we are to those people, not individual beings with hopes and dreams and wants and needs. We can't escape being their gods. But to Me, Hera… My love… You are *My* goddess."

She smiled against His chest. They stayed like that for a long moment, the clouds drifting soft and slow around Olympus, the world below getting on without Them—for once.

Then She pulled back just enough to look at Him, with that impish smile He'd first noticed so many millennia ago He'd lost count. "Go ahead, Zeus. You know You want to."

"I have no idea what You're—"

"Zeus. Fix it."

He cocked His head. "Do You mean—"

"Yes. Fix it."

"He doesn't want a tail, Hera. He never did."

She gave him the look She'd been perfecting since the dawn of time. "Not. That."

He waited.

"Unconditional Immortality, Zeus. No provisos, no conditions, no secrets. The man has earned it."

He opened His mouth.

"Don't." She picked up some baklava. "You know I'm right."

He didn't argue. He picked up the iPad and did what should have been done a long time ago.

~~~

The Allotment

Nalowale Atoll was not what he'd expected.

Sonny looked at the empty expanse—for lack of a better term—of hardscrabble land. When Captain Kam had informed him—on that rocky prison before escorting him off with all the largesse of a superior officer who had better things to do than deal with the consequences of his catastrophically bad judgment—that his allotment was being reassigned, Sonny had braced himself. A barren rock off the Aleutians, maybe. An ice shelf somewhere south of nowhere. Something with a lot of wind and very little to eat, which would have been fair, all things considered.

Instead, he'd received a small scrap of coral and sand barely big enough to pace across, a scraggly cluster of shrubs that would do for nesting if he didn't look too closely, and a hill of driftwood and Human garbage that was going to take him the better part of a breeding season to clear out. It wasn't the best by far, but it also wasn't what he *should have* gotten for what he'd done, and he definitely wasn't going to look a gift frigatebird in the beak.

It wasn't luxury, but it was his. While it was going to take some work to make it worth something, he could live with that because at least he *was* living…
~~~

Quetzal's squad had already arrived, tentacles waving from the shallows like a welcoming committee. Sonny gave them a nod he hoped communicated both *Thank you* and *Don't push it.*

Sunny was perched on the highest point of the atoll, her feathers catching the late afternoon light. She didn't move when he landed beside her, just looked at him with those dark eyes that always made him feel like she could see straight through his gular sac to whatever he was actually thinking.

"You're late," she said.

"I know."

"You look terrible."

"I know." He reached into the pouch he'd fashioned from kelp on his way back and produced three shells. Not the prettiest ones he'd ever seen. Certainly not the ones he'd imagined bringing her when he'd first hatched his whole disastrous plan. But they were real, and they were his, and he'd collected every one of them himself on the long flight. "It's not what I promised but I'm going to get you more. Better ones. It'll just take some time. I've got connections now—royal ones, if you can believe it—and once things settle down I'll—"

"Sonny."

"—find the best ones in the Pacific, the kind with the pink insides you always liked, and I'll—"

"*Sonny.*"

He stopped.

Sunny looked at the shells for a long moment, then at him. "You absolute idiot." She leaned against his shoulder. "I didn't want the shells. I don't need them. I never did. I only said so to my girlfriends because it seemed so important to you for you to be someone important. It was never like that for me. I wanted to support you, but, really? I just wanted you home. With me. Forever."

Sonny stood very still and let that land.

Below them, the shoals were thick and the thermals were strong and Nalowale Atoll stretched out in every direction.

It turned out to be enough.

~~~

The Volcano

The anglerfish had gone back to their posts.

Poki was asleep at her feet.

Pele sat in the quiet of her chamber. Again.

Jace was alive. His brother diminished. Her secret safe.

For now.

She stroked Poki's ear and looked up at the magma veins threading the walls, the slow pulse of them like a heartbeat she'd long since stopped hearing as anything other than home. She had made her peace with this place. Mostly.

But Zeus had promised her *soon*.

She'd petitioned Him for her life back and while He hadn't said no, He'd given her a *not yet*. Which was not the same thing.

The world isn't ready, he'd said.

Which world? The Human one, the Mer one, or Nāmaka's? Her sister had always lived in her own world—which was, in the end, the whole problem."

Poki stirred.
~~~

At least she had him to keep her company. She'd tried other names over the centuries—more dignified ones, names befitting a goddess's companion—but he'd only ever responded to *Poki*. Small Dog. Not exactly the stuff of legend, but then, neither was hiding in a volcano.

She'd almost lost him one summer when Humans had descended on her islands in droves, eyes glued to their little screens, chasing creatures called Pokémon. The word had echoed through her caves so many times that Poki had nearly trotted straight out toward a particularly persistent group of them before she'd grabbed him by the scruff. She still didn't know what a Pokémon was. She didn't want to.

Poki settled back to sleep, comfortable in this place.

She looked around. *Soon.* Not *never*. She guessed she could wait.

After all, she'd been waiting this long already.

~~~

The Rock

The Rock stood tall despite its crumbling façade, Mariana's hard work slumped around it.

The princess had had such grandiose plans.

She'd seen them through, though not as The Rock—nor she—had envisioned.

A light flickered in the obsidian still embedded where one of the face's eyes had been. The tsunami may have taken its structure, but The Rock stood firm. Like love, its foundation may have been shaken, but the light inside remained.
~~~

The Rock surveyed the sea. Calm now, the tsunami had spent its energy, but the sea was always changing. The world was always changing; the one constant in this world the gods had created *was* change. Sometimes it was for good, other times, not so much, but life, like love, continued with a sense of hope.

It was that hope that had brought Jace and Mariana together, and their love that would continue through the ages.

The Rock looked forward to seeing where their journey went.

~ Fin ~

Thanks for reading! Please help other readers find my books by leaving a review where you purchased it. And if you'd like to see more of my stories, turn the page!

JUDI FENNELL
I dream of genies

I Dream of Genies
Chapter 1

Scheherazade, the famed Arabian storyteller, had had to come up with a thousand and one nights' worth of tales to save herself.

Eden should have it so easy.

But at least her life wasn't on the line like Scheherazade's, so that was a plus. Her mind, though, was another matter. There was only so much magic a genie could do to pass three thousand years of confinement and not go mad.

Unwilling to succumb to such madness, Eden circled flicked her wrists and snapped her fingers, her magic sending the butterflies, hummingbirds, and twirling glass balls she'd bewitched toward the ceiling of her bottle so she could have a better view through the hazy saffron glass. The rain of yet another Pacific Northwest storm streaked the storefront display window she'd inhabited for the last forty-five years, two months, and thirteen days. If the Arabian weaver of tales had used Eden's last half century as the basis of the stories that had saved her life, the poor woman would have been dead before her first sunrise.

"Mornin', babe." Obo, the cat she'd been cursed—or blessed, depending on one's viewpoint—to share this latest part of her penance with, leapt onto the shelf beside her bottle, licking his Egg McMuffin breakfast from his whiskers. The cat was a master forager. "Whatcha lookin' at?"

"Wilson." Eden nodded to the tree in front of the store. She'd watched it grow from a sapling to its current block-the-rest-of-the-world-from-view size for so long that she'd named it.

"Kind of pitiful that you named a tree after a volleyball."

"It worked for Tom Hanks."

"Yeah, but he was stranded on a deserted island. You've got the bustle of the city and hundreds of people right in front of you to keep you company."

Hundreds of people she couldn't interact with. She was on the outside looking in—well, actually, she was on the inside and wanting to *get* out. But the High Master had sealed her bottle with so much magic that nothing short of an explosion would set her free.

"And me, of course." The cat winked at her, his yellow eyes against his black fur making the motion noticeable. "You've always got me. I know I'm the bright spot in your day."

"In your dreams, Romeo."

"Speaking of lover-boy, has he been by yet?" Obo nudged the copper ashtray with the mermaid cigarette holder out of the way and curled his tail around her bottle before plunking himself onto his belly. Mr. Murphy, the store owner, hadn't shown up yet, so Obo could get away with it hanging out here. Once the man did, however, all bets were off.

It was a sad state of affairs to look forward to these daily chats with Obo, who was high on her list of Least

Favorite Beings ever since he'd let her take the fall for *his* necklace heist from Ramses II's tomb. It showed just how lonely and bored she was that she even deigned to talk to him, let alone looked forward to it. Other than her thoughts and her magic, she had only him to keep her company.

Oh, and "lover-boy" Matt Ewing. Couldn't forget him. And she didn't. He was pretty unforgettable, and heavens knew, she thought about him more than she should.

"No, he hasn't been by. I guess this weather's keeping him inside." Almost every morning, Matt jogged around the corner of the store in those tight, form-hugging running clothes. The perspiration slicking his face, that sexy curling hair, the controlled, even grace of his movements had fueled her fantasies ever since Mr. Murphy had moved her glass bottle to the front window.

"Or he could have had a hot date last night and it carried over."

Eden curled her legs under her, the curly toes of her slippers catching on the piping around the edge of the new sofa. She propped her elbow on the back cushion and plopped her chin onto her palm. "Thanks, Obo. That's helpful."

The cat licked his paw and swiped it over his ear. "Just callin' it like I see it."

Eden turned to look at him, brushing a wayward hummingbird out of the way, her gold shackle, er, bracelet flashing in the lone weak beam of sunlight that somehow fought its way through Wilson's leaves and the steady rain. "And how *do* you see it, Obo? You've been to his house. What's his world like?"

The cat shuddered and tucked his paws beneath his chest. "A damn sight wetter than yours. You should be thankful you're in this place. It's a monsoon out there."

The cat could be tight-lipped when he wanted to be.

Which was often. All she asked for was news of the outside world and its people, descriptions of the smells and sounds, and the general feeling of being free to come and go as she pleased, but other than getting Matt's name out of Obo, the cat barely shared anything else. He had no idea how lucky he was to have the ability to go where and when he wanted.

She definitely didn't understand why he chose to be *here*. In this musty old shop, surrounded by things other people wanted to get rid of. How Mr. Murphy stayed in business was beyond her, because most of the stuff had been here as long as she had, and there certainly hadn't been any runs on antique plant stands or tarnished brass headboards.

Flicking her wrists again with the accompanying finger-snap that completed her Way of doing her magic, Eden arced a rainbow from one side of her bottle to the other, the purple ray disappearing into the shadow of the bottle's neck. The butterflies immediately began flying through it, and the hummingbirds raced along the ribbons of color that matched their wings.

She snapped her fingers again, and Humphrey *poofed* onto her arm like a trained parrot. The dragonlet, a baby dragon about the size of her palm and her latest "foster child," reminded her of Bogart in his early movies, with a long face, high forehead, and large eyes, hence the name, though the dragon's eyes were blue to Bogart's brown.

In that, Humphrey reminded her of the High Master, but Adham was such a lofty name for such a tiny thing. And, besides, like the Humphrey of those on-demand movies, this Humphrey was on loan, too—until he reached unmanageable proportions, which, with a dragon, was usually around the one month mark, meaning she had about five days left with this one before the hormones kicked in.

She stroked Humphrey's golden scales, then pointed to the rainbow. He gave her the tiniest nip on her palm—full blown dragon love could be really painful—then fluttered his little wings, his strength increasing daily. Today was probably the last day he could fly with the butterflies. The hummingbirds were fast enough to evade his beak-like jaws, but the butterflies wouldn't be a match; they'd more likely be lunch. But for today, he could play among the colors with them. Dragons loved rainbows.

She did, too, because of the happiness they innately engendered, especially on dreary days like today. But rainbows were infrequent manifestations for her because, while Mr. Murphy couldn't see in and most things couldn't pass through the magical barrier of her bottle walls without her. Okay, rainbows required an inordinate amount of light and, therefore, could be seen. Light shining from a dusty, and supposedly empty, old bottle would definitely be noticed.

"Uh, babe?" The gentle *whoosh* of Obo's fur thrummed softly along the ribbed lower portion of her bottle as he brushed his tail against the outside. "The rain might be murder on pedestrian traffic, but it's upped the vehicular kind. And the traffic light is red. A couple of interested kids, and your beacon there is going to get some notice."

Eden sighed, hating that he was right, but flicked her wrists anyway. The rainbow dissipated, leaving traces behind on the winged creatures. Humphrey sported a green stripe down the ridge of his back, and one of the iridescent Blue Morpho butterflies was going to have to change its name to Purple Morpho.

"Why are you here again, Obo? With the free run you have of this town, I'd think this has to be the most boring place you could be."

Obo's tail paused mid-flick, and his ear twitched. "Ah, well, you know… I, uh, can't talk to mortals without freaking them out, and none of the animals in this country have been on the planet as long as me. Who else can I share the good ol' days with? You're the closest I get to normal, babe."

Which was sad, because nothing in her life had been *normal* from the moment she'd gone to live with the High Master over two thousand years ago following her parents' death.

Eden sighed and gathered her magic to summon a pomegranate smoothie on the teak inlay table next to the lime green sectional she'd ordered last month. The persimmon-colored pillows weren't pulling the whole look together as she'd hoped. While she loved color, the backdrop of the saffron bottle made her art deco a little too avant-garde. Ah, well, she'd do some redecorating today to keep herself occupied. The satellite dish Faruq had given her for her birthday a few years ago came in handy.

Not that she'd ever admit it to Faruq. The High Master's vizier, charged with monitoring Genie Compliance, already had too much control of—and too much interest in—her life.

She sipped the smoothie. The dish, and the high-def TV that had replaced the antiquated electronics she'd accumulated over the years, were gods-sends. Much easier to shop, teach herself new languages, keep abreast of changing societies and customs, and learn all about new technology and the selling power of J.D. Power and & Associates. Not to mention, how to make smoothies.

And with her bottle's magical ability to alter its interior without changing the dimensions on the outside, she could order up a swimming pool and Mr. Murphy would never know the difference.

Actually, maybe she'd do that. She'd like to hear Faruq's comment when he found out he was going to have to magick up a couple thousand gallons of water. And as for getting it through the magic channels to her, well, that ought to give him a few fits.

She took another sip of her smoothie. Such were the pleasures of her life.

"Hey, that looks good." Obo peered into her bottle, the tapered neck distorting his yellow irises until he looked like the Cyclops she'd seen off the coast of Crete that last summer she'd been on the outside. "Can you conjure one up for me?"

Eden set her treat down on the Egyptian brazier topped with a circular mosaic tile platter she called an end table. Nothing like combining Old World and New. "Sorry, Obo, but my magic won't leave the bottle for the mortal world while the stopper's in." Otherwise she would have zapped herself somewhere warm and sandy years ago.

"Well, could you calm the butterflies down then? Their flapping wings are driving me nuts. And the dragon…" He shuddered and dropped his head onto his paws. "I don't get *that* at all."

Humphrey did a loop-the-loop above her head, and Eden held out her hand for him to land on as a reward. Baby dragons were so lovable and eager to please. Until they hit that unmanageable milestone—then their fiery heritage took over. It was a treat to be able to enjoy them at this stage, one far too rare for her liking.

As for her other co-inhabitants, they were the only living things Faruq approved to be in her bottle. She'd tried to talk him into a kitten after a few hundred years of solitude, but he'd refused. Said kittens would grow up to be cats, and cats were sneaky. That any cat he gave her might be able to figure a way out of the bottle.

It didn't speak well to the High Master's magic if his own vizier thought a cat could undo it, but Eden didn't buy Faruq's argument for one minute. Just one more thing he wanted to control about her.

So she'd volunteered to foster orphan dragonlets and hadn't complained when Obo had shown up. Not that the cat had any interest in helping her out of her bottle. Knowing where to find her so he could "share the good ol' days" was incentive enough, apparently, for him to make sure she stayed put. Probably worried what she'd do to him after he'd abandoned her during that necklace fiasco. A few hundred years ago, she might have done something, but, nowadays, she was just thankful for the companionship. She'd told him so and had even tried bribing him into tipping the bottle off the shelf with promises of making all his wishes come true, but the cat had turned her down.

She hadn't held out any great hope of a fall breaking her bottle anyway. She'd been dropped many times over the years as her bottle had changed hands—sometimes on purpose—but nothing had budged that stopper.

She conjured up an acacia seedpod for Humphrey, and his blue tongue flicked out to taste it. A bunch of cooing ensued, complete with little claw marks up her arm as he hunched into his "don't take my food" position over the pod. He happily munched away on the outer casing. Nothing like the throaty rumblings of a contented dragonlet. "What time is it, Obo?"

Obo didn't even look at the cuckoo clock hanging on the wall by the shop's door. "Matt's not coming, Eden. You wore your sexy little outfit for nothing." He opened one eye, and the black slit of pupil thinned even more. "Thinking of auditioning for a TV show, are we?"

Eden shrugged. The costumes hadn't been purchased specifically with Matt in mind, but if the opportunity ever presented itself, well, hey, she had urges just as much as the next person. And after being cooped up so long with only Obo and Faruq to talk to, those urges were teetering on the brink of meltdown.

But she'd just *had* to buy the harem girl outfits, one in every color, after watching that genie on the television show. She didn't know who'd ratted out her race, but that Mr. Sydney Sheldon had gotten almost every detail right. Except the costume. No self-respecting genie would be caught dead in this little get-up while in The Service. But it was comfortable and it was colorful. And there was no one but her to see her in it.

"I wonder where Mr. Murphy is? He's usually here by now."

Obo sighed and rolled onto his side, his tail whispering along her bottle again. "Probably rowing his canoe in. I'm beginning to wonder if Noah's up to his old tricks."

Eden smiled. Crotchety and full of complaints—and a liar and a thief—Obo might be, but he was right; they didn't have anyone but each other to share the old times with. Unless she counted Faruq. And she wasn't about to.

But then the bells over the service door jingled, and Obo jumped to his paws so fast it was a wonder he didn't knock her bottle over. He ducked behind the black marble obelisk on the shelf next to her.

"If you're counting on the lack of sunlight to hide you, it's not working," she whispered, flicking the butterflies and hummingbirds onto the gardenia and honeysuckle bushes in her flower garden, and Humphrey onto the mini acacia tree he used as a perch when she let him fly around. The twirling glass balls went into the padded box that prevented them from breaking whenever someone moved the bottle. "You better get out of here, Obo."

"Tell me something I don't know." The cat wiggled his butt trying to shrink into the shadows. "I have to go out the way he's coming in, so we'll need to distract him."

"Keep talking and that ought to do it," she whispered, using her magic to clean up a spot of yellow the rainbow had left behind.

Mr. Murphy walked into the room, but didn't flip over the OPEN sign like usual. Instead, he went behind a French Provincial sideboard beneath a Baroque mirror and brought out a large cardboard box—an empty one— that he soon started filling with every knick-knack from the top of the sideboard. And from the bookcase next to that. And the top of the retro refrigerator next to that.

Eden ducked behind the big stone marker Hadrian had given her as thanks for the carpet ride all those years ago when he'd surveyed the land for his wall. True, Mr. Murphy wouldn't be able to see her spying on him, but years of habits weren't so easily forgotten, no matter how rarely utilized those habits were. "This doesn't look good."

"Gee, ya think?" Obo muttered, his back end tiptoeing toward the edge of the shelf. "I'm outta here, babe." With that, Obo executed the perfect stealthy leap cats were known for, hit the floor running, and was into the back room before Mr. Murphy heard anything.

Lucky Obo. Eden could only sit and worry.

***

Obo nudged his way out of the back of the shop. Skulking in the shadows again. Story of his life—and one he was heartily sick of.

296

For years, over two thousand of them, he'd been hiding. First from the assassins, then from tomb raiders, then from anyone who wanted a "pet kitty." He'd lived a life of luxury before being on the run, and while pâté and room service were heavenly, the plotting and backstabbing by usurpers was anything but. He'd been done with that life when his mistress had ended hers, and he hadn't looked back. Obo looked out for one thing and one thing only: his own life.

With the end of it approaching—nine magical lives could only take a cat so far—he had to look out for his Afterlife now.

Walking along the back of the store, Obo tried to keep his paws out of the puddles. Futile, but worth a shot because nothing was worse than soggy paws. Well, except burning ones. He might complain about the weather here, but it definitely beat the hot sands of the desert. If he never saw a desert again, it'd be too soon.

Getting out of that part of the world had been an added bonus to Bastet's offer: keep an eye on Eden and balance the heavenly scales for a good number of his transgressions. He had a *lot* of transgressions to make up for, so this seemed to be a simple enough task.

All he'd had to do was pack up his meager belongings and get himself to this part of the world, then provide monthly reports via the mocking bird the goddess had sent to, well, *mock* him. A *bird* was her messenger? Seriously? Bastet was a cat goddess, and she sent a bird to collect her reports? There was probably some sort of test in that, too: don't kill the messenger and knock off two extra bad deeds from his celestial tally.

However the goddess was keeping tabs, Obo was in.

A gutter groaned overhead, and its contents gushed down in front of him, a good portion splashing off the concrete and soaking his fur. He wouldn't mind being *in* right now, but any of his regulars—mortals who took in stray cats—lived far enough from Eden's store that he'd be just as soaked anyway.

Obo shook the rain water off and rounded the end of the building. Maybe Wilson would provide some cover. At least he could hang out in the branches to keep his paws somewhat dry.

He dragged himself into the crook of Wilson's lowest branch just as Mr. Murphy walked out of his store and dumped that cardboard box on top of a garbage can by the curb, then he ran back inside and adjusted the CLOSED sign.

What was the mortal up to? Why was he tossing things he'd been trying to sell? Cardboard dissolved in this much rain. It didn't make any sense.

Then a trash truck turned the corner, and it suddenly did.

Except—

Son of a bichon! The top of Eden's bottle was sticking out of that box!

~ * ~

Books by Judi Fennell

ROYALLY SUNK SERIES
Mermen and mermaids are just mythology, right?
Try telling that to the unsuspecting humans who fall
head-over-heels for those who don't always have heels...

In Over Her Head

Reel's a merman without a tail, and Erica's terrified of the ocean. Only one thing could get her into the water: a gun. And only one thing could keep her there: the sexy merman who saves her life, only to risk his own.

Wild Blue Under

Valerie's a mer princess landlocked in the middle of the country. Rod is the prince who sets out to rescue her. But can they dodge a usurper's plot and make it back to the ocean before his tail—and his claim to the throne—disappear forever?

Catch of a Lifetime

Logan ran *away* from the circus; all he wants is for his life to be normal. The naked woman who shows up on his boat is anything *but* normal. Especially when Angel turns out to be a mermaid—with an angry sea monstress after her.

Love on the Rocks

Princess Mariana isn't a poser; she really *is* an artist which she's about to prove with the statue she's carving on a deserted island. Problem is, Jace is hiding out there so the one thing that will set Mariana free from her royal prison is the one thing that will get Jace killed. Romance is rough enough, but when there's a tsunami in the weather forecast, love is on the rocks.

Making Waves ~ Outtakes

Read about The Incident that made Erica terrified of the ocean, the reason Valerie, the lost princess, was found, and how Logan's young son Michael found a mermaid The stories *before* the stories.

~~~

BOTTLED MAGIC SERIES

Careful what you wish for... it just might come true!
As these humans come to find out when a magical genie
ends up their laps—literally—before they're whisked off
to the most magical adventure of all... falling in love.

I Dream of Genies

Matt's luck has finally changed when genie Eden escapes her bottle and lands in his lap. Literally. And she vows never to go back in. Unfortunately for both of them, the guy who put her in there wants her back and he'll stop at nothing to get her.

Genie Knows Best

Samantha inherits her father's estate, complete with a genie who has one last master to serve before his indentured servitude is up. Sam's more than willing to set Kal free—until her greedy ex has decided that if he can't have Sam, no one can.
~~~

My Fair Genie

Zane's inherited the family mansion which he can't rid of quick enough to put the rumors of his family's crazy history to rest. Too bad the genie who's been the cause of those rumors has been set free to run amok once more. Only this time, it's his heart she's messing with.

Your Wish Is His Command ~ Outtakes

Find out how Kal came to be imprisoned in his lantern and why he needs to serve 1001 masters. It's the story before the story.

~~~

ONCE-UPON-A-TIME ROMANCE SERIES

Once Upon A Time sounds good in a fairy tale,
but real life isn't like that.
Or... is it?
With the help of a guardian-angel-in-training, these
lucky couples will find that falling in love is the greatest
tale of all!

Beauty and The Best

Jolie is a personal chef by day and a romance writer by night. So when she gets a gig for the hot reclusive artist, Todd, she has the perfect hero for her book. Until Todd finds out and kicks her out of his kitchen, his home, *and* his heart.

If The Shoe Fits

Once upon a time, a long time ago, in a land far, far away, there lived a girl by the name of Cinderella. This is not her story. *This* is the story of Lucinda Isabella Casteleoni, who, like her namesake, has a
~~~

wicked stepmother, two tacky stepsisters, and countless hours of hard work to (not) look forward to. But unlike that fairy tale princess, Bella's Prince Charming is nowhere to be found. Until a little old man with sparkling green eyes opens a shoe store down the street. Then the magic begins...

Through The Leaded Glass (prequel)

An accidental trip to medieval England has ad exec Kate scrambling for a way home… But can she bring the hot knight in shining armor she's fallen in love with back with her?

<center>~~~</center>

BEEFCAKE, INC. SERIES
Girls' Night Out never tasted so good!
Magic Mike has nothing on these guys.
Sit back and enjoy the show as the guys of BeefCake,
Inc. show you how it's done...

Beefcake & Cupcakes

Lara wants her cupcakes to be a success. Exotic dancer Gage wouldn't mind sampling them, but his work schedule to pay off his nephew's hospital bills doesn't leave him time to do so. Until a party where beefcake meets cupcakes and, *oh*, is it delicious!

Beefcake & Mistakes

When Bryan mistakes Jenna for a hooker and she realizes he's her adopted son's father, the mistakes and misunderstandings start to grow. But something else is growing between them, too. Sometimes, one wrong turn can be oh so right…

Beefcake & Retakes

Tanner wants his ex-wife to be out of his life forever, but when her grandmother has a stroke and he has to pretend to still be in love with Juliet, can he risk a retake on the one woman who never stopped loving him?

Beefcake & Snowflakes

Gina's had a crush on Darien since forever—until the day he humiliated her in school. Fifteen years later, he leaves her cold. Exotic dancer Darien has come back to town to set a few things to rights. One is the mess he made for Gina years ago… and *maybe* rekindle the flames they'd once had. But the only way to melt the snow around Gina's heart is to turn up the heat, both on the job… and off.

~~~

MANLEY MAIDS SERIES

What happens when three irresistibly sexy brothers lose a poker bet to their enterprising sister? They get hired out for her housecleaning venture. Now, the Manley Maids are at your service. Satisfaction guaranteed.

What A Woman Wants

Resort owner Sean plans to buy an historic estate, making a name for himself and making millions, so he moves in under the guise of cleaning the place to thwart the one condition of the inheritance. But heir Olivia and her menagerie get under his skin, and he finds that the poker bet that got him into this mess isn't the only game-changer.
~~~

What A Woman Needs

Movie star Bryan wants fame and fortune, not a repeat of his penny-pinching "normal" childhood. After the publicity surrounding of her husband's death, Beth needs is a normal life for herself and her children, and the movie star who lost a bet to clean her house—with paparazzi in tow—isn't it. But as flirtation turns into seduction, Bryan needs to convince Beth he's more man than a maid. Or actor. Because he's playing the lead in a reverse Cinderella story, and it might just be the role of a lifetime.

What A Woman Gets

Liam has no patience for women who spend a man's money without giving a thought to any actual work. But to make good on his bet, Liam must not only tolerate socialite, Cassidy, he'll have to clean up after her when her father cuts her off. With no money and no home for Liam to clean, Cassidy has no choice but to accept a job offer—as Liam's new maid. But when sparks fly between them, will it be true love or just another messy affair?

What A Woman

MaryAlice Catherine is all set to clean her grandmother's friend's house, only to find the woman's cocky grandson whom she'd had a crush on growing up—and he'd known all along—is living there and she's mortified. Jared remembers it differently; Mac was always a bossy little thing, but he's not going to let her call the shots now. But with the two of them living in one house, there's no telling who's going to come out swinging.

What A Guy Wants

Beckett is ready to pay up for his lost poker bet. He just didn't realize he'd have to do it with his heart. Jennifer is the one who got away and now she's right here in front of him. In her house. That he's here to clean. Jennifer can't believe the bad boy from high school she'd had a major crush on is in her home, but if there's one thing her ex-husband taught her, it's that she can't count on the bad boy. Until Beckett lays all his cards on the table and he turns out to be someone Jennifer can bet on after all.

Here's Judi!

Award-winning, best-selling author Judi Fennell loves to laugh and loves love, so it's no surprise there's a little bit of each in every book she writes. Check out her fairy tales with a twist for a taste of her light-hearted, tongue-in-cheek paranormal and romantic comedies. From mermen off the coast of the Jersey Shore, to genies with magic carpets, to male strippers à la Magic Mike, and manly maids whose motto is *Satisfaction Guaranteed*, there's always a laugh and love to be had.

And, in her copious (?) amounts of spare time, she helps authors with all aspects of writing and indie-publishing with her formatting, cover and promotional design, editorial, consultation, and audiobook company, www.formatting4U.com.

Judi lives in suburban Philadelphia with a menagerie of four-legged friends, and the minute those creatures start A) singing, B) sewing clothing, or C) cleaning the house will be the day she retires from writing…!

Judi loves to hear from her readers, so find her at:

www.JudiFennell.com
https://www.facebook.com/JudiFennell.Author/

Sign up for my newsletter at:
http://JudiFennell.com/newsletter-signup/